There's o

HENRY
GREEN

Leon Hopkins

Pyla Publishing
England

ISBN 978-1-8380540-2-1

Non-fiction books by the same author include:
The Hundredth Year
The Audit Report
The Landlord's Handbook

Cover design: Reece Hopkins

Pyla Publishing
Treth Gwel, TR12 6TB
www.pylapublishing.co.uk

For Jo

Pre-Match Notes

Northern Ireland Press report
September 1971

Sectarian violence reached new heights this week when a home just off Belfast's Lower Malone Road was destroyed by a car bomb. The three people inside the house were all killed.

No warning was given and responsibility for the bombing has not been claimed, although the RUC said the attack had all the hallmarks of a Provisional IRA operation.

'This was a cowardly attack which killed three innocent people with no known political affiliations', said Chief Inspector Arthur Brennan. 'We are determined that whoever committed this crime will be brought to justice'.

The three people killed were George Grimond (52), his wife Martha (46), and their son Henry (20).

Mr Grimond was a senior civil servant, on secondment from Whitehall and attached to the Ministry of Agriculture. His wife of 20 years was heavily involved in charity work, and Henry was a student studying at the Belfast School of Art. He had just returned home from the cinema when the bomb exploded.

Witnesses, who said they preferred not to be named, said a large white van had entered the driveway of the property, stopping close to the front door. The driver had jumped out and run back into the road where a motor-cyclist was waiting, engine running.

The two men, thought to be in their early twenties, sped off in the direction of central Belfast. The explosion followed almost immediately.

'This was a substantial property but the damage was so great that it will now have to be demolished', said CI Brennan. 'A great deal of explosive was used and the perpetrators must have known those inside would be killed. Nobody could have walked out of there alive'.

Houses nearby were also damaged by the explosion, mainly sustaining broken windows. Three neighbours were admitted to hospital with glass-cut injuries – two are in a serious condition. The road has been closed until further notice while the police conduct searches and make a detailed forensic examination of the little that remains of the van.

Kick off

London 2001

| *One* |

Saturday afternoon. Football. Home game, Albert Pertwee Stand.

'OO are YER? OO are YER?'

It was the usual chant when we scored against a top team, or anybody above us in the league - so just about any other team really. Who do you think you are, coming here with your high and mighty attitude, lording it over us? You are just nonentities really, just like us.

'OO are YER?'

It wasn't high on the football rudeometer, coming somewhere near 'Get yerself to Specsavers' and 'Yer don't know what yer doing'. When the other team's supporters went quiet, we'd chant: 'Shall we sing a song for YOU?' And when they left early in disgust: 'We can see yer GO-ing, We can see yer GO-ing'.

But it was 'OO are YER?' that seemed most apt that afternoon.

I didn't join in. I listened. I watched. And I reflected.

It seemed it had started up again. I might have worried but I have a strict 'no worrying' policy. Even so, I couldn't help but go over the events of the morning in my mind.

I had gone to the dentist. I don't like the dentist – not that I see him much. I don't go for check-ups; I only go when something hurts. My teeth are OK, so they don't hurt that often – maybe once every five or ten years. But when I do go, I have to go quickly. I was lucky this time. I had got an emergency appointment for only six weeks on Saturday. That was today.

I was going to the dentist – which was unusual for me – and I'd arrived early – which was even more unusual. It meant I had 15 minutes to spare – 15 minutes. They were 15 minutes that would be lost forever, wasted. And it was raining.

I didn't want to go and sit in the dentist's waiting room, reading Haberdashers Weekly, or National Geographic, or back copies of Women's Own or Gerbil Keepers' Gazette, so I decided to go for a coffee at that Costas in the High Street.

It was busy – and steamy. People who had come in to get out of the rain, dripped as they drank. I bought a cappuccino, just a small one – so it was only three times the size of a normal-sized cup – and looked for somewhere to sit.

The only place seemed to be in a booth with high-backed padded benches and a fixed Formica-topped table in the middle. A smartly dressed woman sat one side of the table. She was in her forties. She wore a dark blue raincoat. Her carefully coloured hair was cut short. To her right, on the seat, was a black briefcase, and, propped up in the corner, a wet umbrella. It dribbled tiny rivulets of rain onto the pleated leather-style seat.

On the table, next to her coffee, were a dark blue rain hat and a pair of black calfskin gloves.

She was hunched over her mobile; texting, or playing some game, or perhaps using the Internet. She might even have been about to make an actual phone call.

'May I sit here?' I asked, pointing to the seat opposite her?

She put the mobile down and looked up.

'Certainly. Terrible, isn't it?'

'What's that?'

'The news. It's terrible. Always is. But how are you anyway?'

This seemed a touch forward - to start a conversation with a personal enquiry. No mention of the weather, MPs' expenses, cricket, or anything like that. Perhaps she was lonely, or lost, and wanted to talk.

'Very well, thank you'.

'Except your tooth'.

'Pardon'.

'You're very well, except for your toothache'.

She said it as if I was old and a little gaga and she was my carer. My mouth must have been swollen or something. It was worse than I thought. I nodded agreement.

'And how is Stephi?'

'Excuse me'.

'Stephi, that Australian girl you are with. How is she?'

She knew Stephi somehow. I didn't recognise this woman but she must be a neighbour or something. Perhaps Stephi talked to her now and then? Perhaps she was a stalker? Not too likely.

'She's fine. Had to work this morning, but otherwise OK'.

'At the clinic, is she?'

She knew her name AND where she worked. Perhaps she was her boss? A doctor or head of the haematology lab? No, she was too smart for that; too well groomed. Her fingernails were too clean and there were no nicotine stains on her fingers.

Perhaps she was a patient? Perhaps Stephi had stabbed her in the arm with her needle and leeched her blood, or whatever she did?

'And your boys? I hope all that nasty business is forgotten now'.

This was getting to me. 'Sorry', I said. 'I don't mean to be rude but do I know you?'

'No, I don't think so'.

'So how do you know all this?'

'I just do'.

'You just do?'

'Yes. Why, am I wrong about anything?'

'No'.

'No, thought not. So, you'd say everything was well with you and Stephi?'

It must have looked as if I was attempting an imitation of Goldie, the goldfish I once owned for two days before he, she or it was flushed down the lavatory. I gave an open-mouthed nod.

'Good', she said. 'Look, the rain's easing off and I've got to be somewhere. You had better get going too or you'll be late for that appointment at the dentist. Nice meeting you Henry'.

And with that she was up and out, clattering across the tiled floor on her high heels, and neatly sidestepping the yellow 'warning, wet floor' cones. I watched her walk off past the window, down the road. I even gave a little wave as she passed.

I might have been flattered by the attention had I not been bewildered; bewildered and a little cross. But she was right about the time, so I, too, hurried out and across the road to my dentist.

I say 'my dentist'. It was the same practice all right, but the personnel had all changed since I was last there. The dentist himself looked about twelve.

'Hi Henry', he said. 'Take a seat'. He ushered me into his chair and moved behind me to pull a lever or two so I was entirely at his mercy.

'So, you've got a toothache, let's have a look. It's not so bad that you can't drink hot coffee'.

I flinched. 'Excuse me, but how do you know my name? How do you know I've got a toothache? And how do you know about the coffee?'

'Easy, the first two are written down here. Mr Hitchen, the dentist I took over from, kept very good records. See, it says here "Henry Green, only comes when he has a toothache". And the coffee I can smell on your breath'.

'Sorry. About the breath I mean'.

'Don't worry, I'm used to much worse. At least you're not chewing gum. At least you're not a smoker'.

This was getting too much. 'How do you know that?'

'Only need to look at your teeth. Wouldn't take a Sherlock Holmes to work that one out'.

'Spose not'.

I got my filling and went home. Stephi would not be back until the evening. I made myself an omelette – nothing too chewy while my newly drilled tooth settled down – and went off to football.

It got to half time and by some miracle we were still in the lead. They had had their chances – 'they' being the other lot. A twinkle-toed winger, new from some German club and costing eight million according to the programme, delivered complete with gold boots, had run our full back ragged. Ollie Wilson was his name – the full back that is.

Golden boots danced past him once too often. Ollie clattered into him, kicking his legs away. The Saddlers Wells impostor fell headfirst into our defender's knee, rolled over once and was still. Blood burst from his nose.

'Dive, Dive, Dive', shouted the crowd. 'Cheat, Cheat, Cheat'. 'What a waste of Mon-EEE, What a waste of Mon-EEE'.

The Ref advanced towards Ollie, who stood with his arms raised, shaking his head. He had the look of a choirboy. He was sent off. Still shaking his bowed head, he left the pitch.

'Ollie, Ollie, Ollie', cried the crowd. 'There's only one Ollie Wil-son, one Ollie Wil-son'.

At half time I got to chat to Iain. That was the rule. We had sat in adjacent seats for the past seven years. Both season ticket holders, we came on our own. At half time we had a sort of bloke's chat. 'Good game, thought the Ref was a bit harsh' – that sort of thing. Except that it was more often: 'Bloody awful game. Bout time we got a decent striker'.

I didn't know too much about Iain. I didn't think he knew too much about me either. All I knew was his first name, that he lived in Welling, had a wife and two kids and worked shifts. And that when his Dad had died, he and his brother had asked to have his Dad's ashes scattered on the pitch. They'd told him he couldn't do that. That the best they could do was to allow them to be emptied behind the goal – North Stand, of course. But when nobody was looking Iain had tossed a handful of ashes onto the pitch anyway.

Obviously, he was just the person to confide in.

'Had a strange experience this morning', I told him. 'I went for a coffee and sat down opposite this woman who seemed to know all about me'.

'Like what?'

'Like personal stuff. Like the name of my girlfriend and where she worked, that she was Australian, that I had a dental appointment'.

'Facebook', he said.

'What about it?'

'That's where she found out about you. Looked on your Facebook page'.

'I haven't got a Facebook page. I haven't even got a mobile. Email's about my limit'.

'Then it was somebody else's Facebook page. Probably your girlfriend's'.

'How does that work? Surely people can't read personal stuff about me on somebody else's Facebook page?'

'Depends what's put on there and how it's set up. Whoever put it up there might not have gone for their privacy options. Or this woman might be their Facebook friend'.

'And that would do it?'

'Yes, that would do it. It's surprising what people say about themselves. And it's surprising what they say about people they know. And it's surprising what you can find out about anybody with a few clicks of a mouse'.

'So how do you know about this stuff Iain? Somebody been spying on you?'

'No, I'm in the Police. Cybercrime, that's me. I don't tell many people because some get funny when you tell them you're a copper'.

The second half started.

The Waste-of-Mon-ee got the ball. He was immediately booed – no wonder, having exaggerated an innocent coming together with so much bleeding all over the pitch.

He raced down the wing, cut inside and rifled home an unstoppable shot from 20 yards. Our goalkeeper did his Margot Fontaine swan dive impression as a tribute to the Waste's dancing skills.

'U-boat, 'U-boat, U-boat', shouted the crowd. 'Dive, dive, dive'.

We lost four-one. Iain and I left five minutes before the end. Enough was enough.

'OO are YER? OO are YER? Their supporters chanted. 'Shall we sing a song for you?

'We can see yer GO-ing, we can see yer GO-ing'.

| *Two* |

Saturday, early evening. Back home.

I hadn't told Iain, but the incident in the coffee shop was hardly a one-off. Similar things had happened to me before. People I don't know seem to recognise me. They think they know me and stuff about me. Sometimes they do.

This, I think you'll agree, is very inconvenient when I'm trying to keep a low profile, not be recognised, not be noticed. Yet still it happens. I don't know why. There's no reason. I must have one of those faces.

Of course, when I was with Jane, she always thought the people who looked our way were staring at her. Some might have been. 'They must have seen my picture in the paper when we gave that cheque to Llamas for Ethiopia', she'd say, or something similar. She was in public relations for a garage chain. They were always giving something to somebody and claiming the publicity.

But it had happened long before I met Jane, and it happened after we split up. Just a nudge to a friend here, a knowing look there. They rarely came up and spoke to me, although I might hear them say something about me as I walked past.

'Isn't that the chap from Life on Mars?' it might be. Or 'wasn't he in Casualty the other week?' 'No. He's an MP or something. I think he was one of those who fiddled his expenses', they'd say as they worked their way through their business expense-paid lunches.

That's what spooked me about the woman in Costas. She'd struck up a conversation with me. That had only really happened three times before. Once was when Stephi came up to me in the pub, and the other two were within a few minutes of each other and had resulted in my worse-than-my-worst nightmare – and quite a few other people's worse-than-worst nightmares too.

Stephi still wasn't back when I got home. She'd had a long day. She pretended to be all Aussie and tough, not bothered about such things, but I knew she'd want to have a hot bath and a drink when she got in, and then be spoilt with some nice food – sitting at the table and everything. What she got was something different.

'Have you got a Facebook page?' I asked her as she came in through the door. She'd expected more sympathy, a hug perhaps, and a steaming cup of tea.

'You know I have'. She was already offended, already on the defensive. Being Australian her defence was of the Ollie Wilson variety.

I didn't care. I was reckless in the face of imminent hurricane-force danger. I pressed on.

'Do you write about me on there?'

'Who'd want to write about you? Haven't you forgotten your wife of thirteen years divorced you for being too boring?'

'No, she didn't. She wanted to move on, do things she'd always wanted to try. Things she didn't want to do with me'. Now it was my turn to become defensive and prickly. 'Hasn't done her much good, has it?'

'She chucked you because you were boring. She told me'.

'You've spoken to her?' This wasn't going the way I wanted at all. We were charging off at a tangent.

'Of course, I have. You don't think I'd go with some bloke who'd been married without first checking that his wife wasn't still on the scene.

'Blokes are like that. They tell you it's all over with their exes and then you find out they're all cozied up together in some love shack in Primrose Hill. Except he goes off on Wednesdays to shag his bit on the side. Somebody whose so desperate she even goes out with the ugly ones, and the really, really boring ones'.

'So, you're telling me that you think I'm boring too?'

'I'm telling you I spoke to Jane soon after I met you. I asked if it was true you were divorced. She said it was, and that I was welcome to you. And I'm telling you I'm bloody tired and I don't want to stand in the hall any more while we shout at each other about bloody nothing just because your sodding team lost'.

'It's not nothing', I said as I padded off to run her a bath. 'We should have won'.

After she got into the bath, I brought her a glass of wine and sat on the side.

'Bad day?'

'Bloody chipper'.

'What would you like for dinner? I've got steak in the fridge'. As I don't work, I do the shopping and the cooking.

'That would be nice'.

'How did you find her?'

'Who?'

'Jane. How did you find her?'

'You're not still on about that? Google, if you must know'.

'Google?' I'm astonished. 'What, for heaven's sake has Jane got to do with Google? I don't understand'.

'I simply typed her name, address and date of birth into Google. It's not rocket science'.

'But how did you know all that in the first place?' Stephi looked a little uncomfortable, as if she had been caught out. But she looked proud of herself as well.

'I looked it up'.

'Looked it up? Where, for Christ sakes?'

'If you must know, I went to the records office. I looked up your marriage certificate and found her name, her full name and her maiden name. And her date of birth. Bit young for you, wasn't she?'

'Only five years. So, what else did you do?'

'I looked up your birth certificate, your children's birth certificates, and your divorce certificate'.

She wasn't uncomfortable any more, she was just proud. It was me that was feeling uncomfortable – a little hot under the collar.

I may not worry about things but, on the whole, I would very much rather remain anonymous. News that anybody, even Stephi, had been digging into my past was not welcome.

'But why would you do that?'

'Why do you think, drongo. I've been caught out by lying bastards too often before. I started doing it for all the blokes I met. And I liked it. It's interesting.

'Anyway, I thought I liked you a lot – THEN. So, it was worth the trouble. I just went to the records office one lunch-time, found the references and ordered the certificates. It doesn't take long. You can do that sort of thing online now'.

'And then you Googled her?'

'Yes, then I searched her name. It's a very common name, but with the other bits, I tracked her down. Found a mention of her in her local paper'.

'What mention?'

'It was the divorce. There was all that trouble about her and the boys. It got into the paper. She was interviewed. Told them what a rotten sod you were and all that.

'That way I got her new name and her address. After that, it was easy. I emailed her, and then I rang her'.

I tried to smile but I could feel the corner of my mouth twitching. At last I asked: 'And what did she say?'

'You're so bloody up yourself. What did you expect her to say? That you were the best husband in the world and how kicking you out was the biggest mistake of her life? All she said was you were stifling her. You were bloody boring and I was welcome to you.

'She wished me good luck, in a way that sort of implied I'd need it. Anyway, it turns out you're not Henry Green'.

'What do you mean by that?'

'Well, I told you I looked up your birth certificate. I know you tell everybody your name is "Henry" but it turns out you're not "Henry" after all. Your real name is "Horace". Horace Henry Green.

'I don't blame you. If I had a name like "Horace" I'd probably want to be called "Henry" too'.

I should have left it at that. But I didn't. 'It's not like that', I told her. My Dad was called "Horace" so everybody called me "Henry" so there was no confusion. That's all'.

Stephi had that look she had when I explained why I was late back from the pub – rampant disbelief. 'I don't remember any other "Horaces" in the bits I looked up'.

'That's because "Horace" wasn't his real name. He was "John", but his Dad was named "John" so they called him "Horace". It was a sort of family joke'.

'Have I got this right? You're called "Henry" because your father's father was called "John".

'Exactly'.

'And you're complaining because I checked up on you. Get over it. It's not just you, it's your whole family. You're all so up yourselves. If I'd known how boring and how up yourself you were before I agreed to let you move in, I wouldn't have bothered'.

She said the last bit with a sort of grin, so I knew we were even now, things were OK. So, I didn't tell her about the woman in the coffee shop. I thought I'd leave that for another day. If I told her now, she'd only think I was paranoid or even more up myself than she already realised.

I went off to start on dinner.

'We know your name, your name. It's not the same, the same. It's Horace, Horace, Horace'.

| *Three* |

Sunday morning breakfast. We're sitting at the table in the kitchen; our only table.

Stephi had bought the flat 15 years ago - 1987. I'd been living there for the last six. It was the basement of a Victorian house in Charlton – 'West Greenwich' we called it. There were four rooms: a kitchen large enough for a scrubbed pine table that could take four people, six at a push, a bedroom, living room and bathroom. The front door was down a few steps from the street, you had to open a wrought iron gate in the railings to get access. The kitchen was at the back and had French doors opening onto a tiny courtyard. A few steps led up was the garden, which was ours – well Stephi's.

Stephi is wearing that nightshirt thing she has – powder blue – and her long fairish hair is loose and tussled, so that a few strands fall over her face and softened her sharp Australian features.

She has sharp Australian eyes too, greyish blue, but not so sharp they didn't need the help of a pair of glasses. She favours the fairly heavy, dark rimmed type.

She is what you might call 'handsome' rather than a beauty. She is not too tall but has an elegant way about her. Not polite elegant, more animal, loose-limbed elegant – a sort of boyish confidence.

We were eating bacon butties, mine smeared with mustard, hers with vegemite, newly imported from earls court.

'She had you followed'.

I was in mid bite. Stephi obviously saw the bewildered look in my eyes, magnified as they were by my spec-saver two-for-one specials.

'Jane. She had you followed. By a detective agency'.

I almost choked. 'When?'

'Before she spilt up with you.

'She told me. She thought you were too happy. She thought there must be something wrong. She thought you must be having an affair'.

'Too bloody happy? How long did this go on? Not me being too happy, her having me followed'.

'About a month, she said. She couldn't afford any more. Anyway, she knew enough by then. Bugged your studio, took pictures and everything'.

I was suddenly angry. How dare she?

'Studio? You mean that summerhouse thing in the garden?' it was more of a shed, a large-ish shed with big windows.

'I don't know, it's just how these people described it. "Your studio", they said'.

'And what did these people say they found out? What constituted grounds for divorce for heaven's sake?' I didn't know why I was cross with Stephi about this. But I knew I had to be cross with somebody.

'They said you gave people lifts to hospital one day a week, helped in a charity shop another, and visited an old people's home on another. Apart from that you sat in your studio, painting.

'As far as they could tell you weren't seeing anybody else. You had money coming in every month from a blind trust in Lichtenstein, and plenty in the bank. They said Jane had no reason to think you weren't happily married'.

It was true. I was happily married.

I hadn't worked since before I met Jane. In truth, I'd never worked. perhaps to ease my conscience a little – maybe so I didn't look like a complete waste of space - I did some charity work, looked after the house, and dabbled with painting.

The painting started after I bought a box of old oil paints at a boot fair. There were over a hundred, of all sizes and a great many colours. You couldn't tell what most of the colours were until you unscrewed the top because all the labels had come off, although a few had a smear or two of their contents around the caps.

The paints came with a box of brushes, an easel and a couple of old canvases. There was no excuse not to have a go. After all, hadn't I been to art school?

I was happy with Jane. She was a bit moody, occasionally spiteful, but on the whole she was OK. I didn't get on with her as well as with Stephi, but then I didn't know Stephi then, so I didn't know what I was missing.

I was good at the charity work too. People seemed to like me. At the old people's home, I got some of them who had been all but gaga to talk to me – sensibly and sensitively. My favourite was Agnes.

She couldn't remember her own name, but she remembered mine.

'Are you my son', she asked one day?'

'No Agnes', I told her. 'You know I'm not. Your son's in America'.

'Fancy that', she said. 'But I seem to know you so well'.

I was pleased with that.

I might not have had a studio then, just a shed, but I had one now. I bought it after Jane kicked me out. Well, she didn't have to do too much kicking really. She just said she'd had enough of me and I'd better leave. So, I left.

I bought somewhere else to live and to paint in. It had been an industrial building of some sort, perhaps an old print works or small factory – very small factory. It came with a house on the side. in Greenwich.

I gutted the inside, replaced the windows with some you could actually see through and made it into the large open space I called my studio. The factory/studio bit had its own frontage, its own gates and a small courtyard where I kept my car – a Volvo estate that was appreciated by the people I took to hospital.

I lived in the house to start with. I'd been living there when I met Stephi. Now I rented it out. In fact, I had just found new tenants after the last chap moved out. He was fine, didn't give me any trouble, just kept himself to himself. No wild parties or anything. He'd even paid me six month's rent in advance – in cash.

I went to the studio a couple of days each week while Stephi was at work – usually Thursdays when she stayed on for her tai chi class, and Fridays when she went straight to her drama group.

We ate late those days, sometimes out, sometimes a takeaway.

'What is a "blind trust" anyway?' Stephi asked.

'It's a legal thing. Somebody puts money into it and a lawyer looks after it. Nobody knows who owns it. In Lichtenstein it's against the law for lawyers to disclose information about it and only people who get paid out know it exists. It's a sort of tax thing. It's the type of thing Robert Maxwell used'.

I thought perhaps I'd said too much, so I stopped.

'Dodgy, you mean?'

'No, not dodgy at all. All legal and above board'.

'Except that it's in Lichtenstein and not above board. It's hidden strictly below board'.

'Well, yes, to an extent, I suppose. But legal, and very convenient, especially if you get divorced. Meant Jane couldn't clear me out entirely'.

'So, you were planning on getting divorced all along?'

'No, course not'.

'How did you end up with money in a blind trust then?'

'Well I struck lucky.

'I must've told you this'. Stephi shook her head. I knew she was right. I was operating on a strictly 'need to know' strategy – or whatever it is spies, bankers and chief executives say.

'When I left school, I didn't have any qualifications, so I started a tyre company. Bit like kwick-fit but not so big – and not so quick. Just a shed, another shed, on a bit of waste ground, a high wire fence, a guard dog and a lot of tyres.

'We charged less than anybody else and got along OK. Always busy, always queues. Then a supermarket decided it wanted to build a depot behind my bit of land, and it needed access for its lorries. It made me an offer for the lot. A very good offer.

'I was 20 and I retired on the proceeds. Cool'. I thought saying 'cool' sounded very cool. My mistake.

'Course, I'm not saying that it was me that paid money into that trust. An adviser sorted everything out for me. My accountant. That's all. Some money was paid in and I get paid out something every month'.

'Ooo'.

'Anyway, how do you know all this?'

'She gave me the report. Jane said when she got it, she realised just how boring you really were. Not just mediocre boring, world class boring. How could anybody be that happy with nothing to do except potter around and visit old people? That's why she got shot of you. She didn't need the report any more, so she gave it to me'.

'To you? And you kept it to yourself all this time – or did you pass it around to all your friends. All have a good laugh? Or perhaps I can look it up on your Facebook page?'

'Course not. I hid it away'.

'You still have it. Where is it?'

'In a file, if you must know. In my knicker drawer with all the other stuff'.

'What other stuff?'

'All the other bits I've collected about you. More a scrap book than a file'.

I think she added the last bit to make it sound better, less intrusive. Calm me down a little. It didn't work.

It was shocking, it really was. There I am, minding my own business, trying to be obscure, hoping to slip into and out of life quietly, without being noticed, and there were all these people checking up on me. People who were supposed to love me, understand me. It was a bloody outrage.

'A crap book more like. How could you do it? Don't you think it's all an invasion of privacy? My privacy'

'Don't blame me, my little drongo. It was Jane who hired those people'.

'But you did some checking up as well, you told me'.

'Well if you didn't want people to know your business you shouldn't have told it to that dating agency'.

'What dating agency? What now? I've never told anybody my business, I've kept it to myself. Man of mystery, that's me. It's like when people say you should never take all your clothes off – keep some allure. I like to keep a bit of me to myself'.

Stephi almost laughed. Guffawed would be more accurate.

'Well it's not bloody alluring. It's bloody annoying. No wonder Jane ditched you and your boring secrets. And anyway, it was one of the things I liked about you best. You were so open. That's why I went along when the dating agency set us up'.

'I thought you just wanted my body'.

'frrr, dream on'.

'Anyway, the dating agency didn't set us up. I just met you in a pub, that one down by the river. I was standing there all alone, staring at the water, and you came up and made some remark'.

This was a bit of a lie. I'd watched her come in. And I watched the younger bloke by the bar look her up and down. He was pretending to read a newspaper. But as soon as Stephi came in, he finished his drink and walked out, carefully staring at the floor all the way.

I guessed then it was a dateline date and Stephi had lied a bit about her age. She probably usually got away with it. Probably the blokes lied too. Probably they'd both lied about their age, but she'd lied more.

'I said "hello Henry", not a bad chat up line as it turned out', said Stephi. 'Hello Henry, you don't look much like your photo.

'And you said "it's a photo of somebody else". I thought that was so open. So, I said, "I suppose the details are wrong as well". And you said of course they were'.

'Well they were. I didn't go to any agency. I wouldn't. I never have. I certainly wouldn't have given them anything about myself, or who I was looking for, for that matter. Because I wasn't looking for anybody.

'You just came along and started chatting and that was that. It was just something else that happened to me. Things just happen. I don't look for them, they just happen. You were there and it was obvious that something had happened'.

The truth is I don't like having my photo taken, never have. I avoid it. The only pictures I have of me are the one I use on my driving licence – and that doesn't look too much like me anyway – and one other. Me with my parents.

'Stop being so pompous. Of course you told the agency, how else would I have known all about you?'

'You didn't. You didn't know anything about me, not a sausage. All you knew was that I didn't look like the photo you had and the details were wrong as well. You probably even had a different name'.

'I did'.

'Then why did you call me Henry?' In fact, it didn't faze me that she knew my name. Lots of people seem to guess it. I must just look like a Henry. I've grown into it, I guess.

'I just knew your name was Henry. It wasn't so odd that it wasn't the one the agency gave me. Lots of people lie about their names just in case the person they're paired up with turns out to be a nutter or a stalker. They lie about their name, their age, everything. It's just that you admitted it. It was kind of refreshing'.

'You just knew it?'

'Yes, I just knew it. and you misled me'.

'How?'

'By telling the bloody truth, that's how. Bastard. I bet you spent your nights lurking in that pub looking for vulnerable women to mislead with your truths'.

We stopped for a while then so we could go back to bed, tell each other some more lies, a few truths, and show each other just how vulnerable we thought we were.

'The only sight I wanna view, is that wonderful picture of you. Of you. You. You.'

| *Four* |

Later.

'Can I see it? That "scrapbook" you have. Can I see it?'

'No. It's personal'.

'Yes, personal to me. You've got things about me and you won't let me see? If you were a business, I would be able to pay you five shillings or something and you'd have to let me see. Otherwise I'd report you to the data czar or whatever he's called. You'd get severely told off'.

'Well I'm not a business, am I? And you tell me off all the time anyway'.

'No, I don't. I've never told you off – despite everything'.

She knew it was a sort of joke – the 'everything'.

'Bastard. I'll think about it'.

She did – think about it. And then she went into the bedroom and came back with a plastic concertina file and slapped it on the coffee table.

'There, you can read about yourself all you want now. Check up on just how wonderful you are'.

This was said in a way that led me to think I'd have to do a lot of checking to find anything like that.

I flicked through. The detective agency's report looked a bit thick. I thought I'd read that some other time.

But I was amazed to see a dozen or so photos included. They were 10 by 8 and obviously taken by somebody with a camera with a very long lens. They were good quality but a bit grainy.

There was one of me getting into my Volvo, another of me arriving at somebody's house: Margaret Bartram who I had taken each month to have her eye appointment.

There was one of me painting, taken through the window some sunny afternoon. Whoever had taken it had position himself so there was no reflection from the glass. It got me with my back slightly turned so you could see the canvas I was working on quite clearly.

The newspaper clipping looked more manageable as a Sunday lunchtime read than the report, so I decided to look through it.

Local mother of two, Jane Green, 36, was this week jailed for seven days after uproar at the divorce hearing she was attending.

She had already been branded an 'uncaring mother' in a bitter dispute over custody of her two children, George, 15 and David 17.

The Judge, Mr Justice Bosterman, said he had been astonished to find the case had not been about who should keep the two boys, but who should not have custody of them.

Mrs Green's husband, Henry Green, had, said the judge, made the selfless decision that they would be better off with their natural mother. He said it was better they did not live with him.

But Mrs Green said she did not want them. She planned to travel and said they would be an 'inconvenience'.

The financial settlement proposed by Mr Green had been particularly generous, said the judge.

He had offered Mrs Green outright ownership of the house that had been their matrimonial home – even though he had owned this prior to their marriage – and he proposed a substantial 'clean break' cash settlement that meant she and her sons would be very well provided for. On top of this, Mr Green had said he had no objection to Mrs Green taking their sons travelling and that he would pay their travelling costs.

'All in all, I believe Mr Green has the best interests of the family at heart and you have not', the judge told Mrs Green. 'It seems to me that you brought these divorce proceedings for no good reason other than your own selfish whims and that you are nothing more than an uncaring mother who now wishes to shrug off her responsibilities for her sons.

'We are told that in divorced families, children are most often better off with their mother. I might have had cause to doubt this to be so in this case. However, Mr Green has shown himself to be a very reasonable person who has presented well-argued reasons that you should be given sole custody of these two children. I therefore have no hesitation in deciding this issue in favour of Mr Green'.

At this point Mrs Green stood up and started shouting at the judge.

'You don't know what he's like', she said. 'You're another fxxxxxx bastard just like him. Another bloody man'.

The judge held her in contempt of court and jailed her for seven days.

Mr Green left the court without comment.

There was a picture of Jane entering the court building with her 'hurt wife' look. Underneath was the caption 'Uncaring mother'.

I didn't care about the house or the money. Money had always come easy. I was sure some more would come along. As for the boys, well they were better off with her. I'd already put them in enough danger and they'd soon be men anyway, when they could make their own decisions. They were better without me. They probably wouldn't understand, I couldn't tell them, or anybody else, the real reason.

Anyway, although I hadn't made anything of it, I was not their natural father. Jane already had them both when we married.

She wasn't sure who David's father was. He'd apparently been conceived at a party and Jane had never known the name of the bloke she'd fancied so much while under the influence and whom she'd never seen again.

George was the result of a short fling with a married man from work who'd dumped her as soon as she got pregnant.

I met her when I went to buy my first Volvo. She seemed nice enough and I could see she was struggling a bit, being a single mother with two young children. And she liked the idea of me being a painter. Of course, she didn't like it so much when she found out I had to spend hours doing it. But that was later.

It just seemed so convenient. A nice woman with a ready-made family all ready to move in. So, we got married and I adopted the boys.

There was another cutting, from the same newspaper. There was a photo of Jane outside the prison gates and a news item alongside. It read:

Jane Green of Applebey Court Gardens risked further imprisonment last week when she insulted the judge who had jailed her for contempt of court.

Mrs Green, pictured right, was in defiant mood when leaving Holloway Prison last week. She accused Mr Justice Bosterman, who had granted her custody of her two sons, of 'typical male insensitivity' and of adopting a 'bullying attitude' towards her.

'Who does he think he fxxxxxx is? Frankly I don't think he's fit to be a judge. He clearly doesn't know what he's doing.

'Yer don't know what yer DOO-ING. Don't know what yer DOO-ING'.

| *Five* |

Two weeks later. Football. Half time. Score 0-0.

'Bloody awful weather, bloody awful game'. This was Iain. It was a cup match and we were playing some team from a lower league.

'OO are YER, OO are YER?'

It was cold and wet and it was clear most of our players would rather be at home in the warm watching television. And so would we.

'Bunch of prima donnas if you ask me. Bout time they put a decent shift in like the rest of us'. Iain again.

'Don't know why we put ourselves through it', I said. This was a common theme.

'Anyhow, it wasn't Facebook. That woman I was telling you about, the one that seemed to know all about me. She couldn't have found out on Facebook. I asked Stephi. She showed me. She has an account but she hardly ever says anything about me. Says I'm too boring. And there's definitely no pictures.

'So, it's still a mystery'.

'Phishing', said Iain.

'Fishing? What's catching fish got to do with it?'

'Nothing. Not fishing, phishing with a "ph". People get information out of you by phishing'.

'What, like those emails from Africa where everybody is related to a late dictator and needs to move five billion out of the country fast and can you help for a suitably large commission? All you need to do is to send them your bank details'.

'That's sort of it, but your version is a bit old hat now. People have cottoned on. But it's along those lines, but automated'.

'You mean I wouldn't know?'

'You would if you were wise to it. They send you an email that looks as if it's from a big company – say E-Bay, or Barclays Bank. They're easy to mock up. Whoever sends them asks you to confirm your account details by answering a few questions. Things like address, date of birth, bank account details. Everything they would need to get some money out of you.

'It's big business'.

'But I don't have an E-Bay account, and I don't use Barclays'.

'Doesn't matter to the phishers. If they send out enough emails, they'll certainly reach some people that do have those accounts. And some of those will reply. It happens all the time'.

'So, you think I fell for something like that and gave away all that information? I don't think so'.

'You're in denial. It's the usual response. Other people fall for it, but not me.

'Or if it's not phishing it's pharming'.

'What's that when it's at home?'

'Same sort of thing except this time it's a fake website. You get directed there by an email and when you click onto it, you're asked to register. Then you fill in all the details they want'.

'I know you're a wiz at this and all that, but I don't think it makes sense in my case. That woman knew about Stephi, her name and where she came from. She knew about my divorce. And she knew about my toothache. I'm not likely to put all that on a form, am I? And even if I had, she would hardly let me know that she knew, would she?'

'Well I'm just saying people give away lots of information about themselves without realising it until it's too late'.

The second half started and we left it there.

'What a load of RUB-BISH', their lot chanted. I could only agree.

It got near the end.

'You know what's going to happen now, don't you? It'll get to the last minute and they'll nick a penalty or something, and that will be that', said Iain. 'Shall we go?'

I don't know why we always leave together, but we do. Perhaps it's for moral support among deserters.

I nodded my agreement and stood up to leave.

Just at that moment the ball came flying my way. My arms were already up and I simply stretched out and caught it. One of the photographers by the side of the pitch turned around to see what was happening. He had a fancy camera with a very large lens and one of those support rods sticking out the bottom. He raised the camera to his eye, aimed it at me and clicked away. My moment was captured for all time. It was too late to do anything about it now, I'd been digitally recorded, probably dozens of times, in the blink of a fisheye.

Ollie Wilson plodded towards the side line. I tossed the ball to him.

It all happened so quickly nobody, especially the other team, seemed to be paying attention.

Within a second Ollie had thrown the ball to Kumoo Ratti, and he had rolled it back to Ollie, who booted it up the field towards their penalty box. A new seventeen-year-old whose name I didn't know, only just put on as a substitute and still young enough to actually have some enthusiasm for the game, dashed down the wing and pinged a neat side-foot kick between the keeper's legs.

The Ref blew for the goal and then for full time. We had won.

'I don't suppose we'll see Rafina playing for us again. Too good for us', said Iain.

'OO AH Rafeeena. OO AH Rafeeena'.

| *Six* |

Late Sunday morning. Stephi wearing her blue nightshirt again, but this time with bed socks and a loose-knit baggy cardigan. The full works. She is sitting on the sofa with her legs tucked under her, reading the Sunday newspapers.

'Screw my granny, look at that'.

She waves the paper she had folded over and was just about to throw on top of the pile on the floor. Section 98 of 1,437 no doubt. I ignore the attempt at an Australianism – she's not too good at those. Hardly a 'strewth' to be heard in our house.

'Something good?'

'Something bloody amazing. Look at that'.

I take the newspaper. It's the sports section. And there I am on the back page. Full frontal, the centre of the picture. I'm standing with my arms outstretched above my head holding the ball.

Fan power wafts United through, was the headline.

A quick-thinking fan returned the ball so swiftly to the feet of United's Ollie Wilson that he was able to deliver a killer pass before the other team had time to react, read the story.

I threw the paper down and skulked off to the kitchen to make a cup of tea.

'I knew you couldn't believe what you read in the papers', shouted Stephi. 'They said you were quick thinking'.

She thought it a joke. But I hadn't wanted by photo taken, let alone published in the papers. I'd been violated, my image had been stolen and held up for all to see. I went to football to be part of the crowd, as anonymous as one of those Starlings in a flock that rises and falls, dives and wheels in seeming formation – each bird losing itself in the identity of the crowd. A murmuration, that's what they call it. A murmuration of Starlings. And now I was expected to accept my picture being published without a murmur. In truth there was little else I could do. At least they hadn't got my name.

Even so.

I must have been quiet after that because about six o'clock Stephi told me to 'snap out of it' and that I could bloody well take her out for a meal. So that's what we did. We walked down to Greenwich so we could have spicy chicken while scanning the Thames.

Being a cold, wet, Sunday, the restaurant wasn't too busy. There were plenty of people eating but we didn't have to queue. We just walked straight in and sat down. Our order included two large glasses of wine, and we sat sipping these while we waited for the food.

'Have you noticed that woman behind you?' asked Stephi.

'No, why?'

'Because she keeps staring at you. I noticed when we came in. And when you got up to order and get the wine, her eyes followed you all the time'.

It was one of those places where you order at a bar and pay in advance.

'She's not that woman from Costas I told you about?'

'How would I know? More likely a past conquest. Or your bit on the side. Some other dumb mug like me. She said this with a mock pout. It was supposed to be a cue for me to say something nice – like 'your more than enough for anybody'. But I didn't, so after a pause and a meaningful look, Stephi carried on.

'Anyway, she's talking and looking the other way now, so just turn around and have a quick look. You might recognise her'.

I snatched a look. At that moment she glanced up and saw me looking her way. I didn't know who she was, but I swear she turned a little red. She was with two other women, all three in their thirties, I'd say, and she nudged the one nearest her who sat with her back to me, and said something. They all started giggling and the third woman took the chance to look my way.

'I don't know what they're bloody looking at you for', huffed Stephi. 'It's not like you're Brad Pitt or anything. One stupid picture in the paper and you think you're a bloody celebrity. You probably paid that photographer anyway. Otherwise who'd want a picture of you?'

I agreed. But I didn't say so. Instead I put on what I thought might be an urbane smile. That didn't go down too well either.

We spent the rest of the meal in small talk, with me feeling guilty for something that had nothing to do with me.

We were about to leave when somebody from the restaurant came up. He was a little older than most of the other waiters and waitresses and I took him to be the manager, or at least the assistant manager's assistant. He was carrying two large glasses of wine and a slip of paper.

'Thank you so much for eating here', he said. 'We are honoured you should choose us. Please accept this wine as a little gift from us. And here is your credit card receipt. I've cancelled the payment. This meal is on the house'.

I didn't know what to say. I didn't understand what it was he was doing or saying. It just seemed bizarre.

Stephi was a little more alert though. She wasn't the sort of person to turn down a free meal when it was offered. 'That's very good of you', she said. 'We've enjoyed the meal very much. Would you like some sort of recommendation? A photograph perhaps?'

'I don't like to. I don't want to intrude on your evening, I'm sure you must dread this sort of thing'.

'No worries', said Stephi.

A waiter was summoned. A mobile phone was produced and pictures were taken. I didn't like the idea but I could see by the look in Stephi's eyes that resistance would have unpleasant consequences. Crocodiles might be involved – or at the very least crocodile tears.

The women from the table behind me had also taken their mobiles from their handbags and snapped away.

They waved as we left. 'Who do you think he was with?' I heard one say as we walked by. 'Probably some model'.

Several people stood up and clapped as we walked out.

'And all that because you caught a bloody football', said Stephi.

'He's big, he's tall. He caught the ball. Henry. Henry. Henry'.

| *Seven* |

Friday.

I woke up grumpy with myself. It was to do with a dream. It had a recurring theme – not particular events, just a feeling. I was young and expectant. I was excited about life and what it might hold. I thought I might be a lawyer, or a doctor, perhaps a politician. Even an explorer. I might do something to be noticed, to be somebody. Perhaps I'd be an actor, a celebrity even. No chance of being a footballer. But perhaps a racing driver, dicing with death, burning up tracks around the world. It was all to come, all to unfold.

My long dead parents were there. Friends were there. We were all the same age we were when I was twenty or so. We were full of ideas and ideals. No stopping us.

And then I woke up. I woke up. Here I was, coming up to fifty – I'm 33 days older than Stephi (she calls me her 'sugar daddy'). All those things I had dreamed of had passed me by. My life had drifted along to where I was now, all but gone.

It was not that I was unhappy with my life. It was good. But the chances of being world heavyweight boxing champion, or of being Formula One world champion, had long gone. I was what I was, and that was that. In fact, I wasn't even what I was. It made me angry.

I didn't mind this. Friday was a painting day, and I painted better when I was angry. I'd go off to my studio and attack a canvas or two, splash and smear, run my fingers through the oily pigments. I might cut the canvas even – I'd done that before - or go to work with a pallet knife.

The colours I'd use would be whatever they turned out to be when I opened one of the original unlabelled tubes – I still had a few left and I usually started by picking one out of the box. The first thing I did whenever I bought new paints was to tear the labels off. That meant that, by the time I came to use them, I wouldn't have a clue what colour was inside. That's why I favoured the old-fashioned oil paints in lead tubes with paper labels - none of your acrylics in pre-printed plastic see-through tubes.

I should explain, I am an expressive painter, what people call a 'modern' artist.

Really, I just make patterns on canvas, using paint. I do it because it pleases me. I don't think about it. I just start with a daub of this or that, and work from there. Sometimes I splash or drip the paint on. Sometimes I use heavy brushstrokes; sometimes I use my hands and fingers. Sometimes I just squeeze the tube of paint and smear it directly onto the canvass. Sometimes all five. I do whatever comes to me at the time. It's messy but very liberating. You should try it.

If, after an hour or so, sometimes two, I have something that looks arresting, I put it to one side and start another.

It's been like that for years. I have quite a collection.

I sell some too.

It started as a sort of joke, a challenge to myself.

I had a few cards printed up. 'Henry Green, art dealer and artists' agent', they said. Expensive too. Gold lettering on a dark green background, best quality board, and varnished so they looked the real McCoy. I took one of my paintings and went to an art gallery in Bond Street.

They were pretty snooty but I got to see the owner, or at least the manager. And in a roundabout way I asked if he'd like to take one of my paintings.

He looked at the canvas.

'This is by Verdu you say?'

I'd always signed my paintings 'Verdu'. Again, it was a bit of a joke, a reference to 'Green' without giving too much away. In case Jane burst into my shed and told me the paintings were rubbish – which she'd probably do in more graphic terms – I could turn around and say 'Oh those. They're just a few old canvasses by somebody called Verdu'. Of course, it never happened.

'Didn't he have an exhibition in Venice last year Henry?' We were already on first name terms, Arthur and me. He seemed to like me.

'I'm not too sure', I told him. 'Verdu is very secretive, he keeps himself to himself – something of a recluse. I'm only his UK agent. All my dealings with him are by email, and occasionally I get a canvas by special delivery, of course. But I thought the standard of the work stood out so much that I could hardly turn him down. What do you think?'

Arthur pursed his lips a little while staring at the canvas, which was resting at one end of his desk, leant up against the wall. He stared hard at it and nodded.

Everything about Arthur looked expensive, from his Saville Row pinstripe suit to his silk tie and hand-made leather shoes. His watch looked as if it would do everything an international rally driver, airline pilot or SAS commando might demand of it.

'I'll tell what I'll do', he said. 'Let me display this for a week or two, see what interest there is. If people seem to like it, I'll keep it on the wall and if I sell it, I'll pay you 50 per cent. You'll take your commission out of that and pay the rest to Verdu. Is it a deal?'

He held his hand out in that horizontal way people sometimes do.

'Perhaps. But what sort of price would you put on it? I wouldn't want it to go for too little. After all, Verdu's got to eat'.

We both laughed at the thought of a starving artist in his garret – a sort of 'people in the know' laugh.

'Quite. I had in mind £4,500 to start with. A sort of come and get me price. We could see how that goes'.

I told you things happen to me.

Not being a rejection, and being slightly more than the £50 I thought in my wildest dreams I might be offered, I tried hard not to give away my feelings. I simply extended my hand in the same affected manner, and we shook on the deal.

A week later he was on the phone. 'Henry, your Verdu seems quite popular. Could have sold the little piece you brought me several times over. You don't have any more by any chance?'

Did I have any more? I had a studio full of the things.

'I'll send Verdu an email, see what he says. He was a bit disappointed by the price and his cut, I think we might have to do something about that'.

'Quite', said Arthur. 'Very understandable. For the right piece I think we could ask, say, £10k. And now we know more about Verdu, I think we could reduce our fees to 35 per cent. How does that strike you?'

'It seems fair to me, but of course I'll have to ask Verdu'.

I wasn't surprised when Verdu agreed right away, and since then I had been delivering one, two, and sometimes three new canvasses every month. I had to register for VAT and everything.

A few months ago, Arthur arranged an exhibition. The whole gallery was given over to Verdu for a couple of weeks. I provided 30 of Verdu's favourite pieces. The biggest was priced at £75,000.

There was an opening night, canapés, champagne, the lot. The Press were invited and so was Verdu - although unfortunately he couldn't make it. I went along though. So did Stephi.

I didn't tell her I'd done the paintings. I said I was helping out this friend of mine by selling his work for him.

'Another of your charity cases I suppose', was all she said.

It went well. There were a few write-ups, mainly good.

Sheridan Boblemheim was particularly gushing.

Even the name 'Verdu' speaks of verity and truth; of a nature that cuts to the bone.

'The Bee' is an outstanding piece. It is a post-industrial memorial of staggering emotional impact. Drive wheels and cogs of various sizes are seen behind a veil of bright sunlight, suggesting a tussle with nature in which there can only be one winner. What might be a bee, no doubt a worker bee, lies dead at the foot of this mechanical colossus, its industry at an end.

A charred and sooty corner of the canvas bears witness to violent industrial collapse.

The piece speaks volumes of the ravages of global warming while the bizarre pallet of colours adds further to the post apocalypse eeriness that pervades the whole painting.

Well. It certainly helped sell the paintings. Every one was bought within a week. Verdu was delighted.

He was a little mystified by Sheridan Boblemheim's description of what had started out as the spokes of a couple of wheels but which he then began to think of as flowers. They were painted in pale colours because that was what came out when that day's unlabelled tubes were opened.

Old Boblemheim was right about the blob at the bottom though. It was a bee. It had got into the shed and landed on the canvas when the paint was still wet. I had to squash it with pallet knife and then paint over it with some darker paint by way of a disguise.

That's why I called it 'The Bee'. It seemed to fit in with the flowers idea.

He was right about the char and soot as well.

The painting was one of my earlier attempts. As it happened it was the very canvas I was working on when that detective person took my photo.

When I moved out, I left my painting stuff in the shed for a while. It was a bit of a mistake.

After our court case Jane went a bit wild. She couldn't find any of my old clothes to shred or bleach, so she attacked the shed. She tried to set fire to it.

Fortunately, Mrs Blakely, who lived in the house that backed onto us, noticed the flames almost before they were alight. She called the Fire Brigade who turned up in no time and swamped the shed, the garden, and part of the kitchen, with several hundred gallons of water.

I arranged for the contents of the shed to be brought over to my new studio a few days later.

'The Bee' had survived – not the actual Bee but the canvas that had become his mausoleum. A few others made it too, including one that Jane had managed to slash with a kitchen knife.

I put that in the exhibition too. I called it 'Rage'.

Sheridan Boblemheim was beside himself with superlatives:

Three deep cuts run diagonally across the canvass, forcing the viewer to contemplate the horrors of a claw strike by the wildest and most dangerous of beasts. Here the raw edges of the canvas curl inwards to reveal their crimson edges and the darker innards that have been revealed beneath.

It sold for £80,000.

After my day's painting I felt much happier. I met Stephi after her drama group meeting and we went for a meal. As before, one or two people started looking our way and nudging their partners. A small boy came across and asked me for my autograph. I squiggled something on his menu. As before, we were applauded when we left.

'Didn't know so many people liked football', said Stephi.

'Bee, bee, buzzy bee. What a glorious thing to be. Bee, bee, buzzy bee'.

| *Eight* |

Tuesday. 8.00 am. I'm sitting at the table in my dressing gown and pyjamas drinking coffee. Stephi is in her work clothes and rushing out the door.

'There's mail for you', she called out as she left.

I heard her shut the door behind her and clatter up the steps to the street. The gate clanged shut behind her.

This was a first. All my mail usually went to the Studio. I'd only just got around to having it re-directed by the Post Office.

I wandered out to the hall and picked up the official-looking window envelope. There was a logo on the outside I didn't recognise. Probably somebody trying to sell me something – health insurance, double glazing, a holiday. I took it back to the kitchen and tore it open.

It was from an 'Internet loan company'.

'We are sorry to tell you', it read, 'that your loan application has not been approved'.

There was more stuff about how reasonable they were, where I could write if I wanted to check on my credit rating, and how they looked forward to my business in the future.

I didn't bother reading it in full. I hadn't applied for a loan. Obviously, a mistake. Then I remembered what Iain had said about phishing. I ripped the letter and form in two and tossed them in the bin. Bloody cheek. I reminded myself to tell Iain how sensible I had been.

Wednesday. Same time. Same thing.

'There's more mail for you'. It was Stephi again. She left and I retrieved the letters, two of them, both in window envelopes, both with logos printed on the front – two new logos, one I recognised as a major supermarket chain.

'Dear Mr Green, Thank you for your application. We are sorry to tell you that your request to open a personal buying account has been refused'.

The second letter, from the supermarket which was apparently now also a bank, was similar except that I had been turned down for a savings account into which I had apparently agreed to pay £50 a month.

It told me that they had been trying to reach me by telephone but I hadn't been available.

Things had got a bit scary.

I telephoned the supermarket that was a bank. The switchboard was as automated as its check-out tills. I was told to enter an account number to proceed.

I didn't want to admit to an application number. I hadn't asked for one and I didn't want one. I didn't want to give it any credence. But after pressing various buttons – hash, star several times, one-one-one and others - and getting nowhere, I had to admit defeat. I entered the number.

Then I held on for the obligatory three or four minutes before a voice, a living person's voice, asked me for my application number.

I explained. I explained to both companies. I explained I had not contacted them. I had not asked for an account. I had not asked for a loan. I had not agreed to pay them anything and I didn't intend to pay them anything.

In both cases I was transferred to somebody who dealt with fraud. They asked for the application numbers. I gave them.

I explained. I explained I had not contacted either company in person, online or by telephone, until today. I had not filled in any application form. I had not asked for an account. I had not asked for a loan. I had not agreed to pay them anything and I didn't intend to pay them anything.

They asked me to confirm the application number.

They told me the applications had been turned down so there was nothing to worry about. I asked them to write confirming our conversations. They said they would. They said they would report everything I had said to something called CIFAS. It apparently has some sort of register. If I made any other applications, they would have to write to me to ask if it was really me.

I said I hadn't made any applications so how could I make any 'other' ones, but it was comforting to know. Was there anything else I should do? I asked the supermarket cum bank. No, they said, I hadn't lost anything. They had done what was needed. I just needed to be careful – especially as I was so well known. It was surprising this sort of thing hadn't happened before.

'Well known? I said.

'Yes. You are THE Henry Green, aren't you?'

'Well I'm the only one I know'.

'Exactly. You must attract a lot of attention'.

Then a thought struck me. 'Why are you turning me down then?'

'Couldn't say, sir. Might be your credit records. Might just be a mistake in the application. Perhaps you're behind with a credit card or your mortgage?

'But I haven't got a credit card or a mortgage. As far as I know I haven't got a credit record'.

'There you are then. If you haven't borrowed anything you won't have a credit record. And if you haven't got a credit record, it's not easy to get a loan'.

I thanked them and rung off.

'You're a bank that sells beans, sells beans. You sell beans, you don't care about Greens, Greens'.

| *Nine* |

Saturday. Football. Crunch match. First local derby on the 2001-2002 season, both teams at the foot of the table.

The teams were announced over the sound system. They had one of our former players in their team – Georgie Makersby. He had played for us for seven years and been our captain for two. He'd been sold for a healthy profit.

'We welcome back today Georgie Makersby', shouted the announcer. 'He scored 63 goals for us. GEORGE MAKERSBY'.

Georgie had been popular. He was a bit heavier these days, but still recognisable as the old Georgie. The crowd cheered. 'Georgie, Georgie, Georgie', they sang.

'There's only one Georgie Makersby, one Georgie Makersby. GM, MM, GM, MM'.

We settled down for the game. They booted the ball down the field for GM to chase. He reached it at the same time as Ollie Wilson, just back from suspension. There was an almighty collision and tangle of legs. Ollie collapse in a heap holding his face.

'Off, Off, Off', the crowd chanted. 'Off, Off, Off. Re-JECT, Re-JECT. Off, Off, Off.

Ollie got booked for confusing his leg with his face. Honest mistake.

Next time Georgie got the ball he was boo-ed, and the time after, and the time after that.

'Cheat, Cheat, Cheat'.

At half time we were two-nil down – Georgie had scored both goals.

'I've been getting letters', I told Iain.

'What kind of letters?'

'Letters telling me I've been turned down for loans I haven't applied for and don't want'.

I told him the whole story.

'Sounds like somebody has been playing games with you', said Iain. 'You have to be careful and all that. But this doesn't sound too bad. It's not like they've got your bank account details or anything. No money's changed hands'.

'But what should I do?'

'You've done the right thing by contacting those companies. If you get any more letters do the same'.

'Should I go to the police?'

'It's difficult. You haven't lost anything, nor have those companies. We're snowed under with stuff. I doubt this would get much priority even though you're so well known'.

'I'm not well known'.

'Don't be so modest. In fact, I was going to ask you to sign a couple of programmes for me. One for my little girl – she's a big fan – and one for the lads down the station. They don't believe I know you or that I sit next to you at footie'.

I signed his programmes. Don't ask me why he wanted them.

'You check your bank statements, don't you?'

'Now and then', I told him.

'You should always check them to make sure nothing's going out that shouldn't. And you should get a credit report on yourself every few months'.

'On myself? But I don't want to borrow anything from myself. Why would I do that?'

'Because it will tell you if anybody has been checking on your credit - either because they want to know if you are worth fleecing or because somebody has made a loan application in your name. It will also tell you who you owe money too – what's outstanding'.

'But I don't owe anybody anything'.

'Let's hope your credit report says the same thing'.

The second half started. It was as bad as the first. Georgie boy ran rings round us and their big striker nodded home another goal. We lost three-nil.

'Who are YOU?' shouted their supporters. They were a posh lot. 'Who are YOU? We can see you go-ING'

We went.

'Sorry Hen', said Stephi when I got home. 'I'm taking you out to cheer you up. We're going to that swish new restaurant up the road.

It had been mentioned in some television cookery show and since then it seemed to be full to overflowing every night.

We waltzed in about 8.30.

'Have you booked?' asked the poncy besuited man who patrolled the entrance.

'Yes. I booked earlier today', said Stephi.

The guardian of the tables lifted an eyebrow as if to suggest two or three years' notice was the usual requirement.

'And your name madam?'

'Lady Brisbanette', said Stephi in her best imitation of the sort of accent she imagined might fall from the lips of somebody whose thieving ancestors booked a cross channel ferry with Bill Conqueror.

I coughed, mainly to hide the fact that I was choking.

We were shown to our table – one well positioned in the corner, away from any doors and providing a view over the ordinary people eating in the restaurant.

'What are you doing? Lady Brisbanette! Isn't that illegal?'

'Course not. I do it sometimes. Especially when they're as up themselves as this place. So long as you don't use somebody else's real name you can call yourself whatever you like. It's their look-

out if they fall for it'.

'And there's no real Lady Brisbanette?'

'What do you think? I'll call them over and tell them I made a mistake, if you like. I tell them I'm Lady Kangaroo and that later I might jump you'.

We drank a very expensive Australian wine in celebration. One does like Australian wine so much these days, I find. Don't you know.

It was when we were eating our pudding – crème crème with crème stuffing and a blow-torched burnt sugar design on the top – that I overheard the conversation on the next table. There were four people, two couples it seemed. One of the women was leaning over towards the other.

'Yes, I'm sure it's him', she said. 'That chap, you know. I can't think what he's in, but it's certainly him. And the waiter called that girl he's with Lady something or other. And they got all that special treatment. It's certainly him, should we go over?'

I hurried to pay the bill, stopping only briefly to wonder whether I should reconsider about one of those loans I hadn't been approved for. We left.

As we walked out there was a chap on the pavement holding a camera pointing in our direction. His flash went off as he clicked away and I put my hand up to shield my eyes from the light. Nothing was said. We walked on.

'I may not be a Lady, but I think I could get fond of living like one', said Stephi.

'He's big. He's round. He shakes the ground. Georgie. Georgie. Georgie'.

| *Ten* |

Wednesday morning.

'More post for you', shouted Stephi as she left.

It was the PIN numbers I had been waiting for.

I had taken Iain's advice and bought myself a credit report – on me. Well more than one. I did it online, but I couldn't get into the report until they sent me a PIN number. Of course, by now I had forgotten the usernames I had chosen and the passwords also, so I had to look them up.

I have two or three passwords I use all the time, which Iain told me is dangerous, so I made up new ones for the credit report people. And now I had forgotten them. But fortunately, I'd been super efficient – for me – and written them down on the back of an envelope. It only took me twenty minutes or so to find the envelope. But at last I had it.

I logged in to the first report. This was for 'Henry Green' living at Stephi's address.

My credit rating was negative. I didn't have any outstanding credit card balances or any loans, so I hadn't repaid any – which apparently was bad. And I wasn't on the electoral register, which also seemed to be bad.

There had been four credit searches. But, apart from that, the company didn't seem to know anything about me – which, as far as I was concerned, was very good, but which.as far as my credit rating was concerned, was very bad.

I looked at the second report. This was in the name of Horace Henry Green living at the old house next to the studio – I had never bothered to change my address on anything official when I moved. It didn't seem to be necessary as the tenants had always pushed any post that came for me through the studio door.

I suppose I should have told the driving licence people, my doctor, Mr Hitchen or his twelve-year-old successor, and a few others, but it had all seemed such a fag and not necessary.

The report said my credit rating was good, more than good – a moment of pride.

I was on the electoral register, which was good.

I looked down the list of recent credit checks and outstanding loans. They should have been blank. They weren't.

There had been eight recent credit checks – EIGHT.

And it said I owed money. Not a little bit, A LOT.

The house and studio had a GREAT BIG mortgage, taken out only two months ago. And there was a credit card debt too.

These were nothing to do with me.

I telephoned the credit check people to tell them the mistake.

They didn't make mistakes like that, they said. They simply recorded what finance people told them. I definitely owed what the report said I owed. If I had evidence to the contrary, I should write to them so they could investigate. And I could tell the police.

I told the police.

They were snowed under. But it sounded serious and they would treat it as a matter of urgency and would be round in a few days, two weeks at most. A FEW DAYS? TWO WEEKS.

Yes, nobody had been hurt had they? But in the meantime, I should telephone the mortgage company and the credit card company and tell them my concerns. MY CONCERNS?

'Yes, sir', said the sergeant taking down the details. I made that up. I only imagined he was a sergeant. He could have been my dentist's younger brother for all I knew.

'Could you give me your name again and your address please?'

I did.

'Henry Green. No relation I suppose?'

'No relation to who? To whom, I should say?'

'To THE Henry Green', he said as if I were from another planet.

'I am the only Henry Green I know although I am sure there must be others'.

I could hear him calling across to a colleague. His voice was muffled as if he had put his hand across the mouthpiece, but I could still hear him.

'Here, I've only got Henry Green on the line. Thinks he's been diddled. Right snooty he is. Told me he only knows one Henry Green. He's right up himself'.

He must have taken his hand away because he suddenly became louder and his tone was more formal.

'Right Mr Green. As I said, this is clearly serious and a matter of urgency. We'll have somebody round to you in the next hour or two, if that's convenient.

Mr Green said it was convenient.

'Ello, ello, ello. He wasn't there. He didn't do it. Ello, ello, ello'.

| *Eleven* |

Two of them came.

I was expecting a detective: somebody in a suit and a long coat, Trilby hat, the lot. What I got was two police people dressed for a riot – a man and a woman in navy blue, trousers gathered at the ankles just above impressive rubber-soled boots, and belts loaded with enough equipment to weigh down two mules at the very least. They wore caps and had radios attached to their shoulders and earphones plugged in their ears. No doubt they could have Tasered me at the drop of a hat.

'Mr Green?'

'Yes'

'Nice to meet you sir, we've come about your reported crime. I am police constable Britmouse and this is Police constable Morpeth'.

Constable Britmouse must have been all of 22, but constable Morpeth, who was at least eighteen years his senior, had a most becoming sternness about her.

I told them all I knew. That it looked like somebody had mortgaged my house. That it wasn't me, and that I hadn't had a sniff of the money. That somebody had taken out a credit card in my name and bought lots of things. That it wasn't me that did that either. Nothing that had been bought had come my way.

I told them about the letter I had received about other accounts I hadn't opened and that I had telephoned the companies, the supermarket that thinks it's a bank and the other one, to tell them it wasn't me.

I told them about the something called CIFAS and the credit check. I showed them the credit check. I fumed, I got hot under the collar, I probably turned red and became what passed for excited in the world of Henry Green.

I finished.

Constable Morpeth stood by the door, legs apart in a 'nobody shall pass' stance. Britmouse stood nearer. He frowned.

'And you can prove all this, can you sir?'

I was taken aback.

'I just have. I've shown you the letters and the credit checks'.

'You've shown us evidence that accounts have been opened and loans have been made. You've shown us evidence that there is a new credit card in your name. But you haven't shown us any evidence that the money didn't come to you. Or that you didn't make those purchases on your credit card'.

I was stunned. Was he accusing me of some scam or other?

'Philosophically speaking, I don't think it's possible to prove a negative', I mumbled.

'Philosophically speaking, you'd be better off answering the question', said PC Britmouse in a show of bristles for which he must have come top of his class in bristle showing at Hendon.

'This is a serious matter and we've no way of knowing at this stage whether you're simply trying to wriggle out of your debts. It's no good showing me some piece of paper saying how good your credit rating is when there is clear evidence that you owe considerable amounts'.

I got out my laptop and called up my bank accounts. I showed him.

There were two accounts: 'Henry Green', and 'H Green business account'. The last I used for my 'Verdu' sales. The first had a credit balance of £3,587,307.31. The second had £5,745,089.63.

PC Britmouse looked at the screen, looked up at the ceiling, and then back to the screen. He looked at me. He looked at the formidable PC Morpeth. She stared straight ahead.

'Amy, could you come here a moment please'.

Amy could. She came and looked at the screen. She looked at PC Britmouse, she looked at me, she looked at the ceiling, she looked back at the screen. PC Britmouse cleared his throat.

'You seem to have a substantial amount of money in your bank accounts Mr Green. Can you explain how this could be?'

'It could be because I put it there'.

'So much. I know you are a celebrity and everything, but most people don't have so much money. And if they do, they don't keep it in a current account. Can you explain how you have so much money in your current accounts. You haven't, for example banked any mortgage money recently'.

'No, you can see I haven't', I said, scrolling down the screen so he could scan the last couple of month's transactions.

'And no, I can't explain why it's there and not somewhere else earning nought-point- nought-one percent interest. I just like it like that. I like to have money available to me. It's not worth the effort of putting it anywhere else. This way it's easy to get at'.

'So, it would seem', said PC Britmouse. 'But unexplained large amounts of money are always suspicious. How do we know this hasn't all come from loans that you say have been taken out by people who were not you?

'How do we know this is not some giant money-laundering operation that you're fronting?'

'Because it hasn't and it isn't. Because it's not unexplained. Some comes from a trust fund that was set up for me years ago – that's in the Henry Green account – and some comes from the sale of my paintings. That's in the H Green business account. And I have to pay VAT and tax on everything that goes into the account, so it's not all mine anyway'.

'How much tax and VAT?'

'Well at the moment I probably owe about £45,000'.

'So, not a lot in the scheme of things', said PC Britmouse. I had to agree.

'And you're a well-known artist, are you?'

'No. Not exactly', I told him. 'It's my alto ego that's well known'.

He looked at me blankly.

'I sell paintings by somebody called "Verdu". He's well known. But it's me that actually does the painting. In my studio, in Greenwich. I dash them out and then I sell them'.

'You forge them?' He had the satisfied look of somebody who has just tricked a serial killer into a confession (but I never mentioned that the victim was stabbed – that sort of thing).

'No, I don't. I don't pretend they are by somebody else'.

'But you said you did. This Verdu person. I image he might be a little put out'.

I'm sure my face took on a guilty complexion. I could feel it. 'There is no such person', I said in a very reasonably loud voice. 'Verdu is a nom de plume so to speak. A stage name, if you want'.

I imagined him back at the station. 'Hark at him. Nom de plume. They're so up themselves, these people'.

'Pays well, does it, sir?' He must have given up the serial killer line of enquiry for the time being.

'Not too bad. Can't complain'.

'Another thing, sir. The mortgage and loans are to "Horace Green". But your name is "Henry Green". How do you explain that?'

I told him about my father and my grandfather.

'So, you're saying "Henry Green" is another of your stage names. Is that right? Perhaps there are some others you would like to mention?'

'No. No, I don't have a stage name. My name is "Henry Green". That's what everybody calls me. "Horace" just slipped in because it was written on some official documents'.

'Well I'm not too happy about this. It all looks a bit odd to me. I'll have to report all this to my commanding officer. I should imagine he'd like to ask you some more questions'.

'And what about the person who is opening accounts in my name?'

He looked at PC Morpeth.

'That's not for me to say, sir. This all looks a lot more involved than we thought. As I said, I'll have to report this to my superiors'.

They left.

'He's not as tall as you'd think', I heard PC Britmouse say as he walked out the door. 'And with all that money you'd have thought he'd have bought himself some better clothes. There's definitely something not quite right there'.

He might have been right about the clothes. I like the 'casual' look. In other words, I don't care too much so long as my clothes are comfortable.

'He's not tall, at all – tall at all. He's not tall at all, and his head's too big'.

| *Twelve* |

Saturday. Football.

We have a new manager. The old one didn't last the season out. He'd come in full of hope and spent all the money on some players with names we didn't know and couldn't pronounce, let alone spell. He had a dressing room full of stars. But they were not a well-oiled machine, more an expensive collection of good quality but ill matched components. Some were a little rusty.

We were in a dire position. It was time for action. He had to go. We'd told him.

'You don't know what yer do-ing. You don't know what yer do-ing.

'OUT. OUT. OUT.

'We want Clive. We want Clive'.

We didn't really want Clive. He managed our bitter rivals. But they were above us in the table and 'we want Clive' sounded conveniently like 'we want five' which only a mere 30 or so years ago we had chanted when we had scored four goals against those very same rivals.

We hadn't been there of course, the current supporters, that is. But we knew about it because the old manager had conveniently mentioned it in his match-day programme notes.

Of course, there was no money left for a well-known replacement manager. That's why they appointed Roddy Snoades. He'd been with the club for years. He'd once been an apprentice player. He gave that up and became a kit room manager, then a physio, then the youth team manager, a scout, and now manager. He was known as a NICE MAN. 'Snoozy Snoades' they called him because he basked in an atmosphere of goodwill and well-being that went wherever he went. Thoroughly good bloke, liked by everybody – until now, of course.

The team we played liked him a lot. Snoozy didn't want any unpleasantness, so he fielded a team they could beat with the minimum of fuss.

We, in turn, were super polite. We clapped their mastery of the game, we agreed with the penalties they were awarded, we sympathised with their injuries. We lost very nicely.

'Your lot that came round looked like traffic cops', I told Iain at half time. 'I expected Morse and I got Motorway Cop'.

'They were traffic'.

I looked at him. It was a 'why the hell would traffic cops turn up to investigate a mortgage fraud' look. He understood.

'They won the draw'.

'The draw?'

'Yes, when they heard it was you, they all wanted to go. Chance to meet you, maybe even a high-profile arrest. That sort of thing. So, they all put their names in the hat. Britmouse and Morpeth won'.

'They accused me of trying to get out of a loan'.

'They would, wouldn't they. It's been known. Specially you celebrity types. Living beyond your means and all that.

'Course it didn't seem to apply with you. What with you having a shit load of money laying around in your bank accounts'.

'They told you that?'

'They told everybody. It was the talk of the station, how loaded you are. They'll probably have to ask you about that. Where you got it all from'.

'Isn't that my business?'

'Not if it's ill-gotten gains. And it's not too easy to get that kind of money any other way. Unless you won the lottery or you're a banker. Which is theft by another name.

'You didn't win the lottery, did you?'

'No nothing like that'.

'Anyway, a word to the wise. It's not too clever leaving all that dosh floating around in a current account. For one thing it's not earning anything. For another, it's a target. If anybody knows about it, they might start thinking of ways of getting their hands on it. And if the bank goes bust, you're only covered for the first eight five grand. If I was you, I'd do something about it sharpish'.

'What now everybody knows about it, you mean?'

'Well, not everybody, just the North East Kent and South London police'.

'Exactly. Anyway, it's my policy in life not to worry about money. It's not real. It's mainly just numbers on a piece of paper. I don't worry about it'.

Iain looked shocked. It was as if I'd told him I'd joined a cult. His eyes narrowed in a look he must have practiced in front of the mirror just in case his name ever came out the hat and he was given the task of questioning a master criminal. It all sounded VERY SUSPICIOUS.

'Everybody worries about money', he said. 'Even the Queen worries about money. And she's got enough. You can't tell me you wouldn't be upset if somebody dipped into your little nest egg – well big nest egg?'

'I didn't say I wouldn't be upset. I just said I don't worry about it. If it happens, it happens. I'd just have to get some more from somewhere. It just seems to come my way'.

Iain was getting flustered. Flustered and excited. I guessed he was about to start arguing with me. Luckily enough the second half started then, so I could switch my attention to an ordeal of a different sort.

It was a good result. We only lost by three goals, the only ones of the match.

'Snoozy's captain of our ship, We're a-l-l sinking, a-l-l sinking'.

| *Thirteen* |

Monday evening.

'Look at that', said Stephi. She slapped a newspaper on the kitchen table. It was the Mirror, not a paper she often bought.

'What?'

'Page five. You won't believe it. Somebody showed it to me at work, so I went out and bought a copy'.

She looked indignant, but a little pleased all at the same time.

I picked up the newspaper and turned to page five. It was a picture of Stephi and me leaving that fancy new restaurant the Saturday before last. Stephi looked great, even if her eyelids drooped a little over her glazed eyes. That's Australian wine for you – far too strong.

The picture of me wasn't so good – thank goodness. I had my hand up, partly covering my face, and the part that was showing was distorted by the flash or the nearness of the camera. But there was no mistaking that it was me, the caption said so.

Henry Green leaves London's latest must-be-seen-in restaurant, Quatraponi's in Greenwich. His companion for the night was Australian socialite Lady Brisbanette. Since Henry's divorce he has often been seen in the company of the aspiring actress and martial arts expert.

'Where did they get all that stuff? And what do they mean "his companion for the night". Have there been other nights with other "companions"?'

'No there haven't', I told her. 'Of course not. I expect they asked around in the restaurant, found out where her ladyship lived. That sort of thing.

'Anyway, what's all this "martial arts expert" stuff. First I knew about it'.

'Yep, that's me alright. Any more of this "companion for the night" shit and I'll show you. You'll have to watch all my best Tai Chi moves'.

'I thought it was some sort of fancy exercise'.

'It is. But it's like slow motion karate. So, watch out. Don't stand still for more than five seconds or you'll get bashed'.

The banter was OK, and I could see Stephi seemed quite pleased with her 15 minutes of fame. But I was upset. Upset and bewildered.

'Why's this all happening', I asked her. 'It's gone a bit too far'.

'You just have one of those faces. You know you do. People think they know you when they don't. They trust you. It's instinctive. Instinctive but misleading. Bloody misleading and totally unfair.

'The goods aren't always what it says on the package. Look at Jane. She thought she knew you. Thought you were a pushover.

'Look at me. One spur of the moment thing and I'm stuck with my little drongo for life'. She put on her actressy wounded convict look, hurt and defiant at the same time.

'I don't know about life. But a couple of weeks or so more may be bearable', I told her.

She gave a stage 'huff' and slumped down in the kitchen chair.

'Trouble is you're too nice. So nice you're bound to offer me a mug of tea any moment, and something good to eat. Or has all this fame gone to your head?'

Nice like Roddy Snoades, I thought. He was already being called 'Shoddy Roddy'.

'We're going down, going down. Que Sera, Sera, whatever will be will be, we're not going to Wem-berly, Que sera, sera - Shoddy Roddy... Shoddy Roddy'.

| *Fourteen* |

Next morning.

'There's a heap of mail for you, bigger than a Kangaroo's dump', Stephi called out as she left for work.

She wasn't wrong. Now I'd had my mail re-directed it seemed I'd instigated a deluge.

There must have been thirty or forty letters, quite apart from the usual junk.

One with a police logo on the front looked important, so I opened it first. It was from a Detective Inspector Simmons – Peter Simmons, he signed it. Could I give him a call and arrange to come to the local Police Station for an interview?

I could, and I did. We arranged for me to go in on Friday; 11.am. It was a bit early for me and a painting day as well. But then I might be angry afterwards so Verdu would be at his most creative.

'I could come later today if you prefer', I'd told DI Simmons – I would have said Peter but he was being very formal.

'That won't be necessary Mr Green. Besides I want to give you time to make your arrangements'.

'Arrangements? What arrangements are those?'

'Well I'd like you to bring copies of all your bank statements, for say the last three years. And a list of your investments. And some proof of identity, say your passport. I might also be asking you about Miss Klevity'.

It took me a minute or two to register that he was talking about Stephi.

'Excuse me? You want me to prove who I am? You want a passport?'

'Of course. It's standard procedure in these cases. I know you're very well-known but we can't give you any special treatment because of that. I want to do everything strictly by the book'.

'I haven't got a passport'.

'I find that hard to believe; a man in your position. It doesn't have to be in date'.

'I haven't got a passport and I've never had one'.

It wasn't quite true. I had had passports in the past – those temporary ones you used to be able to get from the Post Office. They lasted six months and you didn't need a photograph. But they were alright for most of Europe and all of the places I ever went.

One of the things I liked about Stephi was that despite her roots, she had no interest in going abroad. She was quite happy going to Cornwall, or Devon, or Scotland. To her they all seemed exotic and a lot less hassle than having to get up at five in the morning to lug a suitcase through Heathrow so they could tell you your flight was six hours behind schedule but here were some tokens for coffee.

'Mr Green, you're stretching my patience a little here. I'm sure you can produce some proof of identity.

'And by the way, I should advise you that you have a right to have a solicitor present'.

I seemed to have slipped into an alternative universe in which I was Ronnie Biggs' Uncle.

'Are you being serious. A solicitor? Do I need one?'

'You tell me, Mr Green. As I said, I want to make sure we do everything by the book. I know you can afford a fancy lawyer and I don't want him tripping us up over some technical detail, like not informing you of your rights at the earliest opportunity'.

An image of Charlie Aulderton flashed up in my mind. 'Fancy' certainly wasn't the word for him. I wondered if I should trouble him with this. Perhaps he wasn't the right man for the job. And then I remembered the other things he had done for me – the divorce, the conveyancing, the change of identity, and everything else. And then I remembered that there was no reason for me to feel this guilty, except for Peter's insinuations. I tried to imagine him in his underpants wearing old-man tartan slippers – not so prissy then, eh. It helped.

'I'll be in on Friday', I told him.

I looked at the other mail. One letter was from the credit card company telling me my payment was overdue but, being reasonable people, they had only charged me £78.50 for writing to tell me that a late payment charge had been applied and would I please not use my card until the arrears had been settled.

Another was from a building society telling me that it was about time I made at least one mortgage repayment. Being very reasonable people, they would not foreclose – 'start possession proceedings' was the phrase they used – provided I put my account 'in order'.

I put both letters in a new folder I had opened by writing 'POLICE' in a mauve felt pen on the front.

I phoned Charlie. I got put through right away. This is what usually happened.

Charlie speaks in that clipped way the military do, with a hint of an upper-class accent which probably doesn't come naturally to them after being dragged up in Birmingham, or Liverpool, or Newcastle. Its purpose, no doubt, was to convey authority and efficiency. It encourages people to talk back in the same manner.

I told him as succinctly as I could about the letters from the supermarket that thinks it's a bank, and the others. I told him about Iain and his advice. I told him about the credit checks. I told him about the mortgage and credit card that weren't mine. I told him about PC Morpeth and PC Britmouse. I told him about DI Peter Simmons and his request that I present myself at the police station for interview.

'You'd better come in', he said. 'How you fixed for tomorrow morning, 8.30?'

Eight thirty! In London!

'Fine', I said. 'I'll be there'.

I trusted Charlie, and if he thought I should go and see him, he must have thought things were serious enough for me to get up early.

Stephi breezed in earlier than usual. She'd had a good day, saved somebody from an in-growing toenail or something. This meant she wasn't really listening when I told her a building society was chasing me for a few hundred grand. 'That's nice', she said. She wasn't really listening when I told her about Peter Simmons and his steaming underpants.

But she certainly was listening when I mentioned that DI Pants would be asking about her own involvement.

'Involvement? What bloody involvement? You know I don't have anything to do with your affairs. When you offered a joint account, I said I was quite happy as I was. You told me we had money enough, and that was good enough for me. Just because you're generous enough to give me extra spending money each month doesn't make me "involved". You tell him that.

'Don't you go dragging me into your dodgy dealings. You can tell that rat-arsed rosser to mind his own bloody business'.

I thought this might be a little over the top, considering it was me that went to the police in the first place.

'I can take it, then, that Lady Brisbanette won't be accompanying me to the police station on Friday'.

'No, she bloody won't'.

We had a tense evening. And I had a tense night waiting for the alarm to ring at a time no human being should be expected to walk the earth.

'Gotta get up, gotta get up in the morning'.

| *Fifteen* |

Next morning.

By some miracle of weather – no leaves on the line, no wrong sort of rain, or snow - I arrived at Charlie's office on time.

It was in one of those narrow lanes behind Cheapside; between the Bank of England and Guildhall. It had probably been built by some eighteenth-century property developer and was now worth more than the whole of the National Debt at the time brick was first laid upon brick.

Once it had been a home. Now, like all those around it, it was an office. The façade was black-painted brick. The door, a high gloss dark green, bore the only signage - a polished brass plate declaring the name 'Chaucer & Co'. I had no idea who 'Chaucer' might be (except he or she was obviously not the medieval chic-lit author), let alone '& Co', or what they did. But I knew Charlie worked here.

I rang and entered. The door opened directly from the pavement onto a reasonably sized room dominated by a large mahogany desk. Besides this there was a large and well-used leather Chesterfield sofa and not much else.

Behind the desk sat a large and polished man wearing something between a well-tailored suit and a uniform. The nod towards martiality was enough to convey more than a hint of authority.

'Mr Green', he said without prompting. 'Please go up. Mr Aulderton is expecting you. He will meet you at the top of the stairs'. He pressed a brass button on his desk, which I assumed alerted Charlie to my arrival.

This was how it always happened. I never saw anybody else, only the gatekeeper and Charlie. They might have been the only two people who worked there for all I knew, perhaps they were.

I trotted up the wide, shallow, red-carpeted steps. Charlie, as always, was standing at the top waiting.

He was a tall man of about sixty-five or so and walked with a slight stoop less he bang into door frames or low hanging branches. He had long legs and arm – of the latter he had only one, his right hand and forearm had been blown off when he was attempting to dismantle a bomb.

The device had also taken away his right eye, the wound now covered with a black patch – not the sort you might find on a pirate, but one that managed to convey a tailored look; a very expensive tailored look.

He retained a military air, because he, like the man downstairs, was immaculately dressed. His shoes shone and beneath his Saville Row suit, the right arm of which was neatly pinned up, he wore a crisp white shirt. His tie was silk and tied in a discreetly small knot.

How he achieved such sartorial elegance with only one arm and a constant shake was something of a mystery.

He held out his left hand for me to shake and led me into his office. This was a similar room to that directly beneath it. It too was sparsely furnished and extremely polished.

The walls were oak-panelled, the carpet red. The only furniture in the room was an even larger desk that the one downstairs, three upright chairs that might have been knocked up by Chippendale, and a small table on which was placed a silver tray bearing a large decanter half full of what looked like Scotch, and two cut glass tumblers that were large enough to hold a magnum or two. Charlie's swivel chair was placed one side of his desk, and one of other chairs opposite. The other two chairs were against the wall.

The vast expanse of desktop was empty except for a silver box I knew to contain cigarettes, a silver desk lighter and a suitably large glass ash tray.

Charlie was a smoker, and a drinker. It wasn't clear whether this was the cause of his constant shaking, or whether his tremble was the aftermath of the bomb that took away his hand, arm and sight in his right eye.

He signalled me to take the upright chair while pouring us both a gallon or two of Scotch. There was no prospect of dilution with ice or water, so I simply nodded my thanks as he took residence behind the desk.

He lit a cigarette.

I told him again about the letters from the supermarket that thinks it's a bank, and the others. I told him about Iain and his advice. I told him about the credit checks. I told him about the mortgage and credit card that weren't mine. I told him about PC Morpeth and PC Britmouse. I told him about DI Peter Simmons and his request that I present myself for interview.

He listened quietly. When I had finished, he lit another cigarette, took a sheet of paper from a drawer and asked me to repeat the names. He wrote these down, the top of his shaking fountain pen pointing towards me in the back to front way people are obliged to write when left-handed – or lacking a right hand.

He asked me about my studio and my letting arrangements. He asked me about my tenants, and wrote their names down too.

He lit another cigarette.

'OK', he said. 'Leave it with me. I'll meet you at the Police Station on Friday',

'Should I be worried', I asked him. 'Are they going to charge me with something. Possession of a deadly bank account, perhaps?'.

He smiled in the way a parent might indulge a child. 'I shouldn't think so'.

That was it. I had been dismissed. I padded down the stairs, out onto the street and off home.

'Here's to you Henry Green, here's to you. Charlie loves you more than you will know, woa-woah'.

| *Sixteen* |

Next morning.

'There's a heap of mail for you', Stephi called out as she left for work.

Again, there must have been thirteen or fourteen letters, quite apart from the usual junk.

The first I opened was a formal looking letter from a firm that went by the name of Grigson and Hope, 'representatives and agents'. I didn't know what this meant but I read the letter anyway.

The gist of it was that a Mr Conway Grigson was asking me whether I had 'representation'. If not, I really should, he said. And Grigson and Hope were the best in the business.

What 'representation' might be, and why I would want it, wasn't explained, but Conway promised to telephone me later to discuss everything his firm could do for me. It sounded like the last thing in the world I would want.

Then there were some hand-written envelopes. Five were in the same hand. The address was simply 'Henry Green, Greenwich'. How they had got to me I had no idea.

Most of the others were similarly addressed.

I opened the first.

Dear Henry, may I call you Henry, I feel I know you so well?

I just HAD to right otherwise I mite EXPLODE.

I know your single, or divorced or something, and you see that Australian woman. She doesn't look rite for you. What does she do to herself to look so hard? I just KNOW she doesn't treat you as well as I could.

That's why Im writting. I know there is an age differance but I just looked at you and new I had to marry you.

You don't have to say yes rite away. You can try before you buy. I'm here, waiting for you. I'll do anything, anything, ANYTHING. You just have to say.

I want to make you happy, so happy. I want your children. I know you had to give up your first family. That was so noble of you. What a bitch your first wife was. I wont be anything like her.

Let me give you more children. Lots of them. Five or six at least.

I want to look after you, wash your Y fronts, iron your vests, cook your favourite meals, scrub your floors.

And what I'd do in bed you wouldn't believe.

Please, please give me a call, or just a note so I know your thinking of me. I KNOW you are.

Lucy

The others were all the same, or similar. They all gave me mobile numbers. Some contained photos of topless or naked girls. Some looked 16, some 30. One looked about 60. Her offer was the most graphic.

I was wondering what to do when the Phone range. Thank goodness it was a man's voice that spoke. It was Conway. He had the tone of an estate agent.

I obviously needed his services, he said. He could do wonders, he could make me even more famous, and he could make me a fortune.

'Thank you for calling, but you are wasting your time. I don't need publicity. I've already got too much'.

'You can never have too much. But if you think yours is going off message, we can handle that too. We can make sure people see you in the right way. That way we can get you only the choice bookings, those you really want, and maximise your earnings'.

'I don't want any bookings. I don't want to maximise my earnings. I just want to be left alone'.

'Well, we can help there too. But I can't believe you're not interested in making some money. Everybody is.

'If you don't cash in on your name, others soon will. There are already some looki-likies out there'.

'What are looki-likies?'

'You know. People who look a bit like you. They hire themselves out to functions and things. They dress up like you and pretend to be you. After all, let's face it, it doesn't cost much to dress up like you'.

'But what do they do?'

'Give a little talk. Say something about themselves – about you, that is. They give a few celeb insights, talk about their – your – childhood, things you have done. Why let them get all the money. You're the real thing. Think what you could charge. Maybe 20k or 30k, or even 100k – every day of the week'.

'But I haven't done anything. There's nothing to talk about'.

'Don't be so modest Henry. There's lots. There's that Australian lady you're with for a start. And I think her career would benefit from a bit of exposure as well. Reflected glory and all that.

'Anyway, we could work something up for you. It wouldn't have to be long. Just 15 or 20 minutes. Throw in a few names, let them shake your hand, sign a few autographs. That sort of thing. They'd be as happy as Larry'.

I felt as if I'd swallowed a radioactive rock and it was eating its way through my stomach, throwing off heat in all directions. My head was hot, my ears burned. If it were possible, they might have given off steam.

'Look, thank you for contacting me but really I don't want any of this. I think we're just wasting each other's time'.

Conway sounded as if he didn't usually get turned down – not by potential clients, anyway. He didn't give up.

'Well, you're missing an opportunity. And you'll need us when that article by your wife hits the Sundays'.

'I haven't got a wife. And what article?'

'Your ex-wife then. Jane. She's got herself an agent and she's sold her story. They're writing it for her now. Sexing it up a bit so it's worth the money.

'You'll want to respond. Better still, get your retaliation in first. We can do that'.

'How do you know this? Who told you she was writing an article?'

'Well, we keep our ear to the ground. We've got our contacts. There's that. Also, we're acting for her. It's all ethical though, it's not me that's handling her. It's somebody else.

'But just think of it. We could spin it out for weeks. She says something, you reply. She replies to your reply and so on. You'd be everywhere. Everybody would want a piece of the action. You might get your own TV show. You'd both make a mint'.

'But I don't want to make a mint. I certainly don't want to be everywhere, as you say. I'm sorry but I don't want your services'.

'You won't get a better deal with anybody else', said Conway.

'Good bye', I told him.

'I can see what your wife meant now. I thought she was making it all up. But now I see it. You're just a devious control freak. It won't make pleasant reading. And it won't be any good coming to us afterwards. It will be too lake'.

'Good bye'.

'You'll be sorry, oh so sorry. When you feel the pain, you'll be back again. You'll be sorry, oh so sorry'.

| *Seventeen* |

That night.

I told Stephi about the call from Conway – and about Jane's promised article.

'What's she saying now', Stephi asked.

'I don't know. But it can't be good'.

'What can she say? You were the good guy, weren't you?'

She gave me that look, as much to say 'what haven't you told me? Obviously, you were a wife beater and serial adulterer'. It made me feel guilty for what I hadn't done. I was sure I looked guilty; guilty as hell.

'I don't know what she'll say. Conway as good as told me they'd make it up anyway'.

'Well why don't you accept his offer. Make something up yourself'.

'I don't want to. Anyway, we don't know anything about Grigson and Hope. They might be all bullshit. They might have no hope of getting anything published unless I agree to sign up with them'.

'You're so up your own arse. One bit of publicity and you think the whole world revolves around you. I hope she tells the world what you're really like'.

This was said in a sort of mocking way, not entirely serious but even so, just a bit too serious, I thought.

'You're so vain, so vain. You probably think this song is about you, about you, about you'.

| *Eighteen* |

Friday, 2.30pm, at the local Nick. Charlie is already there when I arrive.

We were shown into an interview room and asked to wait.

'I do the talking', said Charlie. This sounded like an order. I nodded. Why not?

It was a sparsely furnished room – Charlie must have felt at home. There were no exterior windows, although the wall between the room and the corridor outside was half glazed. It had a Venetian blind hanging across it. The other walls were blank – no double mirror for hidden observations, no posters; nothing.

In the middle of the room was an office-type table – it had a cheaply veneered 'wooden' top and black metal legs. On either side were two chairs with barely upholstered charcoal-grey backs and seats, and black metal legs.

On the table was a tape recorder, a telephone, a computer screen, keyboard and mouse. Beneath it was a computer.

Charlie and I sat down on the side facing away from the screen. It seemed polite that way.

After a couple of millennia DI Simmons came in. He was holding a file in one hand and a plastic cup with something hot inside in the other. Behind came PC Britmouse, obviously let off traffic duties for the day so he could collect the rest of his prize.

The Inspector looked across at me without smiling. His fingers were as nicotine-stained as Charlie's, so I guessed both were craving a cigarette. But, unlike Charlie's office, health and safety rules applied.

The Inspector was a ferret of a man - all sinew. His shirt collar looked ten sizes too big, and his still-blond hair was thinning, despite evidence of back-combing. His lips were thin and so were his arms and legs. I took an instant dislike to him, despite his meagre long-awaited attempt at a smile.

'Thank you for coming Mr Green. As you know, I invited you here to answer some questions that we have about the alleged fraud that you reported.

'I'm pleased to see you have brought your solicitor – I assume this gentleman is your solicitor?'

'You assume correctly', said Charlie. 'Just as I told your duty sergeant, my name is Charles Aulderton'.

'Thank you', said DI Simmons. 'This is a serious matter, but at this stage we will not be questioning you under caution'.

CAUTION. What was he talking about? I had the same feeling as the previous evening when Stephi implied I had done something wrong, something, anything, but what it was she wasn't quite sure. I was just as certain that I looked as guilty as a serial killer on a bad day.

I glanced at Charlie. He was leaning back in his chair looking quite relaxed. He even seemed to be smiling. Barely a twitch to be seen.

'Not good enough Inspector', he said. 'My client wishes to be interviewed under caution so that he can make a statement, and so that that statement will be recorded. I think that is his right, but if you disagree, I will record the interview anyway'.

He reached down into the airline pilots' case that he had plonked on the floor to the left of his chair and brought out, with a barely shaking hand, a snazzy recorder that might have doubled for a mobile phone, camera and intergalactic teleporter.

Peter Simmons looked a little taken aback but his confidence remained intact – after all there were two people in front of him. One was glowing red with guilt and the other seemed to have a slight tremble of the dipso variety. 'I don't think that will be necessary at this stage', he said.

'Well Inspector, my client does, and I would be grateful if you would do the necessary'.

The Inspector did the necessary. He switched on his recorder, described what was going on, and who was present, and gave me an official warning about how they would use anything I said to put me behind bars for a century or two. My 'don't worry' policy was put to the test.

'Thank you', said Charlie.

'Before you begin your questions, which of course my client will be pleased to answer in full, he would like to make a statement'.

He didn't wait for Simmons to agree. He just pressed on.

'My client wishes to protest in the strongest possible terms about your handling of this case'. This was news to me.

'He brought you details of a fraud that has been perpetrated against him and that is no doubt continuing even as we speak. You have done nothing to investigate this crime other than doubt his word.

'I give you fair warning that your responses may very well, almost certainly will, be used in the compensation claim that we intend to bring against the police and, as is my custom, against those personally involved. Your liability could be substantial'.

Charlie definitely had DI Simmons' attention now. He was probably thinking he had seen it all before. Classic tactic. When you are guilty of something, try and accuse the accuser of something. Couple of tossers. Let them hang themselves with their own rantings.

PC Britmouse, on the other hand, shifted uncomfortably on his chair. It was clear that this wasn't what he had been expecting when he won the station sweepstake. He looked at Simmons as if to say 'it is going to be alright, isn't it?'

'Thank you for the warning Mr Aulderton. But as you don't know what I have done and what I am about to ask, your outburst might be a little pre-mature'.

'Colonel Aulderton', said Charlie.

The Inspector looked nonplussed. 'Excuse me?'

'It's Colonel Aulderton. I think that means I outrank you'.

Charlie said this while reaching down into his bag. He brought out a buff folder which he placed on the desk in front of him. For once his shakes seemed to have entirely disappeared.

'Thank you for your assessment, Inspector. However, whatever you like to say, perhaps even believe, it is clear that a fraud of some kind has been committed and that you have so far failed to address this adequately, still less apprehend the person responsible'.

'Well, we've hardly had time especially since we have serious doubts that Mr Green has in fact lost any money', said Simmons, whose confidence still appeared undented.

'You've certainly had time enough, as you will see.

'As you know, my client owns a studio in Greenwich. There is a house attached in which he once lived. Now he rents it out.

'He has had various tenants. Some eight months ago he let the property to a Dr Christian Obijho. Dr Obijho paid a deposit and six month's rent in advance. Here is a copy of the tenancy agreement'.

Charlie opened his folder took out the top sheet, turned it upside down and placed it with some care directly in front of DI Simmons – who looked down with a certain disinterest, opening his arms and shaking his head so as to indicate 'so what?'

'And here is a photograph of Dr Obijho', said Charlie, repeating his previous performance.

Simmons looked down with slightly more interest.

I looked at both agreement and picture with considerable interest. I had no idea how Charlie had got hold of either or what he was going to say next.

'During his tenancy Dr Obijho applied for a passport in the name of Horace Henry Green. Here is a copy of the application'.

Charlie placed another document in front of Simmons.

'You will notice the picture is not a likeness of my client, but of Dr Obijho. You will also notice that the picture has been attested to be a true likeness of Mr Green by one Dr Obijho. Bit of a coincidence you might think'.

DI Underpants was fingering his collar. Charlie did not pause.

'Four months ago, Dr Obijho mortgaged the Greenwich property in which he was living – Mr Green's property in fact. He made the application through a local financial adviser to whom I have spoken. Dr Obijho made the mortgage application in the name of my client, Mr Green. Here is a copy of that application'.

Charlie placed another document in front of the policeman, who was now looking decidedly pale.

'You will notice that the applicant identified himself by means of a false passport, about which we have already spoken, and various utility bills addressed to Mr Green. You will also notice that Dr Obijho is black and that my client is not. The financial consultant confirms that the man who came to him for a mortgage was black. Here is his signed statement'.

Charlie reached across and placed another document in from of the Detective Inspector.

'You will notice that the application claims Mr Green is a director of Overal Casahof Ltd. As such his income, as confirmed by Overal Casahof Ltd, was more than sufficient to cover the mortgage repayments.

'Overal Casahof Ltd is in fact a £100 company formed six months ago by person or persons unknown – perhaps Dr Obijho, you might suppose. Its address is an accommodation address in central London. You will notice the signature of the director who is supposed to have signed the confirmation of Mr Green's employment, looks suspiciously like that of Dr Obijho on the tenancy agreement'.

Charlie placed a copy of the letter in front of the Inspector who gulped audibly.

'The mortgage was granted to the tune of £120,000 – a fairly modest amount given the value of the property and Mr Green's status and supposed earnings. The sum was paid into a bank account that had been newly opened. Here is the application'.

Charlie slid another document across the table.

'You will notice that this is in the name of my client but the picture and signature on the passport used as identification to open the account look remarkably like those of Dr Obijho. Would you not agree?

'Since the mortgage money was transferred into the account, the sum of £500, the maximum permitted, has been drawn out in cash via a debit card every two or three days. To date some £25,000 has been withdrawn in cash, mainly from cash machines in and around Leicester. By a happy, or indeed unhappy coincidence, depending on your point of view, one such withdrawal was on the very day, almost at the exact time that PC Britmouse here was interviewing my client about his report of a fraud.

'It may interest you to know that since that date, while you did nothing, a further £4,500 has been withdrawn, in cash, from the account'.

DI Simmons was now almost open mouthed. His paleness had given way to a hot flush, while his eyes darted about the room as if looking for a means of escape.

'Let me get this straight Mr...., I mean Colonel Aulderton....'.

'Colonel, Sir Charles Aulderton OBE if you want the full title', said Charlie, who had been looking down at his file. He kept his head tilted and looked DI Simmons in the eyes as if staring at him above a pair of half-spectacles.

The policeman coughed to cover his further confusion.

'Let me get this straight', he began again. 'Your alibi is that a mysterious person who rented Mr Green's house simply pretended to be him and borrowed £120,000? I've heard some desperate stories in my time but this seems to top them all'.

'And the £15,000 run up on a credit card', said Charlie.

'That is precisely what I am saying. And I remind you that this conversation is being recorded. I would have thought your suggestion that my client needs an "alibi", as you put it, is extremely unwise on your part. The use of that word reveals your prejudice against my client. He needs no alibi, he has reported a crime against his property which you seem, for reasons best known to yourself, to be unwilling to investigate'.

'I am unwilling to investigate because I believe him to be telling a cock and ball story', said Simmons, who by the look of him now thought anything but this.

'And explain to me this. Your client is Henry Green. THE Henry Green. Everybody knows him as Henry Green. But this mysterious, possibly non-existent doctor applied for a loan in the name of Horace Henry Green, presumably Mr Green's real name. But how would Dr Phantom know that?'

Simmons thought he had made a good point. He relaxed a little. He leaned back in his chair with a slightly self-satisfied look on his face.

'I am pleased you asked me that', said Charlie, removing another piece of paper from his file. 'It's fairly simple really. Dr Obijho simply searched land Registry online to find out the name of the owner of the property in which he was living. I did it myself this morning, you have the result in front of you. It costs £3.

'Here is a copy of the credit card transaction that Dr Obijho undertook to do the same, a week or so after he moved into Mr Green's house'. Charlie shuffled another piece of paper across the table.

Simmons looked at him as if he were David Blaine on a good day.

'But that also raises another point. Dr Obijho only arrived in the UK a month before this. Here is a copy of his visa application. You will notice the photograph and signature. Here is a copy of his real passport. And here is a copy of his final pay slip from the hospital he was working at in Greenwich.

'You might be interested to know that he stopped working at the hospital a week before he left Mr Green's house. The hospital had previously been asked for a reference from hospital in Leicester. Here is a copy of that reference.

'I expect you will be pleased to know Dr Obijho was diligent and reliable – and far from the "phantom" you believe him to be Inspector'.

Game, set and match.

'So, we have a suspect', said Simmons.

'You seem to have been extremely busy. I am a little surprised by the extent of your resources, especially given our own current restraints. But thank you for what you have done'.

Charlie was deadpan. 'It will not do to hide behind an excuse of limited resources Inspector. You have clearly failed in your duty and I expect a full apology to my client – in writing and signed by somebody senior to yourself – together with your proposals for redress.

'In the meantime, I expect you will wish to apprehend Dr Obijho. Here is his current address'. He slid yet another piece of paper across the desk. The pile had grown while Simmons own had file remained closed.

'Now Inspector, you had some questions, I believe'.

'You don't know what you're do-ing. You don't know what you're doi-ing'.

| *Nineteen* |

Later.

Simmons hadn't had any questions after all. Neither had Britmouse.

Charlie had taken his copy of the tape and we had gone off to the pub: the one down by the river. We sat outside so Charlie could smoke.

I went in and bought four treble whiskies – one for me and three for Charlie.

As I put the tray down on the table, I noticed his shakes had returned. He downed the first Scotch in one go.

'How did you get all that information?'

'Just a phone call or two. If you know who to call, it's easy'.

'Well, thanks anyway. It was impressive'.

'It's what I do', he said. 'Bomb disposal and all that'.

'Were you serious about the compensation?'

'Bit of a frightener for them. Don't want them on your back. I'd say that, given the way you conduct your affairs, you'd be lucky to convince anybody it was anybody's fault but your own'.

'What do you mean by "the way I conduct my affairs"? None of this was my doing'.

Charlie rubbed his cheek with his shaking hand.

'I'd be more worried about looking after my privacy than looking for compensation', he said. 'You've got enough money. Forget about the police. Protect your identity. I don't have to tell you about that.

'And what's all this celebrity business? Thought you wanted to keep a low profile. And there you are in all the newspapers - not just once, but every day it seems. Letting your name be bandied about. Letting other people have access to your personal mail.

'If you move house, for God's sake, don't leave loose ends. At least have your bloody mail re-directed'.

He was right. Iain had been right too. I told him.

'But I'm sorry to tell you that I think you might be reading a bit more about me soon'.

'Why's that'.

'Because that ex-wife of mine has gone to the newspapers. Apparently, she's written some article saying how awful I am. Wife beater or something. Serial adulterer. Abuser of old people. Just the usual'.

Charlie shook his head. 'It's not a joke. Is there anything to any of it? Is there anything she can say?'

'Nothing'.

'When did you find out about this?'

'The day I telephoned you about DI Simmons and his invitation to the local Nick'.

'Well you should have told me straight away. Leave it with me. And a word to the wise – or not so wise in your case – your Aussie girlfriend may not be all she says she is'.

'Stephi. What's she up to? Do I need to be worried?'

'No, not worried. Just be careful. That's all I'm saying'.

I didn't really know what he was saying, so I let it pass. But the words came back to me later when Stephi and I were eating our dinner.

'He sounds good, this Charlie', she said. 'Pretty impressive'.

'Yes, he usually comes up trumps'.

'Expensive?'

'Not realty?'

'Like what?'

'I'm not too sure'.

'You're not sure? Surely you know what you've paid him before. When you bought the studio, for example?

'I didn't take much notice'.

'But he's a bloody lawyer. They're all leeches. He's probably planning to bleed you dry'.

'Well I don't really pay, not directly'.

'You don't pay? What planet are you on? I know we agreed not to make each other account for what we spend, but you don't think I'm stupid enough to think your little charade today didn't cost you an arm and a leg? A leg at least'.

'No. It comes out of my trust fund: the one Charlie's firm set up. I don't think I even see the bills'.

'This is getting stupid. This crocked brief doesn't let you see his bills and the mystery payments he gets from some dodgy fund of yours are on the reasonable side of cheap? And I suppose kangaroos don't jump?

'I know you don't worry about money on principle, but you're way off beam there mate'.

I didn't say anything. There was no point.

'Where'd you get him from anyway?' she asked. She was on her Aussie high horse now.

'I sort of inherited him'.

'From who?'

'Whom', I said. 'Well his firm looked after my dad's affairs. So, when I sold the

tyre business I went to them. Been with them ever since.

'First off, I dealt with somebody else. Then he retired and I got Charlie'.

'Well this one-armed coot sounds dodgy to me'.

I supposed he did, but he always seemed to come through.

'Anyway', said Stephi. 'All this police stuff must have taken its toll. I was thinking we could take a break. Maybe weekend after next'.

'Sounds OK to me. Have you anywhere in mind?

'Well, I was thinking of Outbe, Outbe in Yorkshire'.

I looked at her blankly.

'The place where you were born', she said.

'Why would you want to go there, for heaven's sake?'

'I thought it would be a good break. We could wander around the place, you could show me your old house, and tell me all the scallywaggery you got up to. I'd get to know a bit more about your family and all that'.

'We weren't there very long. My parents moved away when I was a few months old'.

'Well, where did you go next? We'll go there'.

'No, we were always moving. There's nowhere really. Let's just go to Brighton, or something', I suggested.

Stephi wasn't having it. 'Why'd you move so much?'

'My father worked for the railways. Always getting posted to some out-of-the-way place'.

She looked at me a bit quizzically. 'Your birth certificate said he was a doctor'.

'Yes. A doctor for the railways. Sort of corporate doctor. Looked after the employees. All that stuff. He died when I was quite young. I don't know much about it'.

'It's a shame', said Stephi.

'What, me being orphaned?'

'Not just that. Here you are, apparently loved by everybody, a besotted following of pervy women who lust after you, famous for being famous, and you have no close friends, no family, nobody except me. And you won't even take me to see where you were born'.

'Well there's Iain. And there's Charlie'.

'That's what I mean. I ask you who your friends are and all you can come up with are two acquaintances. You're just lucky you've got me'.

'I've always thought the Commonwealth was a good institution', I told her.

'Bloody Pommie bastard'.

'Ain't got no mother, ain't got no friends, ain't got no love, ain't got no name'.

| *Twenty* |

Saturday. Football. It was not yet Christmas and we were already in a relegation match – a six pointer against the team second from bottom.

They score after six minutes. Then they do it again after twelve. They hit the bar, they hit the upright. We get three players booked.

'You're bottom of the league. You're bottom of the league', their lot chants. 'We're staying up, we're staying up'.

Halftime comes as some sort of relief.

'You got Potty SIM Card Simmons in a right state the other day', said Iain.

'Why Potty'.

'Cos he's nuts. Works all hours. Never stops. Got the best arrest rate in the station. And he thought you'd be a nice addition to his CV. Didn't reckon on your brief though. Where'd you get him? And where did he dig up all that stuff about Doctor Death?'

'When we pulled him in, it turns out he'd been struck off in three countries. Spent time inside in one over some drugs scam. So, SIM Card got his arrest. He didn't come off too badly after all – unless your complaint goes any further, of course.

'Are you going to follow it up?'

'No. Charlie, my solicitor, said to let it rest. Said I'd probably get some of the blame for not looking after my mail and personal data properly'.

Iain nodded. 'He's dead right. I was going to warn you that you'd be on a looser. I know publicity is important to you lot and all that. That no news is bad news to you celebrity types. But believe me, if SIM Card thought his career was in danger, he'd go absolutely potty. My life would be a nightmare while we looked at all we had on you. And we'd certainly have to keep digging until we found something big'.

'But there is nothing'.

'Doesn't matter. We'd keep going until there was. At the moment you're quits. Call it a day'.

'I'm not quits. Doctor Death has my money'.

'You'll get it back. No building society or bank wants bad publicity. And shafting you wouldn't exactly be good publicity, would it?'

The second half started. Snoozy Snoades must have woken up for a few minutes because our lot had had a talking too. Some of them actually broke into a trot once or twice.

We scored. It was a goalmouth scramble. It looked like Cecil Grumasci, our latest 'sensation' promoted from the youth team and only just on as a substitute, pushed the ball into the net with his hand. But the Ref didn't spot the foul.

'You don't know what you're DOO-ing. You don't know what you're DOO-ing', the away supporters shouted at the Ref.

The game resumed. By some miracle Grumasci rifled a shot from somewhere outside their penalty box into the back of the net.

'Goal of the season', said Iain.

The goal was disallowed. Offside. Iain stood up, waving his fist at the Ref. 'EFing idiot', he shouted. 'Get some EFing glasses'. And him a policeman.

'You don't know what you're DO-ing', our supporters shouted. 'You don't know what you're DO-ing'.

The Ref waved play on. Ollie passed to Grumasci. 'There's only one Cecil Grumasci, one Cecil Grumasci', the crowd shouted. The chant might have gone on but a big centre half came sliding into the back of him, neatly chopping his legs away and leaving him writhing in the ground.

The centre half was sent off.

'You don't know what you're DO-ing', their supporters shouted. 'You don't know what you're DO-ing'.

Ollie took the free kick. It landed in their penalty box where Cecil was busy admiring the crowd. It bounced on the top of his head. Turning around, uncertain what had happened, his chin brushed the elbow of one of their defenders. He might have been hit by Mike Tyson, the way he went down

The Ref blew for a penalty.

Snoozy woke up and jumped in the air.

None of this went down too well. The other side surrounded Cecil. Somebody kicked him. One of our side kicked the player who kicked Cecil. There was a lot of shirt-pulling and head-to-head rubbing. There was probably some eardrum damage from all the close quarters whistle blowing going on.

Three more players were sent off – one of theirs and two of ours. Snoozy got sent to the stands. We didn't know what for. He must have shouted in his sleep. Or perhaps it was aggressive snoring.

'You don't know what you're DO-ing', the whole crowd shouted. 'You don't know what you're DO-ing'.

The penalty stood. We scored. The game ended two-two. The referee had to be escorted from the ground.

'You're bottom of the league', their supporters shouted. 'You're going down'.

We had to agree.

'Best game in years', said Iain.

'United till I die. United till I die. Two all. Two all'.

| *Twenty-one* |

Sunday. Early. 11.am. We are reading the newspapers in bed.

'Well, I've looked through them all and I can't see anything', said Stephi. 'Which newspaper was it supposed to be in?'

'I don't know'.

'Are you sure it was this week?'

'No. It just sounded imminent. The way that Conway chap was speaking, it sounded imminent'.

'We'll perhaps something more interesting came up. Perhaps she changed her mind'.

'I doubt she'd change her mind if there was a chance for some publicity and a bit of cash involved', I said.

The phone rang. I picked it up.

'You bastard. You utter bastard'.

It was Jane.

'You bloody bastard. You were just so jealous of me getting a bit of recognition for once that you had to stop them. You're behind it, I know you are. Bloody injunction. Throwing your bloody weight about.

'Well let me tell you, it'll get published all right. If not this week, then next. And then there'll be something interesting to say about you for a change – that you are a bloody bully, using all that money you have to stop me writing an article about our mean, boring little life together – so bloody boring that they had to make bits up to make it anywhere near interesting'.

I sensed a milli-second gap in the tirade coming on.

'Hello Jane. Nice to hear from you. I don't know what you are talking about. All I know is some chap called Conway invited me to write an article slagging you off. I refused'.

'Bloody bastard', she shouted and slammed the phone down.

'Seems the article's not being published this week', I told Stephi.

'Shame', she said, snuggling up. 'I was looking forward to finding out what a monster you are, what you're really like'.

'Your sister is your mother, your uncle is your brother – doodly-do…..doodly-do'.

| *Twenty-two* |

Monday morning.

'Post', said Stephi as she left. 'Big envelope for you. Could be your new personality'.

I padded out to the hall and picked up the brown foolscap envelope wedged behind the clock. It was from Charlie. I knew it from the scribbled, shaky, left-handed address. Inside was a scribbled, shaky, left-handed note and a couple of folded sheets.

'Took out injunction to stop article being published. Here's a copy of what it would have said'.

That was it. That was the note. It was not even signed.

I unfolded the A3 sheets. They were photocopied proofs.

'Star's wife left in misery', was the headline.

Beneath was a picture of Jane looking miserable.

I began reading the article.

Jane Green Lopez, the former wife of legend Henry Green, is living a life of misery in a grubby Hither Green bedsit.

'It's been hard since Henry dumped me', said Mrs Lopez. 'If you're married to a celebrity nobody wants to know you for yourself. I was just Henry Green's wife, the woman who supported him so he could loaf around all day'.

Mrs Lopez has found it hard to adjust since the bitter divorce from Henry that left her with two teenage sons to support. First, the former motor industry executive lost her job. Next, a whirlwind romance and marriage to Manuel

Lopez turned sour when the former waiter returned to Spain.

'He took all my money and left me with nothing', said Mrs Lopez.

Even so, she is too proud to beg support from Henry.

'He just doesn't want to know me', she said. 'He never contacts me or asks how I am managing. He just isn't interested.

'I always thought he was cold and uncaring, and now I know it for certain.

'When we were married, he never wanted to do anything interesting. He never even wanted to go abroad. All be wanted to do was sit in his shed with his stupid paints. He was just so boring'.

Mrs Lopez says she is now developing a career as a journalist and television presenter...

And so it went on.

I rang Charlie.

'You caused me some ear ache yesterday', I told him. 'Jane rang and blasted two barrels at me. Apparently, I've strangled her media career at birth. Apparently, I got some sort of injunction. Apparently, I'm a complete bastard.

'I presume this was something to do with you. Something to do with the "leave it with me"?'

'Well some of that's right', said Charlie.

'I am a bastard then?'

'Well, of course. But you did get an injunction. Or at least I got one on your behalf'.

'And that will be an end to it?'

'Well, not exactly. They could probably get it lifted in a week or so. But I don't think they will want to'.

'Why not?'

'Because I gave them a better story. You can read it next week'.

'She'll be sorry, so sorry. She'll be sorry, just you wait'.

| *Twenty-three* |

Sunday. Crack of dawn – 11.am, Stephi and me reading the newspapers in bed.

The sports pages were not good reading. We lost again, away this time. Snoozy shown the door.

Stephi, next to me uttered her weekly obligatory 'strewths'.

'Burn my barbies, look at this'.

She handed me the paper open at the centre spread. A picture of Jane getting into a snazzy BM dominated the page. It was underneath a headline that read: *Star's wife is benefits cheat.*

I read on.

Jane Lopez, former wife of legend Henry Green is a benefits cheat living a life of luxury at the taxpayers' expense.

When they divorced, Henry selflessly gave Mrs Lopez the house they had shared – a property he had owned before they married. He also gave her a handsome 'clean break' cash settlement and set up trust funds for Mrs Lopez's two sons from former relationships.

In the nine years since, Mrs Lopez has blown it all on a frivolous lifestyle including a series of desperate affairs with younger men, flashy cars, and expensive holidays. She has had to sell her house to pay her credit card debts and now scrounges off the state to maintain her in a luxury Hither Green flat, claiming disability allowance for non-existent injuries.

Seen (above) leaving her aerobics session at a local private gym, Mrs Lopez is a regular at local clubs and bars where her outlandish behaviour is well known.

Her sons, now in their twenties, refuse to speak to her. 'She often asked us for money', said one. 'Henry was a great guy. He made sure we were well looked after. Thank goodness he had the good sense to set up trust funds for my brother and me or our mother would have spent that money as well by now'.

Mrs Lopez, who has ambitions of becoming a TV presenter and writer, recently penned an article about her time with Henry which this paper declined to print when it discovered it to be full of sickening lies.

As he did when Jane brought divorce proceedings against him, Henry Green has maintained his dignity throughout, and has refused to comment on his ex-wife's antics.

That was enough. Charlie had obviously been at work again. I didn't know whether to be grateful, pleased, or sorry for Jane.

'Looks like the bitch got what she deserved then', said Stephi. 'Nobody messes with my Henry, Hey? Nobody messes with the legend'.

'So it seems', I said.

'Who's sorry now, who's sorry now. We told you so, told you so'.

| *Twenty-four* |

Monday morning.

I called Jane. The number was easy to find. She was the only Jane Green Lopez listed for Hither Green. No snooping needed.

'I read about you in the newspaper', I told her. 'Sorry to hear you have problems'.

'Phoned to gloat? I suppose you're happy now you've found out I'm having to grovel for a living. Now you've cut short my media career', she shrieked.

'What the one that's based on slagging me off? Not exactly a career. But no, since you asked, I didn't phone to gloat – or argue. I phoned to see if I could help you'.

It was true. Once upon a time we'd been happy together. I didn't hate her, despite everything that had happened. I didn't even dislike her. Well, not very much.

It was just that after she had kicked me out, some of the things she had done caused problems for me.

I moved the phone a foot away from my ear ready for what was coming next.

'Trying to keep up your public image I suppose? Mr Nice Guy. How could you possibly help me? I'm stuck in this shitty flat, I've got no money and now they're threatening to have me sent to Holloway, or probably Broadmoor, and just because some NHS wanker agreed with me that I had a bad back and couldn't work'.

'Well I could send you some money. Perhaps that would help. Not regular amounts, just something to get you on your feet again. Say twenty-five grand. Would that help?'

I could almost hear the cogs turning.

'You think you can buy me off with your filthy money. What is it you want? Some agreement to shut me up, stop me talking about you. Is that it?'

'No. Nothing like that. Just a gift. For old time's sake. You don't have to agree anything. There's nothing to sign. All you have to do is say "yes" and give me your address and I'll send you a cheque'.

'So that's it. You want to find out where I live so you can send somebody round to put me even further up shit creek'.

'Not at all. It's not a secret where you live. I got your phone number easy enough. No doubt if you didn't want to give me your address it wouldn't be that hard to get'.

'Are you threatening me? I'm making notes. I'm recording this. There are laws against stalking, you know'.

'Look Jane, it's up to you. I'm offering you some help, some money. If you want it you can have it. If you don't, that's OK. I understand. You're pissed off with me for some reason I don't understand. That's OK. I tried and that's it'.

I put the phone down. I waited. She rang back.

'How about thirty thousand', she said.

'OK. Thirty thousand. Cheque or transfer. Just a final gift for old time's sake.

'And if you want, I'll see if I can get my lawyer to help with the police. He's quite good and cheap as well. I can't promise, but he might be able to do something'.

When she spoke again her voice was three notches below the normal galactic level.

'We did have good times, didn't we? I sometimes think perhaps we should try again. You know, pick up the pieces. What do you think?'

'After you set your private detectives on me. After what you said in that article?'

Her voice hardened. 'And how do you know what I said on that article?'

'Just a guess', I lied. 'But no, it is too late now to get back together. Much too late'.

I rang off. Wrote her a cheque and telephoned Charlie to see if he could do anything for her. I knew he would be keen to put an end to the publicity about me. I imagined that he might have an agreement or two for her to sign.

'What's it this time? Been nominated for a Nobel Peace Prize, or perhaps an Oscar?'

'No nothing like that', I told him. I was just wondering if it might be a good idea to give Jane a bit of help. Keep her out the courts as well as the newspapers', I told him.

'Not too easy', he said. 'I could get some quack to say she really is suffering from some little-known back disease that can only be treated by nights out drinking and prancing around. But then she'd probably want to sue the newspapers, get them to give some grovelling apologies. And then where would I be?'

'How do you mean? It wouldn't affect you if they had to pay up'.

'Of course it would. Who do you think gave them the story in the first place? They might not be too upset about the money, but if they have to apologise, they'd probably never take anything from me again.

'But you might be right. Leave it with me. I'll see what I can do', he told me.

'Help her if you can I'm feeling dow-wn. Help her get her feet back on the grow-wnd. Won't you ple-ease help Jane'.

| *Twenty-five* |

Monday evening. Sitting at the table, eating supper. Stephi sulky.

'Why do you put up with it?'

'What?'

'All those things they say about me'.

'What things? Who?'

'All those people on your new Facebook page. You must have seen all the comments. Aussie gold digger, Aussie bitch. Fat legs. Squashed nose. All that sort of thing. Why don't you stop them?

'I know you're famous for your "dignity" and everything. But you should get off your dignified ass and give these whackas some of the Jane treatment.

'You don't like it when people slag you off. So why should I?'

I didn't know what she was talking about.

'I haven't got a Facebook page. I haven't got anything like that. No Twitter, nothing. I don't want them, and in any case, I wouldn't know how to set them up'.

'Well somebody has. Look'.

She put her laptop on the table and booted it up.

'There, look. Henry Green. And there are all those comments'.

'Not me, I don't know anything about it. Must be some other Henry Green. You won't find me on there'.

She tapped a few keys.

'Well look at this then. I searched for "Henry Green" and you're everywhere.

'There's "H Green", "Henry Green", "The real Henry Green", "The authentic Henry Green". It goes on.

'Bet you've got a website too. I'll search your name. There you are – Henrycelebritygreen.bz. Look, there's a picture of you and everything. You can't deny it's you.

'Must be you with an up yourself name like that.

'And look at your email address – celebrity@henrycelebritygreen.bz.

'And there's a forum. Let's take a look. Here, there's bloody thousands of posts. Bet there's more about me. Yes – look – same sort of thing. And here: you've replied. Look what you said: "she's not bad for an Aussie, but I'm open to offers".

'Open to offers. Effing slime bag'.

'It's not me'.

'So, you're not called "Henry Green" then?'

'I didn't say that. I said it isn't me behind all this. It's people pretending to be me. Iain warned me about it. Said there is not too much I can do about it except set up my own pages and make sure everybody knows which are the real ones. But I don't want to do that'.

'You'd rather have people slag me off. It's all right for you, all the messages about you say how bloody wonderful you are. All those about me say the opposite'.

'I'll talk to Iain again, see what he says'.

'I bet it's that bloody Charlie behind this'.

'No. It's not Charlie. He told me to cut out the publicity. It can't be him'.

'Well it had better not be'.

'Mind you, I suppose it might be, he's got a better taste in women than me'.

She threw the mouse in my direction. If didn't reach, restrained by its lead. I told her she should have gone cordless.

'You've got fat legs, fat legs. And you stink, stink, stink'.

| *Twenty-six* |

Later, same evening, drinking cocoa in the kitchen.

'So, let's have a look at your Facebook page then. See what comments you get about me'.

'You're so up yourself. Anyway, there's nothing about you. You're about as interesting as Ayers Rock, but not so quick moving'. But as she said it, Stephi had that offhand sort of fake casual tone she uses when she's being a bit lax with the God's own. Or definitely doesn't want to do something.

'Anyway, it's getting late my little drongo', she said.

'What, half past nine?'

'Well I've had a hard day, what with having to read the papers and everything. When you've been brought up in the Bush you don't get to see a newspaper until you're middle aged, let alone read one. If you can read, of course'.

But I kept on, so we looked up her page. As she'd said, nothing much to get excited about - except that her picture had changed. It was far more glamorous, hair waving in the breeze, pouting glossy lips, seductive eyes, slightly suggestive pose. It didn't look like I'd ever seen her before.

'You look like some film star'.

'It's not me'.

'Sorry? It says it's you – right there'.

'It says it, but it's not'.

'What. Somebody's been tampering with your page'.

'No. I put it up there myself. It's just not me'. She was in full shepherdess mode. There was no mistaking the strong smell of sheepishness.

'So?'

'So, I had a call from that Conway Grigson person. You know, the agent. He said he could help me with my career'.

'What they help laboratory technicians. Suppose he can get you guest appearances in a West End operating theatre?'

'No, I know you don't think much of my acting. Always making your little digs. But I think I'm all right at it. And Conway thinks so too. He came along to our rehearsal the other night. Signed me up.

'He told me for a start I should spice up my Facebook page a bit. Make myself look a bit more glamorous.

'I told him I didn't do glamorous, so I hadn't got any suitable pictures.

'And he said not to worry. They'd get me a makeover and a photo shoot and everything. But as that would take a few days to set up he'd send me a picture I could use in the meantime. A sort of stock picture they keep ready for emergencies'.

I thought about saying something about emergency wards, but thought better of it.

'He said it wasn't cheating because it would be just as I would look after the makeover. And the model who was in the picture was happy for it to be used that way. She'd been paid quite a bit and had signed a paper and everything saying it was all right'.

'Sounds more than dodgy to me. What else has he got in mind?'

'He mentioned a blog. And he's trying to get me a newspaper column and perhaps an interview or two in some magazines. I wouldn't actually have to write anything. They'd do it for me. I'd just give them a ring now and then and suggest a few topics. Tell then what we were up to, what you were doing. That sort of thing'.

Seems Conway had done a good selling job. I could see Stephi was more than a little excited. And it didn't seem to be the cocoa that was doing it.

'Well I hope Conway comes through for you'.

Of course, I wasn't happy about all this. It was bad enough me suddenly getting noticed. Now it seemed we were destined to become a celebrity couple. Goodness knows where that would lead. I might have to talk to Charlie again.

'Go, tell it to the birds, the birds. Tell it to the birds'.

| *Twenty-seven* |

Tuesday night. Football. We have a new manager, fresh from the white heat of the Lithuanian second division. He had a name we couldn't pronounce – Petras Petrauskas – so we knew he must be good.

We were up against a mid-table team come for their points.

At half time it was nil – nil. They'd missed three good chances and had one goal disallowed as offside. On the whole things were looking up.

'Old SIM Card's in a right state about your missus'. It was Iain kicking off the half time chat.

'SIM Card? I haven't got a missus or a mobile'.

'No, SIM Card. You know. Potty SIM Card Simmons. Jumped up DI your brief hauled down a peg or two.

'He thought that was bad enough, but now he's come another cropper over your ex. Thought he'd got an easy high-profile collar, and what happens? He gets word from on high to ease up. Seems a warning's enough for the powers that be, and no arguing.

'SIM Card's in a right huff. Glad I'm not on his watch. He's bound to take it out on somebody. And I wouldn't like to be in your shoes either. SIM Card doesn't forget. And he'll probably blame you for being innocent and for getting your missus off. Sorry, your ex. You didn't, did you?'

I looked at Iain to see if I could tell if he was being serious or not. He was a cop, after all. Perhaps he'd been told to find out if I knew anything about Jane getting off with a warning. Perhaps he thought it would earn him a promotion if he could finger me.

'No, sorry. Not me', I told him. 'I haven't seen the woman for years. And the last time I did she told me what a bastard I was'.

That was true enough. Not the allegation, but that that had been what she'd said. Of course, Charlie was almost certainly involved. But I wasn't going to say that.

We thrashed the other lot 1 – 0.

'OO are you. OO are you. There's only one Petras Petrauskas. Only one Peter, Peter'.

'Spose we might just avoid the drop', said Iain as we left.

'Anything's possible'.

'Peter, Peter. You are our Peter, our only Peter. You make us happy when skies are grey. Peter, Peter, Peter'.

| *Twenty-eight* |

Thursday morning. Breakfast table. I had a plan, of sorts. I thought perhaps it was time to move: retire to the country - somewhere quiet like Devon or Cornwall. I would have to break it to Stephi gently, get her used to the idea perhaps. We could take a break and spend a few days in the sort of place we might move to, casually look in a few estate agents' windows, that sort of thing.

'You're not working this weekend, are you? I asked Stephi in as offhand a manner as I could muster.

She was in her work clothes and all business-like, thinking about her day ahead no doubt, all the needles she would jab into people.

'No. But I said I'd do an "on call". You'll be at football anyway, won't you?'

'No, not this weekend. I'd thought I'd give it a rest. Thought perhaps you'd like that weekend away. Nice hotel. Bit of country air. Walk in the woods. Fancy meal. That sort of thing'.

She stopped munching her Muesli and looked up, dribbling a little milk down her chin.

'You didn't seem too keen last time it was mentioned. You don't like going away. You like doing the things you always do. You like being boring. What's up?'

'That's not fair. I just said tramping around some wet Yorkshire moor didn't sound that attractive. I thought a little break would do us good. You know, get away from all that's going on'.

'Nothing's bloody going on. It never does'.

'Yes, it does. All that stuff with the police. And with Jane. And in the restaurants. All those people recognising me'.

'Exactly. Things happen to you, not to me. And just as it seems something might happen to me, you're going to take me off to some pit in the middle of nowhere for a "quiet" weekend'.

'What might happen to you?'

'I might just be going to get a part in film. That's what might happen to me'.

'What "Skippy – the movie"?'

'I thought you'd say something schneidish like that. That's why I didn't tell you straight away. At least Conway isn't so self-obsessed that he can't see that somebody else might have a little talent'.

'What that agent? Conway Grigson? He's actually come up with something? I though he was using you to get to me - because I turned him down'.

I knew that was a mistake as soon as the barbs ripped their way out of my lips. But I'd said it now.

'No. Sorry. I didn't mean you hadn't got talent. It's just that he's in business to exploit people'.

'Fucking pommies are all the same', she said. 'You're all fucking up yourselves'.

'So, you don't like the idea?'

'What fucking idea?'

'Of a weekend away. You know, a romantic couple of days in our secret hideaway. A little fishing village, smell of the sea and all that'.

'No, I fucking don't', she said as she marched out.

Three minutes later she was out the front door. 'There's post', she shouted as she slammed it shut. 'More fucking fan mail for you to piss yourself over'.

It hadn't gone exactly to plan, but if she was serious about the film idea – and Conway was telling the truth, or something near to it – then something had to be done. Perhaps I should move out. I had the studio. It had a kitchen and a bathroom and another room I could use as a bedroom. It would be enough. Stephi could get on with her film career and I could get back to a quiet life. I thought I might tell her that evening, or perhaps the next, I'd think it over.

I mean, I liked her – a lot. But things were spiralling out of control. Something had to be done for both our sakes.

I could just go - leave her a note, or an email, I thought. 'Gone to live at the studio for a while. Needed a break. Good luck with the film. You know where I am if you need me'.

I could have done that, but after six, or was it seven years, of near uninterrupted less than seriously hurtful bantering, I thought I owed her more than a note. So that was all right then, here I was being the good guy, not taking the easy way out. And it was her fault after all, going out of her way to court fame and fortune.

I felt better already. The feeling lasted all of three minutes – the time it took me to pad into the hall and start opening the mail.

The first letter was from a firm of solicitors, heavily embossed with their name - Munroe, Munroe and Belfry.

We act for Geoffrey Porter, they told me.

It is our sad duty to inform you that the well-known painter Verdu died in an accident last week. Mr Porter is the sole beneficiary of Verdu's estate.

It has been brought to our client's notice that you have been acting as Verdu's agent, and have been selling various works of art on the painter's behalf.

In view of this, it is our duty to inform you that our client wishes to terminate this agency forthwith. He requests that, within 14 days, you inform him, via ourselves, of any works of art created by Verdu that remain in your possession and that you make arrangements for their safe return without delay. Our client also requests that you account for all outstanding monies you have received for the sale of Verdu's paintings and that you remit these funds to us, again, without delay.

Any failure to respond to this letter, to return the said works of art, and to remit funds due to the estate of Verdu will be treated as a serious breach of trust on your part and could lead to a claim for substantial damages'.

I went back to the kitchen and made myself a fresh pot of coffee.

Either I was going insane and was threatening to sue myself, or somebody, somebody who didn't know that Henry Green and Verdu were one and the same, was trying to cheat their way to ownership of some valuable daubings and a pile of cash.

Whoever it was couldn't know the details of any fictitious contracts or financial arrangements between 'Verdu' and me. And they obviously didn't know how many paintings I had in stock or how much 'Verdu' had been paid or was owed.

The trouble was, if I owned up to being Verdu there was certain to be more unwanted publicity.

I decided to wait awhile before replying. In the meanwhile, I phoned Arthur at his gallery.

'I'm sorry, Mr Beaumont is with a client and not taking calls', said the voice at the other end of the line.

'Arthur, I know it's you. What are you playing at?'

'I'm sorry Henry. I'm trying to be careful. I shouldn't be speaking to you until this Verdu thing is sorted out'.

It turned out Arthur had also had a letter from Messrs Munroe, Munroe and Belfry, and it had scared him quite badly. It seems it's not too good for business to be seen selling pictures without the owner's permission. Especially when you have been warned that that is what you are doing. And Munroe, Munroe and Belfry had given such a warning in no uncertain terms.

'You've dropped me in a bit of a mess, old boy. Seems you may be investigated, or sued, or something like that. Then how would it look? I'd have clients swarming all over the place wanting their money back, not just for Verdu canvasses, but for any old spur of the moment buys that have turned out to be not as valuable as was first thought.

'I've taken advice. The legal chappie said it would be best if I didn't talk to you, write to you, text you, or have any contact with you until this is sorted out. I know this might all be some sort of scam. I hope to God it is. But until it is settled, I can't take any chances. I'm sure you can see that. It would probably be best if you just paid these people some money to make them go away, that would be my advice. After all, there's plenty more coming provided you don't do something to put authenticity in doubt.

'Sorry old boy'. And he put the phone down.

It's always the same for us struggling artists, just shafted at every corner.

'He's an artist, an artist, he won't look back. He's got everything he needs, and he won't look back. He can take the dark out of the night time and paint the daytime black, BLACK, BLACK. He's an artist, artist, artist'.

| *Twenty-nine* |

Friday morning. 2.30 am. I woke up with a jump. I'd forgotten all about moving out for the time being.

I must have been dreaming about Verdu – the dead one - because suddenly it all seemed very clear. His son, or whatever Geoffrey's relationship with Verdu had been, must really believe this person was the one and only Verdu. Otherwise he surely wouldn't have taken the trouble to go to a firm of solicitors and issue threats. Instead he would have made a quieter, more sly approach.

Verdu – the dead one - must have pretended to be the painter of the same name. Perhaps he said something down the pub and it all got out of hand. Geoffrey had never twigged that he wasn't that renowned painter of abstract and very expensive twaddle.

I thought I had better meet Geoffrey and break the news as soberly as possible. After all, he had lost a relative and now he was going to lose a fortune that he thought was coming to him.

He wouldn't be easy to convince. From his point of view, he was likely to assume I was trying to wriggle out of my responsibilities.

For some reason I thought of those private detectives that Jane had set on me. They seemed to have found out the truth – well most of it – that time. So perhaps I should hire them to check up on the fake Verdu and this Geoffrey Porter. Yes, that's what I would do, I'd phone them in the morning.

I couldn't remember their name, so I'd have to ask Stephi if I could see her file again.

'Who you gonna call? Who you gonna call? Ghostbusters. If there's something weird, who you gonna call? Who you gonna call? Ghostbusters.

| *Thirty* |

Friday morning. Breakfast. Stephi munching on some toast and Vegemite. Me just finished gulping down some hot, too hot, coffee.

'Going to your drama group tonight?' This was my attempt at breaking the sub-zero temperature.

'Yep. Big night. My agent's popping by. Said he was bringing along a producer or something. Said they'd already seen me on Facebook and they were interested'.

'But that's not you'.

'Details. Why are you getting so autistic all of a sudden? Not jealous by any chance? You needn't be. Conway told me they are casting for the part of the village idiot, and you would be perfect. Hardly any acting needed'.

She said this in a matter of fact way, but her eyes had softened from deep frost to light chill, so I knew we were back in normal banter mode, hardly a resentment showing.

'Good luck', I told her as sincerely as I could pretend. And she thought I couldn't act.

'I need to get something under way and I thought I'd use those detectives Jane unleashed on me. Can I have a quick look in that file again, just to get their address?'

'Just checking what a good bloke you are again? It's a bit sad if you have to use detectives to boost your ego. Mind you, it's so high it must be something of an effort to stop it toppling over.

'But be my guest. You know where the file is. Just so you don't use them to check up on me and Conway'.

And with that she was gone, taking her travel bag with her, no doubt stuffed with costumes designed to impress Conway and his 'producer'.

I cleared away the breakfast things and then ambled into our room to rummage in Stephi's knickers draw and fish out the famous file.

I found it soon enough, despite the riot of knickers, socks, tights and bras stuffed inside, and took it out. By accident, when lifting it out, I also picked up a slimmer card folder that was apparently lying underneath.

I rifled through the plastic concertina file and soon found the report from the detective agency. Their name was 'Morpeth and Slim' and they had offices in Deptford – not too far away. I noted the address and the telephone number and went to put everything back. But before doing so, and only out of idle curiosity, I flicked open the buff folder.

Inside was a passport - a UK passport and three official looking certificates.

The passport was in the name of Mrs Stephanie Myers. MRS!

The certificates were a birth certificate for Stephanie Klevity, a marriage certificate for Stephanie and one Bryan Myers, and a divorce certificate for the same.

I didn't like Bryan Myers on first sight of his name. His parents must have thought it witty to spell 'Brian' with a 'Y' to echo that of 'Myers'. I could imagine their front room with its aspidistra and net curtains, Bryan's Dad washing his car every Sunday. He probably polished it too.

Miss Klevity had been born in the year she still claimed - 1952 - but in Southgate, north London, and a good deal north of Sydney, Australia. She had been married in Southgate too, and was apparently living there when she was divorced, some eight years later.

You just can't trust these people from North of the River.

Curiously, the discovery didn't make me cross. After all, we all have our little secrets. I had been forewarned by Charlie to expect some kind of revelation. And now I knew, Stephi seemed a little more mysterious, a little more interesting – and attractive - in a strange sort of way. It also made me feel more powerful. I had something that gave me an advantage, perhaps an unfair advantage. But that would depend on how I used it.

I put everything back into the drawer and promised myself not to say anything about what I had found. Not for now, anyway. Instead I went back to the kitchen with my scrap of paper and called Morpeth and Slim.

Yes, they were still in business. Yes, at the same address. And yes, I could come and see them about a matter of some delicacy. Yes, later that morning would be fine. And by the way, was I THE Henry Green. Because, they said, absolute discretion was assured.

I went along to see them, bumping my Volvo into a dusty industrial estate in Deptford. The place reminded me of the old tyre yard I had described but after the supermarket, probably the supermarket that thought it was a bank, had got its hands on it.

Morpeth and Slim were in what looked like a Portakabin, albeit a double, or even a triple-sized one. Business might not have been too brisk. They could see me at short notice and they worked from a Portakabin. But they were hanging on, still here after at least ten or so years.

I went in. A middle aged, stout-looking woman sat behind a grey metal desk. On it was an open laptop and a fancy looking telephone with more buttons and switches than the cockpit of a Jumbo Jet. On the wall was a selection of framed certificates proving the utter trustworthiness and complete authenticity of the firm. There was also a framed photograph of the same woman I now faced shaking somebody's hand in front of a banner proclaiming 'Detective Weekly sleuth of the year'. I made that bit up, I couldn't read the banner, but it must have been something like that.

'I've come to see Mr Slim', I told her.

She smiled at me in a slightly condescending way, as if to indicate that if I had a brain that worked like hers, I would have already worked out that there was no Mr Slim, and no Mr Morpeth, but that there was a Miss Slim. And she was it.

'I'm Miss Slim', she said. 'Of course, I know you are Mr Green. We spoke of the phone earlier'.

She ushered me into an inner office that had a Venetian blind at the window, another framed picture of Miss Slim shaking hands with somebody, and a low round table, set about by four chairs. These would have been modern when Morpeth and Slim set out on their road to snooping success – bucket seats on slim pedestals supported by large chrome disks. They were not to be moved without the aid of a crane or at least four Miss Slim looki-likies. But the slightly frayed orange upholstered seats were comfortable enough.

Miss Slim produced two coffees from a machine that had been burbling away on a cupboard set against the wall. It, like the table, was white. The carped was a faded purple tufted affair.

Putting on a pair of Harry Palmer spectacles she settled herself opposite me, clipboard in hand.

'First I'd like you to tell me what you would like us to do for you'.

I couldn't help but notice there was not much evidence of an 'us'.

'Not too much detail, just an overview. Then I will tell you whether I think we can help you, and what our terms would be. If you are happy with those, I will ask you to sign an agreement. It's for your protection as much as ours. And then I will take down lots of details about you and the assignment, and we will agree a plan of action and a payment plan.

'Does that sound reasonable to you?'

I said it did. Although my payment plan was to write her a cheque which would keep her going for a couple of years.

I told her about Verdu, the real one. I told her about Arthur and his Bond Street gallery. I told her about Sheridan Boblemheim, about Munroe, Munroe and Belfry, about the Verdu that had died and left all my paintings to Geoffrey Porter.

'And what, exactly, do you want from us?' she asked.

'I want you to find out all you can about Geoffrey Porter and this so-called Verdu – not me, the other one. I think Geoffrey believes his father was the real Verdu, but I need to know for sure. And I need to know what this so called 'Verdu' has been up to besides bragging to his family and friends down the pub. Whether he cut off an ear or killed himself drinking Absinthe – that sort of thing'.

Miss Slim gave a polite 'let's stick to the facts' cough. 'Well it will make a change from the usual divorce cases we get', she said.

So, I told her about Jane and how Morpeth and Slim had compiled a nice fat folder about me for her. We had a laugh about that – a kind of 'we're people of the world but that was another more innocent time', kind of laugh.

Sylvia, for that was Miss Slim's name, offered me another coffee. I signed her form, answered her questions, agreed what she would do, paid her a cheque large enough to ensure her undivided attention, and left her shuffling her papers. No doubt she'd soon be backing her Mini out of the parking space marked 'SS' and driving down to the bank.

'SS' was the only marked parking space. Signs of Morpeth were nowhere to be seen. I thought perhaps I had caught the private eye virus, what with the discoveries about Stephi and Sylvia. But perhaps I was just getting up myself.

'We're on our way, we're on our way. How we get there, we won't say'.

| *Thirty-one* |

Friday night.11.30. Stephi just arriving home from here drama group. Me with Scotch in hand, watching the box.

'Good night?' I asked. She looked a little flustered as she dumped her bag, coat and shoes.

'Bloody awful. Panic at work. Surrounded by morons. Bloody Conway didn't show, nor his producer bloke. Sent me a garbled text message about how one of his best clients had been caught out bragging to an undercover reporter about his coke habit'.

She'd come in and was peering through the curtains as she told me. She seemed more distracted than annoyed.

'Are there are some Press guys out there or are they all busy with Conway's client tonight?'

'No, nobody hoping to catch a glimpse of the Sun God. I just thought I saw somebody I recognised standing across the street, that was all. It's nothing. Got something to eat, I'm starving?'

When I came back with two trays laden with pizza slices, salad and wine, she was still looking out the window.

'Seen anything?'

'No. All quiet on the Western Greenwich front. Anyway, did you hire your private detectives'.

'Private detective', I corrected her. 'Yes. Miss Slim. Although she's not – slim, I mean'.

'What's all that about then?'

So, I told Stephi about the letter from Munroe, Munroe and Belfry, and about the fake Verdu and his son Geoffrey Porter. I told her about how Arthur had cut me off. I told her about Morpeth and Slim.

'Did you sell this Verdu chap's pictures without permission?'

I'd forgotten I hadn't told her of my very close relationship with Verdu.

'Course not. I am Verdu. I painted them all'.

'You didn't tell me that. I stood there in that gallery like a lemon while all that arty farty lot had a laugh because I didn't know it was you all along?'

'No. It wasn't like that. Nobody knew. Not even Arthur. I've never told anybody except you. And Miss Slim. And Charlie. And the Inland Revenue. And the VAT people'.

'Everyone except me then'.

'No. hardly anybody. Other people think Verdu is some recluse living in a mountain hideaway somewhere foreign'.

'Well, they can't sue you for selling your own paintings. So, what's all the fuss about? Tell them to piss off back to their varmint holes'.

I thanked her for her considered legal opinion and returned to pushing bits of pizza into my mouth while gulping down some Chianti that probably came from grapes grown and crushed within a stone's throw of Verdu's imaginary hilltop farmhouse.

'About the weekend', said Stephi. 'You still up for going away? I'm up for it, if you are'.

'What, this weekend? As in tomorrow?'

'Yes. Why not be a little spontaneous for a change, get a little reckless? You might consider buying some new socks too, while you're at it. Some coloured ones'.

'Don't know. I'll have to check the Volvo for fuel. There won't be time to get it serviced or have a practice putting all the luggage in the boot to make sure the cases all fit in. I'll have to download a few maps and things. Names of some likely hotels – no time to book, we'll have to take pot luck'.

'You're saying no; turning down a love-struck Aussie who's forced to live in an alien country miles from home and who is just longing for a weekend alone with her hunk of a man stripped down to his new coloured socks?'

Perhaps she did have some acting skills after all.

'I didn't say that. We'll go'.

So, we did.

'We're all going on a summer holiday, no more work for a day or two. We're going where the sun shines brightly, let's see if it's true'.

| *Thirty-two* |

Saturday.

We didn't go to Devon or Cornwall. When I looked on the map, they seemed further away than they had been the last time I checked. We went to Brighton instead. Just an hour or so down the road. We booked into the Grand Hotel, then went for a saunter along the front in the rain - not your proper stuff but the misty type that soaks you through and through.

Then we went on the beach and kicked a few stones about, and then down the Lanes to find a priceless antique or two.

Stephi was in one of her lovey-dovey moods. Barely an 'up yourself' passed her lips.

We went and changed into some dry clothes. We tried the bed, and then we tried it again. We put the clothes we'd changed into and then taken off, back on again, flicked through the television channels, then, feeling pleased with ourselves, we skipped down the stairs to dinner.

'Good evening Mr Green', said waiter. I might have asked him how he knew my name but there didn't seem much point. Instead we took our places and ordered the most expensive bottle of wine we could find on the wine list. It probably sells for at least £5 in Aldi.

When we got to the pudding, Stephi casually asked if, when looking for the name of Morpeth and Slim, I had come across any other files in her draw.

I might have done, I told her.

Had I looked inside?

I might have done.

'Good', she said. 'I was hoping you would. I've got something to tell you and I didn't quite know how to do it, I'd left it too long, so I put the file there for you to find. Took you long enough'.

It was my fault she hadn't come clean before now.

The gist of it was, she wasn't Australian after all. Pretending to be Australian was part her disguise. 'Disguise?'

Yes. She had been married, to Bryan. He had seemed nice enough at first. But after they married, he got very possessive. He wanted to know where she was all of the time, who she met, who she spoke to. He didn't like her going out on her own in the evening, and he told her to give up her drama classes and other things. When she said she wouldn't, he shouted at her. She shouted back, told him it was her flat and he should leave. He did.

But Bryan wouldn't give up. He used to stand outside the flat for hours. He pestered her with phone calls, texts and emails. He cancelled all her credit cards, generally made life a nightmare.

He must have copied her address book, because, after they divorced, he contacted all of her friends and told them what a bitch she was. After a while, she realised she couldn't stand it anymore. She put the flat up for sale.

On the day the sale went through she handed in her notice at work, said she was owed enough holidays to cover her notice period three times over, and caught the train to Greenwich. She didn't leave a forwarding address.

At first, she stayed in a hotel, then she found a new flat, the flat we shared.

She'd used her maiden name and pretended to be Australian. That way she thought it unlikely Bryan would track her down.

She thought she was safe. But now, she realised, all the publicity we had received had been a mistake. Bryan had found out where she, we, were living. She had seen him standing across the road only yesterday. She was worried about what he might do.

'There's something wrong with him. He just seems obsessed with me. I left him and he didn't like it. Goodness knows what he's thinking'.

'You're so up yourself', I told her.

'I knew you'd be like this. I knew you'd be cross. If you want to dump me, you can. But at least you could try and be a bit more sympathetic. You don't look surprised or even concerned about me'.

I had been trying to look both. 'Sorry, of course I am — sorry for you and concerned about what will happen. This is my sorry and concerned face. I just don't have your thespian skills'.

I did sympathise with her, I really did. But in the scheme of things, Bryan couldn't be such a big problem. I was sure we could do something to make him back off. It might even help persuade Stephi to move to Cornwall — or if not Cornwall, perhaps Brighton.

'It's no joking matter', she said. 'What should we do? He made my life a misery before and he'll probably try and do it again'.

'Where did you meet him?' I asked in my concerned and sorry voice. 'And what about your parents, surely they must be wondering what has happened to you?'

Stephi bit her lip before taking another mouthful of wine. 'The thing is, I don't have any parents. I was abandoned when I was a baby. Nobody owned up to being a parent.

'Apparently, I was adopted, although I never met the people who were supposed to be my parents. They were civil servants and soon after they adopted me, they went off to live abroad – Australia, I think. They left me with a nanny.

'It was all very swish – there wasn't any hardship or anything. I went to a posh school. I had everything I could have wanted – except for parents. There weren't any other kids and the nannies came and went.

'When I was eleven, I got shipped off to boarding school. I didn't go home for the holidays; there was no point.

'When I was eighteen, some man who said he was a friend of my father, came and told me my parents were dead. He gave me some money, enough to buy a flat, and told me that from then on, I had to make my own way in the world.

'He'd arranged for me to become a student nurse. It was a "good start", he said. So, I went along with it all.

'Turns out I was quite good at it. I got qualified, then I got promoted. I took an Open University Degree and went into Haematology. I got promoted again and then I bought the flat with the money he had given me, the first one'.

'All sounds a bit austere. It's amazing you're still sane. Perhaps that explains it all'.

'Beast', she said, but she wasn't cross.

'How did you meet Bryan then?'

'I met him at a demonstration'.

'A demonstration of what?'

'No, not of anything. It was a demonstration against something. Well, for something really. It was an animal rights demonstration'.

'Come on. You'd kick a cat as soon as look at it. You're hardly into animal rights. You're not that good on human rights'.

She ignored the last bit. 'I'm not. I wasn't then either. It's just that this girl I worked with was. I used to go to art classes with her. We got friendly and she asked if I'd like to go to a demo with her. I didn't want to upset her and I thought it would be interesting – a bit of excitement – so I just went along.

'I went with her to some foxhunt. We laid a trail of aniseed buns so the dogs would all run off in the wrong direction. And then we went to some pub where they were all supposed to meet before the hunt so we could make a nuisance of ourselves by shouting out things and getting in the way of the horses.

'Nobody got hurt, although one chap spilt his drink down his nice red jacket.

'There were a few police around. After a while we got fed up and wandered off. And on the way back to the railway station I met this chap. He seemed to know a lot and he was reasonably good looking. And when he asked if I wanted to go for a drink the following week, I said I did.

'After that it all went rather quickly. Within a month he'd moved in. He was some sort of carpenter or builder. A kind of odd job man. He had a van with lots of tools in the back. But he didn't work too hard. He spent most of his time on animal rights'.

'And you married him?'

'Yes. I kind of tricked him really. We went away on this demo in Norfolk. It was against battery farming, and it was my birthday. I told Bryan I had some money saved up – which was true – and that I'd like to spend some of it on a nice hotel for the night.

'He didn't like the idea but he went along with it. The hotel was right next to the town hall. So, as we left the hotel the next morning, I said wouldn't it be great if we just went inside and got married.

'He said it would be but you had to book these things up months in advance and you had to have a licence. I said, 'so, if we had all that, you would marry me right now?'

'He said yes, of course he would. Then I told him that I had booked it up, I had a licence, and we had twenty minutes to spare.

'He made a few excuses about having to have witnesses and how he wasn't dressed for the occasion and he wanted to make me proud – all that stuff. But I told him he would make me proud however he was dressed and that I had everything covered.

'I could see he didn't want to do it. But he had no choice really. So, we went in and I came out as Mrs Stephanie Myers.

'It was all right at first. Good. Then you know what happened'.

'And you said Bryan wanted to control you. Sounds a bit the other way to me', I told her. 'This Bryan doesn't sound too scary. Perhaps I could put Miss Slim onto his case. Or get Charlie to sort him out.

'But I've got something to tell you as well, something that might change things a little, and also something to suggest. And it might be better if I did that in our room', I told her.

She thought I had other things in mind. 'This is serious', she said. 'And all you can do is joke about it. And you haven't even got your new socks yet'.

'I promise you, I'm deadly serious too. Let's go up and raid the mini bar and talk things over. There's something you don't know about me. Not even Morpeth and Slim have an inkling'.

She looked a little dubious. 'I don't think they have mini bars any more. We'll have to take a bottle. I think I could do with another drink'.

We ordered another bottle of the Aldi special, I signed the bill, and we went back to our room.

'So why Australian', I asked.

'I just used to dream that my parents had gone there on one of those £10 tickets but couldn't take me straight away because they knew it would be so awful to start with. They were just getting things ready had forgotten to take me. I imagined they'd send for me as soon as they were established.

'That, and the fact that when I was growing up, I liked Skippy so much the other kids at school said I might as well be Australian'.

'Stephi had a dream – to join her fam-ily – in Australia, Australia'

| *Thirty-three* |

Saturday evening. 9.30. In our room at the Grand.

Stephi kicked off per shoes. 'So, what's all this about then. Are you going to confess to scratching the Volvo, or something even worse? Perhaps the paper shop gave you the wrong change?'

'I haven't been entirely honest with you', I said. 'You had your secret, and I had mine'.

'You've got another woman I suppose. Is that what it's all about. Got fed up with me and found somebody else. I suppose she's younger and prettier. One of your groupies, I expect.

'Fair dinkum. It was good while it lasted. If you want to believe all that stuff they tell you, it's up to you. You can piss off'.

'First', I said in what I imagined to be a dignified but hurt sort of way, 'now we are being honest, perhaps we can cut all that Australian crap. No more "dinkums" or "billabongs" if that's all right. It gets a little wearing.

'Second, there is no other woman. I like being with you. But if you want me to leave, I will, as you say, piss off. Just say the word.

'But if you do want me to go, please tell me now, before I say what I'm going to say'.

She looked a little taken aback. 'Fair do's mate', she said. 'I suppose I could put up with you for a few more weeks'.

I sat on the bed. 'The truth is, I'm not Henry Green'.

'What are you then. One of Conway's looki-likies'.

'No, I am Henry Green, Horace Henry Green in fact. But that was not the name they gave me when I first came bawling and bellowing into this world'.

I could see she still hadn't quite grasped what it was I was trying to tell her.

'Next you'll be telling me you're not called "Henry" because your father was known as "Horace" because your grandfather was called "John".

'You seem very good at saying what you're not called. You're not called Horace or Verdu. Now what is it you're not called'.

I told her my story. I thought it would help and it wouldn't put her in any more danger than she already was from Bryan.

'Horace, Horace, you're so boring. Tell her the story you've been storing'.

| *Thirty-four* |

Friday, 3 September 1971. Belfast.

It had been raining all afternoon – that sort of stodgy rain that Belfast specialises in. Even so, we'd gone to the playing field for a kick-about after college ended.

I have to own up to you now. My father was not Horace Green, my grandfather wasn't John Green either. And I'm not Henry Green. Well I am – now. But I wasn't then. I was Henry Grimond. It might not mean much to you, but it does to some people.

There we were, living in Belfast. I wasn't born there. My parents moved there when I was 15. I was at boarding school at the time, so I didn't see much of the place – or them either – until I was 18 and at art school. By then I was apparently old enough – just – to make my own decisions, so I was allowed to come to Belfast and live with my parents. I'd say 'at home', but it wasn't much of a home really.

For a start, my parents were rarely there. My father was some sort of policeman or soldier. I'm not sure which. He never talked about his work. He didn't wear a uniform but I noticed that when he had people come to the house, usually late at night, they often addressed him as 'Sir'. I sometimes caught other snippets too; usually about 'operations' or 'stop and search', or arrests.

What my mother did, I had no idea. But it also involved strange hours and hardly being home.

They had separate rooms and I noticed the light was often on in my mother's room late into the night.

I was left pretty much to my own devices - which meant plenty of sports and plenty of drinking after classes.

I enjoyed the course. It was a relief to be so free after the confinements of boarding school. The others in my year were all OK. We got on well, although I must have been awkward with the ones wearing skirts – not having seen much of them close up before.

Anyway, it was mid-way through my third year, and as I said, we'd gone to the Rec for a kick-about. Afterwards, three of us went to the pub for a pint or two. It wasn't much of a pub, a bit dingy with the main concession to decoration being the soggy beer mats on each of the tables.

We took possession of a corner table.

Tock, Alfred Clock to you, left after twenty minutes or so. He had a date with one of that skirt-wearing fraternity – or should it be 'maternity'. That left Kieran and me with fresh pints of stout and no particular place to go.

After solving the world's monetary crisis and third world poverty, Kieran decided he had better take a piss. He took himself off to the Gents.

Almost immediately a short swarthy man came through the main doors. He was wearing what I imagined to be seamen's clothes – a navy blue serge reefer and one of those tight-fitting knitted hats, also blue. He was carrying a sports bag. He looked around, saw me, and came over.

'Henry?'

'Yes, you've got your man'. He was not from Belfast, that was for sure. His English was good enough but he spoke in an accent I couldn't quite place. I guessed he had mistaken me for somebody else, it happened all the time.

'Or perhaps it's another Henry you're looking for?' I told him.

'No, the message for Henry. They told me, you go to Fighting Cock pub. There you find Henry and tell him message'.

I wanted him to move on, so I could finish my pint, but he didn't seem too keen on moving.

'Well, I don't think it's me you want. But tell me anyway', I said.

'I understand. It not you. You not here. I never see you. But tell your friends that the place to come is 28 Albermarle Street. It a warehouse near to docks. The gates closes 10.30 at night. You tell them have lorry come just before. If all OK, everything will be put inside, no questions. You don't see us, we don't see you. Just the driver.

'This all clear?'

'Crystal', I said.

'I not understand. All clear, or no?'

'Yes, all clear'. I had no idea what he was talking about.

As he went to move away, I noticed Kieran coming back into the bar. When I looked around the man had gone.

'I'll be off. You coming?'

Our buses went in opposite directions, from different bus stops, so there was no point walking out together.

'No, I'll just finish my pint and follow on'.

I was about to drain the glass when somebody else came into the pub. He was taller than the first stranger, a little older than me and a little awkward in his gangly raw-boned frame. He was also looking around the room.

One mistaken identity a week was quite common, two in one day was not. He obviously didn't know this, because he came straight over and dumped his bag under the table.

'Henry?'

'I'm your man'.

'Good. I was afraid you'd be gone. Sorry I'm late, had to be careful, check-points everywhere. You know how it is. I needed to be careful'.

At that time everybody had to be careful in Belfast.

'Anyway, I'm here now, so no damage done. What's the address?'

'A warehouse in Albermarle Street – number 28', I told him. I was pleased to be able to do a good deed.

'The gates close at 10.30 at night, so the lorry is to be there just before'.

He nodded. 'It'll be there'.

Without another word he picked up his bag and left.

When I went to leave, a few minutes later, I realised the bag under the table wasn't mine. I guessed Kieran had taken mine by mistake. We'd have to swap back again on Monday. No problem. I took the bag and caught the bus home.

I climbed up to the top floor. There were only two other people up there, sitting at the other end.

And I got to thinking that the stranger had been right. It paid to be careful in Belfast. So, I brought the bag onto the seat and unzipped it, just to make sure there wasn't a bomb inside by any chance. There wasn't. It was stuffed full of money. BIG BUNDLES of £50 notes. There must have been at least 200 in each bundle - £10,000. And there must have been about 200 bundles. Two million quid.

I zipped the bag up again and put it carefully down on the floor – more carefully that if there had turned out to be a bomb inside.

The only thing I could think was I had somehow got involved in some shady deal between some very dangerous people.

I remembered hearing my father say the Provisionals had just taken charge of the IRA's munitions, and they hadn't been impressed with what the found. When they came to dig up the promised arsenal, they found that most of the revolvers and rifles were Word War I vintage. And there were not too many of them either, nor explosives stable enough for even the most unstable volunteers to consider fashioning into workable bombs.

The boys were now busy re-arming and the chances were the money I now had under my seat was to pay for a delivery.

My guess was that my second unwanted visitor, the buyer, so to speak, was supposed to have been sitting in the pub before the seaman, the seller, arrived. When he got there, they should have exchanged information and bags, and gone their separate ways, the seaman taking the cash, and the volunteer taking the bag the seaman had been carrying when he arrived – which for appearances sake, was probably stuffed with newspaper.

Because the timing went wrong, and because they both I assumed I was the person they were supposed to meet, the seaman had gone off with a bag stuffed with my sweaty football shirt, shin guards and very muddy books.

The volunteer had left with a bag full of newspaper, and I had gone off with the money – the money that must belong to the Volunteers and intended to restock their Semtex cupboards and gun racks.

It couldn't be good – especially for me. Misunderstanding, mistake or whatever, I didn't think they'd be too amused. I wouldn't be keeping the money. I needed to be handing it back to the boys as soon as possible – or get some serious protection.

When I got back to the house there was, as usual, nobody in. I didn't think I'd stay around too long either. They had my bag and there must be something inside that would lead them to me – to here.

So, I scribbled a note to my father and put it in an envelope and slipped it under his door: this was always locked when he was not there and nobody was allowed inside. I told him there'd been a mistake. Somebody had handed me some money, a lot of money, that was meant for somebody else. And something was happening at 28 Albermarle Street at 10.30 – I didn't know what day, but very soon, probably today.

I went down the garden and put the bag of money into the shed, behind the mower. And then I left. It seemed the best thing to do.

It was now past seven and most things were closed. I was wet and cold, and afraid. I went to the cinema. I couldn't tell you what I saw. I didn't pay attention. I was more interested in the audience – who was coming and going.

Sometime after ten I went back to the house. There were lights on, so I went in. I could hear voices, one of which was my father's. They weren't raised, so I guessed everything was all right.

They heard me come in. My father came out of his office.

'Thank Christ you're back. I was thinking the worst'.

I explained again what had happened and why I had gone out.

'You did right. You did well', said my father.

'Of course, it's bloody inconvenient. That's the end of art school for you. We'll have to whisk you away somewhere. They're bound to think it was a set up and you were in on it. They're not going to let that rest for quite some time.

'Bloody good sting though. You did well. Wish I'd thought of it myself'.

It was all gung-ho, officers' mess stuff. He was almost rubbing his hands in glee

'Sergeant Reynolds here will take you off somewhere safe tonight. I'll come over in the morning and we'll talk this through. Meanwhile we need to recce this Albermarle Street address. That's a new one on us.

'Well done again'.

With that I was dismissed. He turned back to his desk and the two other people in the room. In the hallway was a soldier in full combat dress.

'Come with us', he said. 'We'll fetch all your stuff tomorrow'.

He and another soldier bundled me up the drive towards an armoured personnel carrier. On the way up the drive we met my mother, just back from wherever she'd been.

'You off? Sergeant Reynolds will look after you. See you tomorrow'. She waved in an off-handed way without actually looking round, and disappeared into the house.

'Let's get moving', said Sergeant Reynolds.

That was the last I saw of either of my parents.

They put me in what might have been a cell. It was a bare room with no furniture other than a wooden chair and table, and an iron-framed bed on which lay one of the thinnest mattresses I have ever seen. There were bars across the only window which was high up in the wall – too high to look out of.

They even brought me some food on a tray. It consisted of something that was mainly baked beans in a metal mess can and not too hot, and very sweat tea in an enamelled mug.

Both were still on the table the next morning when some predecessor of Charlie came knocking on my door. He was as well turned out as Charlie but not so mutilated – only a finger or two missing – and not so shaky.

'Bad news', he announced.

'Sodding IRA up to their tricks again. Got your parents. Sorry to say you're an orphan now. They've detailed me to take care of things for now. Put you out of harm's way'.

That was it, as far as sympathy went. I'd got my parents killed and lost the only family I had. It was a shock but, as I hardly knew them, I can't say it was a personal tragedy. I might as well have been an orphan from the word 'go' and was used to looking after myself.

Major Hubon, for this was the name of my new six fingered counsellor, told me what he knew about what had happened.

It seems, a couple of hours after I was given secure board and lodging for the night, a white Ford Transit came speeding around the corner into our road. Without so much as a hand signal or indicator flash, it swerved into our drive, stopping only a foot or two from the garage doors. At this point a man in full IRA combats – black top and balaclava – jumped out and ran to the road and jumped onto the back of a motorbike that had conveniently, and momentarily, slowed down from its former ninety-miles-an-hour to near walking pace.

The motorbike driver didn't greet his passenger with friendly chit chat, nor even wait for him to put on a crash helmet. He simple gunned it down the road before Sergeant Reynolds or any other of his unit had time to shout 'who goes there', or whatever else it is they say on such occasions, or to indulge in any gunnery of their own.

Ten seconds later there was an almighty explosion and our house, or most of it, and my parents, were no more.

But this was war, said Major Hubon. My parents knew the risks they were taking. And they had done so much for their country. Even last night, before the bombing, my father had arranged an operation against the address in Albermarle Street. It had yielded spectacular results.

He had been a brave man. And I, apparently, had done the right thing. I had been extremely 'useful', which was obviously nice to know.

Now they had to do something to spirit me away. After all, we didn't want to hand the IRA any propaganda victories.

I took this to mean it wouldn't look too good if they were allowed to kill me.

They would find me a new identity and a place to live where the IRA would be unable to find me. And I was not to worry. They would make sure I had some money. What with cutbacks and tight budgets and the like, this wouldn't be a fortune but it would be enough to live on –

provided I was careful – at least until I could get onto my own two feet.

I was not to worry, all would be taken care of.

It didn't sound too promising. So, I mentioned the £2m hidden away in the shed which, as it was at the end of the garden at the back of the house, might still be standing. Couldn't, perhaps, that be used to fund my allowance?

'I think that might work', said the Major. 'If anybody asks you, say the money was in the house. They'll like that; the boys blowing up their own money. That way it won't appear in the books and my friends will be able to set something up for you. And it won't be a drain on our budget. Yes, that would definitely work'.

So that's what happened. They found out some family, a doctor, his wife, daughter and son, who was my age, had been killed in a motor accident in Yorkshire. Coincidentally the boy was also called 'Henry' although this had been his middle name. They got a copy of the son's birth certificate, applied for a passport in his name, but with my picture, and gave them both to me. They set up the Lichtenstein blind trust, gave me a telephone number to call in emergencies, took me on an Army transport to Northolt airport and sent me on my way with a train ticked to London.

This was the story I told Stephi some thirty and a bit years later. It was the first time I had told anybody else. Of the people I knew, only Charlie knew the truth.

'You're on the road to nowhere, road to nowhere, nowhere, nowhere'.

| *Thirty-five* |

Saturday evening. 10.30pm in our room at the Grand.

'You bloody bastard', said Stephi.

'I know. I'm sorry. Nothing has happened for such a long time. I didn't think you'd be in any danger. You're not, as far as I can tell. But I should have told you before. As soon as all this publicity thing started'.

'It's not that', she said.

'Well, what is it?'

'It's every time I tell you something, you have to go and top it with some bullshit of your own. Some bloody story that shows how wonderful you are. You're so up yourself'.

I suppose she had a point.

'She's so beautiful, she's so beautiful'.

| *Thirty-six* |

Sunday morning. 2.30 am in bed, in our room at the Grand.

Stephi: 'Do you really think we are in danger?'

'Well, I suppose a little. Not too much. Charlie doesn't seem to be jumping up and down too much. He's just saying I shouldn't keep getting my name in the papers.

'It was all so long ago. There's been the peace process and all that. There must be a few people still around who remember that night, who are still pissed off with me. But whether they've still got the fight and the bitterness in them to do anything about it − even if they do find out where I am − well I doubt it'.

'But it wasn't always like that', said Stephi. 'You must have been more scared than a croc when it sees a handbag, to start with, at least'.

'Well, perhaps for a while. But I soon got fed up with it. I reckoned that if I was going to ruin my life by looking over my shoulder all the time, then they might as well have blown me up that night as well. So, I made a policy decision. I was not going to worry. Not about anything, except football'.

Stephi sat up. It was dark in the room, almost pitch black, so I could just about make out her outline. But I could feel her staring at me.

'What are you talking about? You can't just blot out something like that with a POLICY DECISION. You're nuts'.

'No, look at it my way. I had a new name, plenty of money, people looking out for me. I had Bill Shankly. I was living comfortably, doing whatever I liked doing. So why ruin it all by worrying? If they caught up with me, something nasty would happen for sure. But they might not. And there was nothing I could do about it except keep a low profile. The deed had been done. So why worry?

'Things changed a bit when my name started getting into the papers. When there were pictures to go with the name, when you started being mentioned, and started talking about getting into films. That made me think I should do something to tone things down. But for your sake, not mine'.

'Do what? Ditch me and run off with another new name?'

'No. Nothing like that. I care about you. That's the trouble. I wouldn't blame you if you wanted to leave. I'd understand. But if you want to stay with me, then we need to quieten things down a little.

'I thought we might move. To the country perhaps. You could retire. You don't need to work. We've got more than enough money. We could find some new interests – whatever it is you pretend Aussies like doing these days'.

'Get real', she said. 'We'd stick out like sore thumbs in some country village where everybody knows everybody else's business. We'd be sitting ducks. The best place to be is somewhere crowded, like London.

'Anyway, what's all this about this Bill Shankly character?'

'Legend, please. Manager of Liverpool. FC. About 30 years ago. He made them good. And he said that football is not a matter of life and death. It's much more important than that. So, I thought I'd take his advice and channel my anxiety into football instead of those less important life and death things. Football is serious, life is just a game. That would stop me going mad.

'Didn't work then', she huffed with only the slightest of grins.

'So, you're not leaving me?'

She flopped back down in the bed. 'What and miss all your witty repartee. Miss out on hearing how wonderful you are every five minutes. I'll think about it. I'll let you know my policy decision'.

'We're go-ing to Wem-berley, Wem-berly. We're go-ing to Wem-berly'.

| *Thirty-seven* |

Sunday morning. 3.45 am, in bed, in our room at the Grand.

'So, all that work I did was a complete waste of bloody time'.

It was Stephi again. I didn't know if she'd been back to sleep, but she was wide awake now.

'All what work, light of my life, carrier of my dreams and hopes?'

'Piss off. You know bloody well. All that time I spent in the Family Records Office getting birth certificates, marriage certificates; all that crap. They were all bloody lies, bloody worthless lies.

'Truth is, I don't know you at all'.

'Pot, kettle', I made the mistake of mentioning.

'Don't you bloody pot kettle me mate. I didn't get my parents killed and run off with a couple of million quid'.

She said this in a whisper, but as near to a shout that a whisper can get.

'OK. But there are similarities. Even a bushwhacker would admit that. We were both innocents caught up in something.

'Anyway, you do know me. It's not as if I'm a secret trani, a closet gay, or perhaps a paedo'.

'What, you think that because your sexual orientation matches Mr average that I should be grateful? Do me a favour. You might be more interesting if you were a trani.

At least I could talk about shoes with you. Perhaps I'd even get you to watch Strictly Come Dancing'.

'Now you're being stupid'.

'Why? Because I think it better not to be lied to?'

'No. Thinking I'd ever watch Strictly Come Dancing'.

She had to concede that point.

'No. What I mean is that I am like Popeye. I am what I am and that's all what I am.

'You get what you see. A change of name didn't make me a different person. I'm still me. I still have the same opinions – well almost – I still react the same way. It's just that you didn't know the name I used before, a very long time before I met you.

'I didn't tell you about what happened when I went to the pub one night in 1971. But there was good reason for that. I'm not suddenly a different person because of that.

'Anyway, I don't know you, obviously. All those dark secrets. If I'd known you came from across the river, well things might have been different. Who knows what goes on up there?

'Suppose we try and get to know each other a little better?'

'You're not wheedling into my knickers that way', said Stephi.

'You're not wearing any'.

'That's all right then'.

'Knowing me, knowing you (a-ha), there is nothing we can do'.

| *Thirty-eight* |

Sunday afternoon. 4.30pm, driving home after a lunch at the Grand.

Me: 'So what shall we do then?'

'How do you mean?'

'Well do you want to ditch me? Do you want to run off with me and settle down in the country – forage for food? That sort of thing? Or do you want to carry on as we were?

'Christ. I thought you were the one with the "no worries" policy. Well I've taken a leaf out of your book. I've decided I've no worries either. I'll be just like you. Well, not just like you – obviously nobody would want that.

'No, I'll just let other people sort out my sodding mess and not worry about it. I'll take what comes. Even if it does mean living with a walking disaster for the rest of the few months left to me - a boring walking disaster with a Volvo who pretends to be somebody he's not'.

It was low grade stuff. An attempt at Aussie humour.

'Really?'

'Really. Although I might cool it a bit. I might tell Conway that his sodding Grigson and Hope have got no hope. I'll tell him to forget the film roles and all that Mrs and Mrs stuff'.

'Sorry. What's this about Mr and Mrs. Did he say we should get married? Is this a negative proposal or something?'

'What, you think I would want to not marry you? You must be out of your mind'.

'It's a proposal then?'

'I said I wouldn't worry. I didn't say I was doolally. Mrs and Mrs: it's a television show where they ask couples stupid questions. They're supposed to guess what the other one would say.

'Conway said it would be "good exposure". He said it would help me. He didn't say it would make me look bloody stupid because I didn't know any of the answers'.

'And you thought I'd go along with it; this television malarkey?'

'Well, not now, obviously. Not now I know how much I don't know about you. Course not. You're too boring anyway'.

She was in a jolly mood – relieved, I suppose.

'Pot, kettle', I said. 'It's a negative, negative proposal then?'

'If you like, my little drongo'.

'Then I accept'.

'Good', she said. 'But you'll have to get something done about that ex-husband of mine. Get your own personal minders on to it or something. Nothing too drastic. Just something that will scare the shit out of him and leave him a whimpering wreck'.

'I'll see what I can do'.

'And obviously I want a big wedding. We can sell the pictures to Hello! magazine. We'll be in all the papers'.

'Get lost'.

'Here's to you, Stephi Green, Henry loves you more than you will know'.

Half Time

Meeting in the park

| *One* |

Thursday before Christmas, 6.30 in the evening. Stephi is at her drama group – final rehearsals before the big day - I'm at home opening Christmas cards.

We've been getting about fifty a day and, after the first batch or two, we had been putting them to one side. We had started by opening a few. Most were from people we didn't know. Some even wished us a happy Christmas. The rest were an assortment of begging letters – asking for autographs, pictures, telephone calls, visits, or money – abuse and offers of marriage or sexual favours. A few contained knickers.

We made a decision to throw away all those cards that did not have an exact address – 'Henry Green, London'; 'That bitch that lives with Henry Green'; 'Henry Green', that sort of thing.

That still left us with quite a pile, more than might be accounted for by Stephi's work colleagues, fellow Tia Chiers and amateurs luvvies, or my few acquaintances such as Charlie or Arthur Beaumont , or close friends such as the dentist. People on the hospital run and Iain had handed me cards in person.

It was my job to open all the perfectly addressed cards.

I got on with it. I was diligent. I read the letters inside just to make sure they really did tell us about Sandra and John's trip to the Seychelles with their amazing children who had spent the year passing exams and gaining prizes for their sporting achievements, or about Cedric's million mile walk for charity raising the equivalent of Iceland's national debt.

But at any hint of abuse or obsequiousness, they were on the TBB pile ('to be burnt' – reduced to a pile on unread ash).

All went well until I got to the last card. It came in a square, brown paper envelope that could have come from one of Stephi's eco crazy vegetarian luvvies, had it not been addressed to me and market 'personal and private' – not the sort of thing you usually see on a Christmas card. It was addressed to 'Horace Henry Green' with the exact address and postcode. And it had something embossed on the flap. On close inspection this turned out to be a hammer and sickle.

There wasn't a stamp. Instead the envelope had been franked. It was, apparently, a diplomatic missive that did not have to be paid for. I hoped what was inside would be more diplomatic than some of the cards I had read.

It was. The card showed a snow-covered Red Square with a frosty-looking Kremlin in the background. A printed message told me it had been send to me 'With the compliments of the Russian Embassy'.

Below that was a hand-written note in a scrawl that a five-year-old writing left-handed on the first day of school might not have been proud of.

I have important information for you. Meet me please, mid-day Tuesday after Christmas at Observatory in Greenwich. I will know you. Come please, it is a good present, it said.

The note was signed 'Uncle Vanya'.

I put the card and envelope on the table on the DKWTDW pile. It was a pile of one.

I had the irrational feeling that it might somehow be dangerous. Perhaps I would absorb some fatal chemical from the unusual paper? Perhaps it was a joke? Perhaps I was being set up?

At that moment Stephi came through the front door.

'You're early. Thought you'd all go for a drink'.

'No, there was a big row. Tim, he's the director, told Lucy, she's our leading lady, that she needed to sharpen up her act. She got twitchy and told him she'd spent hours and hours learning the part and thinking about it, and if he didn't like her interpretation, he could stuff it. Then George, he's Lucy's husband, said he'd a good mind to punch Tim on the nose. So, Jud, he's Tim's boyfriend who has made some of the costumes, including an amazing one for Widow Swanky, said that George should be grateful to Tim for giving Lucy the part because she was far too old to be believable as a principal boy and couldn't act to save her life.

'At that point I decided to come home. I don't know if we'll be putting on the performance now, but I expect we will'.

'So just a usual rehearsal then?'

'Exactly. Anyhow, how many real cards did you salvage from that pile?'

'About twenty or so', I told her. 'And that one on the Don't Know What To Do With pile. 'You haven't got an Uncle Vanya I suppose?'

'No, my little drongo', she said. 'Uncle Vanya's a play by Chekhov'.

'Well Uncle Vanya's sent me a Christmas card. What's his play about?'

'It's about some professor bloke who goes to visit his country pile with his new misses. He got it when his first wife died. She was rich but the new one is like one of those kids in the round robin letters people put in their cards. She's good looking, glamorous, clever, the full deal. She makes everybody feel like a Kanga that can't jump – totally inadequate. They all feel like shit and end up living unhappily ever after'.

'Sounds fun', I told her. 'So how do you happen to know this? You haven't been sending me Christmas cards to make me feel so inadequate I'll stomp up on some mega Christmas present?'

'Drongo. I know because that's the play we did last year. I turned down the lead part, of course. That's why I played third woodcutter. You fell asleep half-way through and started snoring. You must remember it'.

I did, vaguely.

'From Russia with love. I will not let it show, in case you say no, no, no'.

| *Two* |

Friday before Christmas. Getting on for lunchtime.

I telephone Charlie. He's on call divert, probably holed up in some country hide-away.

'I had a card', I told him.

'No need to thank me. It's all part of the service. Make you feel wanted, part of the team. All that'.

'No, not your card. Another one. From the Russian Embassy. At least that's what it says. It was signed by Uncle Vanya'.

There was a pause. He was wondering if I was being serious. I had his attention.

'Somebody's pulling your leg. Uncle Vanya's a play by Chekhov…. He's Russian', he added after another pause, or at least he was'.

'I know', I said. 'I know who he was, I mean. 'I'm not that uneducated. I'm living with an Australian who handles all my cultural affairs. But I think the card really was from the Russian Embassy. It's embossed and everything. They want me to meet somebody.

'Do you think it's a set-up? Are our Irish friends likely to be involved, or a Libyan or two?'

There was another pause.

'I'll get somebody round to pick up the card. And the envelope. I'll call you back later. When were you supposed to meet them?'

I told him.

'I'll see to that', said Charlie. 'Plenty of time. We'll come up with something'.

A motor-cycle messenger knocked on the door about half an hour later. At 4.00 in the afternoon Charlie called back.

'It's genuine', he said. 'Seems they really have got something to tell you. We can guess what it is. We don't think you'll be in any danger. But we'll have people there just the same'.

'You think I should go?'

'Yes. It would be useful. We'd like to know who turns up, what they've got to say'.

'Should I come and see you so I can get wired up, or whatever it is you do? Go over the plans?

'No. Better not. The less you know about what we're up to the more natural you'll seem. Don't worry, we'll make sure no harm comes to you. And we don't need any wires or anything like that. That's old hat. We've got better stuff these days.

'You will go? You don't have to. But as I said, it might be useful'.

'"Useful" is my middle name', I said. 'I'll be there. You never know he might give me, perhaps a Faberge egg or some equally valuable Russian bling.

'Do I call you afterwards?'

'No need. We'll know as much about what happens and what is said as you. Probably more'.

I had an empty feeling in my stomach. It felt a little exciting. And then I remembered that I didn't have emotions, not really, not like other people. I was the outsider, the observer looking on. It wasn't excitement I was feeling, it was interest. I was interested to see what happened.

Then I remembered that Uncle Vanya had tried to shoot his brother in law, the professor. He tried twice and missed twice. It was after that, that I fell asleep. It would be interesting to see if my Uncle Vanya had similar intentions, and whether he was any better a shot.

'Meet me at the corner, tell me what to do. Don't ask me who I am, I'm just a modest man'.

| *Three* |

Mid-day, Tuesday after Christmas outside the Greenwich Observatory, standing at the railings overlooking London. I'm wearing the new sweater and scarf (designer label – Marks and Spencer) that Stephi bought me for Christmas. I bought her a new iron. It was a sort of joke – about getting married. She didn't get it.

'Good view', said the man who sauntered up next to me. He was younger than me by fifteen years or so, a bit shorter and rather heavier set. He was wearing a grey coat – the sort you might imagine a civil servant wearing - grey trousers and smartly polished brown shoes. In all, he was more soberly dressed than most of the people there. Some were obviously tourists, many spoke languages other than English, and many had young children with them.

'Not bad', I told him.

'It a little disappointing – your response I mean. I think perhaps you might say something like "good for the time of year when the geese fly home", or perhaps "I prefer the view in Moscow"'.

I looked at him again. He was holding two hot drinks. He must have bought them from the kiosk by the side of the path.

'Are you Uncle Vanya?'

'Just my small joke', he told me. 'You call me Ivan. Ivan, I not so terrible. My brother Peter, and he not so great'.

'Another small joke?'

'Perhaps. Perhaps it not translate too good. But come, we walk. That way the people who watch have to work a little bit. They hear us anyway, but they have to sing for supper'.

He handed me one of the drinks. It was in a paper cup ringed on the outside with a corrugated cardboard sleeve, presumably put there to make any legal action for scalding out of the question. The cup had one of those plastic tops that have various holes and a sort of teat-like protrusion. I'm never sure if you're supposed to make yourself look silly by taking the top off and splashing yourself with coffee, or by sucking the unctuous liquid through the teat.

I did neither. I just held the cup as we walked. The less than scolding liquid inside - coffee I guessed - was already dribbling down the side and onto my hand. It was sticky. As we passed a bin, I threw my cup in. Ivan did the same. He handed me a wet wipe.

'Excuse me, but is that standard issue for spies these days?'

'You make joke too. I see we going to be great friends. Get on like houses on fire.

'But I'm not spy. I'm journalist. Now I'm Press Officer for Embassy. It's not me who keeps secret to myself. I tell everybody everything. This is why we here, you and me. I have something I think you like to hear. It about your mother.

'She a great woman. Sonya is the name we give her. That is why I call myself Uncle Vanya. Perhaps it not funny in English. In play Vanya is uncle of Sonya.

'I want tell you about your mother. Some things you not know, a lot perhaps. You should know all. We want you to know'.

By now we'd walked a little way from the people milling around outside the Observatory. In this part of Greenwich Park there were mainly parents with their children and a few joggers puffing steamy breath. We sat down on one of the park benches.

'Look, it's very kind of you, but I didn't really know my mother too well. I never really lived at home – just the last two-and-a-bit years. And when I did, she was always a bit distant. I don't think she liked children very much. Or perhaps it was just me. Something happened to her. It was a long time ago and it was probably my fault. I don't like to talk about her too much. It's private.

'I came because I thought you might be something to do with what happened to her. I thought you were going to do something to me and I thought if that were the case it would be better if you tried when I knew something was likely to happen and where I had a few friends on hand to look out for me. I can see perhaps I was mistaken. Thank you for the trouble, but I think I'll just go home now'.

'No, no, no. We not hurt you. We thank you. We want you share your mother's success'.

'What success. And who the fuck is "we"?'

'See America not all bad. It give world many things. It teach us to be more casual, slouch about, chew gum. But it also give us "fuck this" and "fuck that", "mother fucker" and all that bullshit. I like be calm. You be calm too. I tell you everything.

'"We" is my country. Russian Federation. Used to be Soviet Federation. Now just Russian Federation. Success is honour placed on your mother'.

'I'm sorry I'm not usually so rude. But I've got no idea what you are talking about'.

'This is what I want to tell you. You listen, please. It not hurt you'.

'Alright, I'll listen. For a while at least.'

I listened.

My mother, it seemed, had been made a 'Hero of the Russian Federation'. It is the highest award the country gives out. It has to be authorised by the President himself. You don't have to be Russian to get it and you certainly don't have to be alive.

'Why?' I asked.

'Your mother great woman. She born in Austria. Her father teach politics and other things at university. He also write many things – books and articles. He also editor of Kapital Ideen. This a radical magazine. The name Capital Ideas was a little joke of his own – good ideas, but not about capitalists, more about Mr Marx perhaps'.

It seemed to be a day for little jokes.

'Your grandfather, he very worried about what happening in Germany. Not because he Jewish but because he see all those Nazi boys taking it out on communists. And he think communists have the only good future.

'In 1935 he bring family to England. They come not together, but three then two. Your mother she come with her mother and sister, and later, not too much later, her father come with his son'.

'Hold on', I told him. 'My mother told me she was adopted. She said she didn't know her parents. She said she hadn't got any family. Now you're telling me she came here with her family. What was their name, where are they now?'

'I come to that', said Ivan.

'Their name Steinitz. There were many Rabbi in Steinitz family. Many clever people.

'Your mother – her name "Martha" – had older brother Karl and younger sister Freda. Your mother 10 when she come to England, her brother 14 and her sister eight. They all live in Hampstead.

'Your Grandfather, he had many friends living here already and they found family an apartment. It place where many people have same ideas. Many writers. That sort. People who like to spend their time eating and drinking and talking to each other. Every night they go to each other's places and eat and smoke and drink and talk. Many times people come to the place of your grandparents and do this. Some German people, some not. Some Russian people and their friends. Some Jewish people, some not.

'And every night your mother listen to what is said. She very clever. And soon she make up her own mind. She know her father right. She know communists know best future.

'Your mother listen and learn. Learn and listen. She study hard and work hard. And when she 18, she get job at Houses of Parliament. She became secretary for member of your Parliament. She helped to get this by people who live in her apartment building. The man she worked for, he go to the apartment often also. He not communist but he a socialist. He what you call a "Champagne socialist". It mean he come from very rich family but have a conscience. So, he become socialist. He a Labour MP.

'Your country very funny. You have class system. You think people better the longer ago they steal their money.

'Families who steal money long time ago called "aristocrats". These are the top class. Those who stole money not so long ago, maybe hundred years or so, they called "middle class". These also good, but not top class. Then you have working class". These people who do work, who make things, who feed everybody else. These the bottom class.

'Well the "champagne socialist" that your mother work for was top class. His family stole everything long time ago – maybe thousand years. They have big house, four hundred years old, all that sort of thing.

'For generations youngest son go into church, next youngest into army, and oldest, he tell everyone else what to do. He in charge of house, of land, of law. He judge and jury too.

'Man your mother work for was oldest son. He everything your mother despise. But she work for him anyway.

'Why? Answer is because she also work for us, for Russia. Not for money, but for future of all world. Somebody at apartment recruit her as agent. And she very good agent. And Freda also but not the brother so much. He leave and go to Russia where he work for a while. He dead now. They all dead now. You the only one'.

This all seemed like a film or something. It certainly didn't seem to match with anything in my world – even if my world was somewhat bizarre at times. Here was this smartly dressed man babbling on about people I was apparently related to. He was telling me I was the son of a traitor, that I was Jewish, that my mother had a surname I'd never heard before. It was too much to take in. It must be like being told you have won the lottery or contracted some dreadful illness. You hear the words but not their meaning.

Ivan must be up to something. Perhaps he was a journalist trying to trick me into confessing something. Or perhaps he was on some sort of revenge mission. I thought I'd better be on my guard.

'So, what was it she did for you? If her boss was already a socialist, she could hardly convert him', I said.

Ivan read my mind.

'So not traitor', he said. 'Your mother not traitor. Russia and Britain allies then. On same side. She just tell us what going on. It only later things got more difficult. Then you came along.

'Labour won election in 1945. All those soldiers coming home wanted different life. Wanted different world. Women too, wanted to be treated more like men, have more to say. Labour won and your champagne charley looked like he could be a big shot in Government. Perhaps a minister. Perhaps defence or foreign affairs. It would be big help if he listened more to us.

'Your mother, she take him to her bed. He married, but he still happy to have your mother for some nice times. That is what happened. And you came along'.

'I don't believe you', I told him. I felt indignant for a mother I didn't know.

He took out a brown A4 envelope from under his coat and drew out a black and white photograph.

'This Sir Matthew Plusmeny, your father. You see he look like you'.

I took the photograph and looked at a picture of somebody who could have been me aged about 30.

'How do I know this is genuine?'

'I don't know. You take or leave. But this might explain why people think they know you. He quite famous at one time. You his "skeleton in his cupboard"', he said looking, rather pointedly I thought, at my oversized frame. Anyway, you keep picture. It another memento'.

'How hell you know — sorry, how the hell do you know that people think they know me?'

'We know lot about you. We watch you grow up. We think you very useful asset, so keep watch.

'After your mother killed, we lost you for while. But then, not so long ago, the man who was Sonya's control — he old now but still have sharp eyes — he see your picture in newspaper. You were at football match. "It him, no doubt", he say. So, we come looking and we find'.

'And I suppose you want me to do something for you? Is that what all this is about?'

'No, no, no', said Ivan. 'You much too famous now to be of use. Anyway, you know nothing. No, water all passed under bridge. We just want tell you about mother. Give you her medal. We've had our money's worth.

'Anyway, I tell you more. Sir Matthew Plusmeny, he know his little affairs with your mother be big scandal if anybody know, especially his wife. To stop cat coming from in the bag he pay for your mother to move to new flat where nobody knew her while she have you. Later, he pay for woman to look after you so mother can still go to work. Later still he paid for you to go boarding school. All kept secret.

'But your mother listen to all he had to say and she tell us. And when we disagree a little we tell her, and she tell him. And he listen, because he scared everyone find out about you. It all go very well. Then his father die and he became a Lord. He have even more reason to be afraid people find out about your mother and you.

'But after he go to the House of Lords, he not so important, so we tell your mother to marry another man and get sent to Northern Ireland. That what she did. Your father help her and husband get job there. I think he pleased to see her go'.

'Wait a minute', I told him. 'This doesn't make sense. My dad, David Grimond – I presume that's who you mean – was some sort of policeman. Why would he want to take on my mother and pretend I was his son?'

Ivan allowed a grin to make itself known – a sort of 'aren't we clever' grin.

'David Grimond also work for us. We tell him what to do also. When you born, we tell mother to put his name on certificate – but she not tell champagne Charlie. She just say all sorted out "for now"'.

'What on earth did they get up to in Ireland – my mother and father?'

'David Grimond was counter intelligence for police. But he also counter counter intelligence. He a double counter. Another joke perhaps?

'Anyway, he tell us all that going on.

'Your mother, she work for Irish MP. She spend a little time in his bed also. And she tell us plenty.

'She also run drop for other agents we have in Ireland. We have one or two quite big men, they make law and all that. Some in army also. They leave little messages in special places only your mother know. She take messages, and in night she set up her little radio and tell us what messages say. So we know all that going on'.

I didn't say a word. I couldn't.

'Then they both killed. Not everybody had wonderful ideas like your mother and David. Not everybody easy to control. It was too bad. But they did plenty good for us, plenty good. So now your mother get her medal'.

Ivan passed me an envelope he had been keeping inside his coat. It was not much bigger than a Christmas card but reasonably heavy.

'What's this?'

'It your mother's gold star. Take please'.

I did.

'Have you got anything else under there?'

'No just bullet proof vest in case your friends get angry. I think you might have one too'.

He patted my stomach. It might have been another joke, perhaps?

We walked off in opposite directions.

'Do you want to know a secret? Do you promise not to tell? Let me whisper in your ear. Say the words you long to hear'.

| *Four* |

Back home after my stroll in the park.

'You're still alive then?' It was Stephi calling from the kitchen. Perhaps she did care – in an Australian sort of way.

'Yes, made it back in one piece – in body if not in mind', I said putting the gold five-pointed star on the table.

'Why? What happened, and what's that? Have you been round that antiques market again?'

'It's not an antique. It may be for things that happened a long time ago, but it's new. It's real'.

'Real brass more like'.

'No, it's a real medal. Probably real gold'.

'They gave you a medal? More secrets I suppose?'

'Yes, more secrets, but not mine. It seems secrecy runs in the family'.

I told her. I told Stephi about my grandparents, about my uncle and aunts, about my mother and her bed hopping, about her reasons and how successful she'd been. About the man I had thought was my father. I told her about the lot.

'And you believe him?'

'Well not about everything. He as good as implied I was on the large side'.

'He got that right'.

'That's very hurtful; I'm a fine figure of a man'.

'Don't worry. Lots of women like their men a little round. They think it makes them look contented, a tribute to home cooking, and that they're not still on the prowl for other women – and even if they were, other women wouldn't fancy them. Doesn't seem to stop you though, by the looks of all those letters you get'.

'Power of the Press', I tell her. 'Anyway, look at this'. And I show her the photo that Ivan had given me.

'So? It's a picture of you before I met you. Do you want me to put it in a frame and kneel before it every morning before I go to work?'

'No, it's not me. It's somebody called Sir Matthew Plusmeny He's the person Ivan says is, was, my real father'.

'Was. What he's not your father any longer?'

'No, he's dead. He became a lord and then he died. We have a long family history you know. A family seat and everything. You might give me a little more respect. I've got blue blood coursing through my veins', I told her.

'That why you gave be an iron – so I can start acting like a serf. You're so up your sodding aristocratic ass. Why don't you slit your wrists to get a look at all that blue blood'?

'But before you do that, I think you'd better phone Charlie and ask about this Ivan character and whether any of this stuff is anything other than bull dust. Because you don't seem like a toff to me'.

'I am the lord of the dance, said he. I'll lead you all, wherever you may be, and I'll lead you all in the Dance, said he'.

| *Five* |

Same day, late afternoon. I am calling Charlie.

'Thought you might call', he tells me. 'Did you enjoy your little tête-à-tête with Ivan? By the way he's not Ivan. He's Andrei Shubkin. Officially he's a naval attaché at the Russian Embassy'.

'You mean he's a spy?'

'You could call him that'.

'And what he said, was it all bullshit?'

'Hard to tell. There's been a few of these medals given out recently. It's meant to confuse. Sometimes it's for a genuine reason, sometimes it's just to make us think that what somebody has done was more important than it actually was.

'When Philby died it was suggested we give him a medal. That way the other side might question the worth of all those things he told them. We didn't do it in the end because somebody else pointed out they already knew that most of it was true', said Charlie.

'You said they do it to make us think somebody was more important than they were, or perhaps their information was more important?'

'Yes'.

'That means my mother was of some importance? She did hand over some information?'

'Well, yes. But it was a long time ago'.

'Long time ago or not, she was an agent?'

Charlie hesitated a moment. I sensed he was adjusting his shake.

'You could say that, with a reasonable amount of certainty', he said.

'And this Plusmeny bloke was my father?'

'Very probably'.

'That makes me a lord then, or at least an aristo?'

'Hardly. Even if you weren't the second son, it's not a matter of genes, it's a matter of paperwork. If it were genes, who knows what havoc there'd be? There'd be a "Bar Sinister" on quite a few of the shields of our so-called leading families – not that most of them are not complete bastards anyway'.

'Excuse me?'

'Bar Sinister – it's a motive used in heraldry to give the nod that somebody was conceived on the wrong side of the sheets'.

'And people are proud to have it?'

'Depends who the father is – if known. If you were the bastard of Charles ll, it was almost obligatory. But the truth is, we all know who our mother is but many of us do not know who our father is, or was – just like you and Plusmeny's other boy'.

I had to think about this a minute or two.

'Are you saying my supposed step-brother, is not related to me at all? That Plusmeny's wife screwed around as much as he did?'

'More I'd say'.

'Then he has got my title?'

'Forget it. As I said, it's a matter of paperwork. He has the paperwork. All you've got is a Bar Sinister and a Gold Star that was given your mother for doing so well. Be satisfied with that'.

'Suppose so. Thanks anyway', I said putting the phone down. On the whole I felt I knew less now than before I met Ivan. It was disappointing.

'Mother, will they drop the bomb? Mother will they like this song?'

Second half

West Greenwich, London

| *One* |

Around dawn – only 9.30 am - and I am on my way to collect Daphne, one of my regulars, for her hospital appointment.

Daphne gets confused and there is talk of finding her a place in an old people's home that specialises in such cases. I knock on the door. There is no reply. This is the usual.

The house is of the sort thrown up by developers in the 1930s: a standard semi-detached with a bay window and a nod towards the Tudor period with some fake beams on a small gable above the bay.

After a few minutes I see Daphne peeping out from behind her net curtains. It is probably the only time see goes into that room, to look out and see who is knocking at the door.

A few minutes later and she is behind the door, peering through the letter box.

'Who is it', she asks. We go through this every time.

'Henry'.

'Don't be silly'.

'Henry, come to give you a lift to the hospital'.

'What do I want to go there for?'

'You've got an appointment. I've come to take you – in my car. The one you like so much because we can raise the seat and you can look out the window'.

'That will be nice'. And she takes the chain off the door and opens it just enough to take a proper look at me.

'Henry you say? Well you don't look like my Henry, but you certainly have a "Henry" look about you.

'I can't be too careful. There's people trying to get in here all the time. When I came down this morning there were two of those asylum seekers sitting on my carpet. They wouldn't go. I think they were cooking something. Or making a bomb. Anyway, they had a fire going.

'Time was when we had plenty of asylums. They put all the mad people there. Then that Thatcher woman closed them all down. It's no wonder there's so many mad people wandering around looking for asylums. They won't find any though'.

She lets me in. I explain again about the appointment. We've plenty of time. She's never ready, so I always arrive early.

Daphne fusses about tidying things up, putting things on, looking round the room. Eventually we are ready.

I take her to the hospital. We go to the psychiatric wing. Daphne notices the sign and I can see she looks as if she's sat on an ant hill – as Stephi would no doubt say. I check in at the desk.

'They won't make me into an asylum seeker, will they?'

I tell Daphne not to worry.

We have an appointment, so we only have to wait an hour or so.

Eventually a small brown man in a white coat appears. He looks friendly – as if he's only administered five or six electric shock treatments and one frontal lobotomy this morning.

'Mrs Hopchurch', he calls.

Agnes jumps up. 'You will come with me?'

I look at the man in the white coat. He looks at me in a knowing sort of way, as if he is sure I have ulterior motives. I'm obviously a granny abuser or I'm on the make, hoping Daphne will leave me her house in her will. But he nods – no more than a flicker of his eyelids really – and I look suitably guilty. I follow them both into a room adjoining the waiting area.

There is no desk, or uncomfortable chairs here. There are three uncomfortable settees instead, arranged in a 'U' shape. In the centre is a coffee table that looks like one of Sylvia Slim's cast-offs.

We each take a settee.

'Well Mrs Hopchurch, perhaps I can call you Agnes (Agnes smiles in an embarrassed sort of way) how can I help you today?'

Agnes looks a little flummoxed. She didn't want to be here, and she doesn't think the good doctor can be of any help. She thinks it's the Government that should do something about the asylum seekers – open a few more mental care institutions. But she was brought up when people were usually polite to doctors and policemen and she doesn't want to offend anybody.

'I'm not sure you can. I'm not sure I need any help. I only came because that woman from the social said I should and before I'd had time to cancel the appointment, so as not to waste anybody's time, I had a lift waiting. Then I thought I'd better come anyway'.

The man in the white coat, who was wearing a badge identifying him as 'Dr Gromwich', leant forward and picked up a clipboard from the table.

'I see'. He leafed through a few of the pages attached to his clipboard.

'And your friend here, who is he?'

'That's Henry', said Daphne. I nodded.

'His second name please?'

'I'm not too sure', said Daphne. 'I always call him Henry'.

'Green', I said, in as helpful a sounding way as I could muster.

'Thank you', said Dr Gromwich. 'Not THE Henry Green?'

He said this as if it couldn't possibly be true, shaking his head and smiling to himself at his little joke. I half expected him to write it down on his pad.

'Yes, that's me. The one and only'.

Dr Gromwich looked up and smiled in a knowing way. He obviously thought we had shared a joke together.

'All right Daphne. Thank you for coming to see me. And please call me David. I just have a few questions to ask you so I can fill out this form for Social Services and let them know how you are getting on and whether there is anything we can arrange for you that will make your life a little easier'.

'I don't need anything else', said Daphne. 'I'm happy as I am living with Henry'.

'You live with Henry', said the good doctor, giving me a less than conspiratorial glance. One joke was enough.

'Oh yes'.

David scribbled a long note on his pad.

'Well just as a start perhaps you can tell me what day it is today?'

'It's the day I have to see you'.

'No Daphne. I meant which day of the week? The date perhaps?'

'Well it IS the day I have to see you. And that's Tuesday 6 February 2002. Or if you're Chinese it's the Year of the Snake – although it changes to the year of the Horse in six days' time'.

David scribbled something else on his clipboard.

'And who is the Prime Minister?'

'Well if you mean of the UK, it's that Tony Blair. But I don't like him. Nor that Gordon Brown. Nor any of them really.

'But if you mean Ireland, then it's Bertie Ahern, although his real title is "Taoiseach"'.

David added some more scribbles to his pad.

'And why would I mean Ireland, Daphne?'

'I've no idea. It's just that your question was rather vague, you didn't say which country you were talking about. And most of them have prime ministers, don't they?'.

David wrote down something else.

'And what is 17 plus 16'.

'That's 33 in most countries', said Daphne.

'There are some where it's not?'

'Well perhaps not now, unless you're a native living in the jungle and can only add up to three. But if you'd been a Roman it would be XXXIII'.

'I see', said David. He was busy writing again.

'And you sleep well'.

'I suppose', said Daphne. 'I'm getting old and that means I have to get up most nights. Have to go down the hall. But I'm up six every morning'.

'And how old are you?'

'I was born 11 June 1910. That makes me 91'.

'And you're star sign?'

Daphne looked at the doctor as if he were asking a trick question – she probably thought they were all trick questions.

'Surely you don't believe in all that? But if you do it would be a Gemini. I have the same birthday as High Laurie you know.

'He's an actor', she added in case David didn't know.

He wrote something else on his pad and finished it off with a stabbing full stop.

'Well Daphne, you seem to be coping very well. I don't think I need to keep you any longer. I'll write to Social Services and tell them you seem to be managing things very well'.

We left. I drove her home. When we were almost there, I asked her:

'Why didn't you tell David about the asylum seekers in your living room?'

'Oh yes, that was terrible. But I didn't want to bother him with that. He's got enough to worry about'.

When we got to her front door there was a cat sitting waiting by the step. 'Come on Henry, she said as she opened the door.

'Memories, memories, drifting back to me'.

| *Two* |

Saturday. Football, at half time.

We were playing the team leading the Championship. They were eight points clear of the second team with a game in hand. We were three points off the bottom with no game in hand.

They had been running rings around us with extravagant passes up and down and across the pitch – passes that left our team stranded, looking like no-hopers. But somehow, they didn't score. All their shots were off target by a millimetre or two. And our keeper was playing a blinder.

One minute to half time and he made yet another miracle save. He booted the ball up field to where Damien Onslow happened to sharing a conversation with one of the opposing team. The ball ran past them. Without even a polite goodbye, Damien pivoted round and chased after the ball. When he caught up with it, he accidentally kicked it forward.

Two of the other side's backs converged on the ball as Damien loped on. Not used to running, he was fast running out of puff and, just inside their penalty box, he tripped over his own feet and went sprawling to the ground.

The referee blew for a penalty.

'Cheat, Cheat, Cheat', shouted the away fans as the players from the opposing team surrounded the Ref. There was an explosion of whistle blowing and finger pointing. A red card was raised and the centre back at whose feet Damien had landed. He was off, off, off.

'Cheat, Cheat, Cheat', shouted the away fans.

'There's only one Damien Onslow, one Damien Onslow', we shouted.

'Onslow's not slow. Onslow's not slow'. Well he is – a bit. But he was on a high. Damien stepped up to take the penalty.

Their keeper did an elaborate dance, jumping one way then the other, arms stretched wide. He even poked his tongue out. If I hadn't known he had been born in Blackburn – it said so in the programme - I would have been certain he was a Maori. But it worked; up to a point. Charlie, mesmerised by the display put on for his amusement, miss-kicked the ball so that instead of sailing harmlessly over the bar, it smashed into the upright and ricocheted into the net.

The Maori warrior had made a spectacular dive in the wrong direction.

The pip in the Ref's whistle was not quite knackered, so he was able to blow for half time and everybody trouped off – with us up one-nil.

'Now we've done it', said Iain. They're not going to let that pass. We'll probably lose by ten or 11 now'.

'Could be', I agreed. 'Shame it was only one player that got sent off. Another two or three and we might have stood a chance'.

'It's a bit like you and SIM Card', said Iain.

'What is?'

''You upsetting him like that'.

'What by being innocent? I'll have to apologise'.

'You've upset him, and he's not going to let it pass. It didn't come from me, but he's got a team of three doing nothing else but checking up on you. I had a word with one of them. He said SIM Card's obsessed with all that money you had in your account. Says you must be up to something and he's going to get you for it.

'So, word to the wise. If there's anything even slightly dodgy about your accounts I'd do something about it pronto, otherwise you'll be paying another visit to the Nick.'

'Thanks', I said. 'But there's nothing dodgy about it'.

The second half started. It was much like the first. They got the ball, they passed the ball, they shot at our goal from all angles. They missed or our keeper made a save of the century. The whistle went and we had won – one nil – and moved four places up the table.

'OO are yer, oo are yer'.

| *Three* |

Saturday evening. Stephi and me eating dinner at the kitchen table. Curried lamb, Stephi's favourite, washed down with a bottle of white (wine, not spirit).

'Whatever you've done, it's worked', she said.

'Sorry. What have I done, and what has worked?'

'Bryan. He's disappeared. I could never get rid of him but you seem to have managed all right. What did you do? Get Conway to offer him a place on Who wants to be a millionaire or Master Chef, or something?'

'I haven't done anything. Honest'.

'It's OK if you don't want to tell me. I don't want to know the gory details'.

'I promise, I haven't done anything. To be honest I'd forgotten all about him. Perhaps he's just given up'.

'Course he has'.

She didn't believe me. She really did think I'd arranged for Bryan to have a change of heart and perhaps a change of walking arrangements too.

'I ask you to do one little thing and what do you do – you forget all about it. You're so wrapped up with yourself. I might have to re-think this marriage thing. Of course, a hefty ring might help me make up my mind'.

'I'll see what I can do. I'll let the Bank of England know I shall be making a large withdrawal'.

We left it at that.

Me: 'What kind of painting did you do?'

'How do you mean?'

'Well, you said you met your animal rights activist friend at painting class. So, what kind of painting did you do? Landscapes? Portraits? Flowers? Modern?'

'And what media did you use?'

'Oh. I didn't really get that far. I just drew a bit. Mainly in charcoal. Mainly animals. That's why Judy thought I might be interested in animal rights'.

'What kangaroos and duckbill platypuses?'

'I suppose you're going to take the piss now, just because I didn't reach your high standards.

'It was chocolate box stuff, if you must know. Drawings of small fluffy animals in adorable positions. Hamsters nibbling carrots, that sort of thing'.

'Not foxes getting torn apart by beagles then?'

'No, not foxes getting torn apart by beagles whipped to a frenzy by people wearing ridiculous clothes. Although I do think what they do is pretty disgusting. More so after I actually went to a hunt.

'That's probably why I took to Bryan so quickly. He seemed to know so much about it. He was really committed. He wanted to do something about it. He had some strident views. He was very deep. He was almost Australian about it'.

'So, you fell for his Manly charms?'

'You're doing it again'.

'What?'

'You're taking the piss. You think I don't know where Manly is.

'Well just because some bloke likes furry animals doesn't make him a back-door bandit. Not everybody's like you. Some people have feelings. They don't go about taking policy decisions to opt out'.

'That's why he treated you so well then?'

'You're so bloody up yourself'.

'Redback, funnel-web, blue-ringed octopus. Stonefish, crocodile, and the box jellyfish. Redback, funnel-web, blue-ringed octopus. Australia, Australia'.

| *Four* |

Wednesday: At an hour no soul should stir – 8.30am – at Daphne's front door. She has an appointment with the eye clinic at 10.30am and I know she will have forgotten and will take at least an hour to get ready.

The usual window and letterbox peeping precedes the door opening by the few millimetres its security chain will allow.

'Oh Henry', she says. 'I knew it would be you'.

I look around for the cat. It is nowhere to be seen.

'Come in. There's somebody in my front room who wants to meet you'.

'Meet me?'

'Yes, he said it was official. I think he might be looking for those asylum seekers. But I haven't seen them for days. Anyway, he knocked at the door and asked if you were here yet. And as you weren't, I said he could wait'.

'But how did you know I was coming today?'

'He told me - that Mr Bredley I told you about. Do you think I'll get into trouble, letting those people into my house?'

'No Daphne, you won't get into trouble'.

I reminded her about her appointment and suggested she started getting ready.

'Yes, and while I do that, go into the front room and talk to Mr Bredley. He seemed a bit shifty to me'.

I went into the room. To my amazement there was actually somebody sitting on Daphne's sofa. He was stroking the cat, which had jumped unto his lap and was pushing its head into his raincoat.

As I entered Mr Bredley stood up, obliging the cat leap to the floor. He held out his hand. 'Bryan Bredley but you will know me better as Bryan Myers', he said. 'You are Stephi's new bloke, Henry – Henry Green – I recognise you from the photographs'.

Something fell into place. This was Stephi's ex-husband, the animal lover, the shouty, shitty, animal lover with Australian ways who had stalked her until she had to run away. But what the fuck was he doing here?

I smiled the smile I kept for tax inspectors, insurance salesmen and health and safety inspectors.

'Pleased to meet you', I said – stretching the elasticity of truth to its full potential. 'Daphne told me you were waiting to see me'.

He was a fairly short man, smartly dressed – he had blue pinstriped trousers and I guessed he was wearing a suit under his raincoat – with dark curly hair, greying and receding at his temples. He looked a little older than Stephi, maybe close to 55, and I could see his fingernails were about as bitten as they could be. The horizontal hold on his eyes, enlarged behind thick-framed spectacles, seemed to have gone. He alternated between quick glances in my direction and detecting stains that might have been left by asylum seekers on the carpet.

'How did you know I would be here?'

'I followed you from your flat last week. When you went into the hospital I trailed along behind, and when you went in, I got close enough to hear Mrs Hopchurch's name called out. Then a day or so later I called the hospital, said I was calling on behalf of Mrs Hopchurch and that she'd lost her appointment card and couldn't remember the time of her next visit? They told me the day and the time and I guessed you would be along to give her a lift. Simple really'.

I wasn't sure if he thought me a dimwit for not realising this straight away, or whether he was waiting for me to congratulate him.

'And?' I said this in as curt a manner as was within my special curtness powers.

'And what?'

'And why did you want to see me so much that it was necessary to trick the National Health Service and also a vulnerable lady who wouldn't mind me saying that she is getting on in years?

'And why are you called Bredley, and not Myers? And why on earth should I want to speak to you after you've taken up stalking Stephi again?'

I could feel myself flushing. But policy is policy, so I did not allow myself to get overly angry. Bryan, though, was shaking worse than Charlie on a bad day.

'Look', he said. 'I came here to apologise and to give you some information that might help you, or Stephi, or both. I don't know'.

'If you want to apologise, why don't you apologise to Stephi. It's her you scared shitless?'

'I know. I know. I was going to. That's why I tracked her down. But if I just knocked on your door she'd freak out or something. I didn't want to upset her or frighten her'.

'It's a bit late for that'.

'I know. I had it all worked out, what I would say. But now I'm getting a bit confused. Can I just say it?'

I let him. I sat down on one of the armchairs and listened while he rambled on.

Bryan's story:

Bryan told me he had been a cop. He'd joined the Met straight from school. He'd always wanted to be a policeman. He wanted to be a detective; solve murders, crack crime gangs, that sort of thing.

It wasn't like that. After a couple of years on the beat he got a desk job with Special Branch, mainly checking up on people thought to be planning civil disorder. He got noticed for his diligence and was invited to join an undercover squad. It was considered a plum job, what with all the overtime it brought.

The squad's task was to infiltrate action groups and find out what plans they had for protests, especially violent protests, so the police could be on hand when they happened.

Bryan grew his hair long, put on some old clothes and wheedled his way into an animal rights action group. It was suggested it would be easier to gain the group's trust if he found himself a girlfriend committed to the cause.

This is where Stephi came in. He didn't tell his wife too much about what he was doing, and nothing about having to find a girlfriend.

He liked Stephi, he liked her a lot. And when she trapped him into getting married, he couldn't see a way out. After all, his assignment was going well, he'd got to know plenty of animal rights activists and he was passing back valuable information.

But Bryan began to have doubts. He kept thinking about the real Bryan Myers – the child who had died at just four years of age and whose identity he had stolen. He thought about Bryan Myers' parents and about Stephi and his real wife and children. And he worried all the time that he would get found out. His nerves began to shatter. He was called in.

But he couldn't just leave. Special Branch didn't want the activists to know they had people working undercover. So, he had to devise a way to walk away without raising suspicions. He got nasty. He got nasty to Stephi and pretended to everybody that he was on the verge of a nervous breakdown – which wasn't far from the truth.

He'd goaded Stephi into a divorce. Then he stalked her for a while until she ran away. After that he told the animal rights people who he knew best that his life might as well be over, so he'd decided to go abroad. He'd disappeared. In fact, he'd gone back to his desk job at the Met.

But for Stephi's revelations about herself, I might have been astounded. But amazingly, I felt quite calm. I only wanted to poke out one of his eyes.

'But what I don't understand is, why have you decided to do this now. Surely you could have tracked her down anytime. You'd only have to enter a National Insurance number or something and her details would pop up?'

In fact, there were lots of things I didn't understand about what I was being told, but this was the first thing that popped into my head.

'Well I couldn't, could I? After I got back to the Met I couldn't settle down. I'd got caught up in all this animal rights stuff and I didn't want to give it up. At the same time, I felt guilty as hell about what I'd done. I'd made some good friends and I'd grassed on them all.

'I really did like Stephi, and I knew I'd let her down. My wife too – although she didn't stay around long after that.

'I had a bit of a breakdown. I couldn't sleep, I was tired all the time, I was on a real downer. I couldn't do my job either. They told me I was schizophrenic.

'I told them it was their fault. They should have given me counselling or something. I said the whole thing stunk and I was thinking of going to the newspapers and telling my story.

'They didn't like that one bit. I got called in and threatened with all sorts of things. Then I was offered a payoff and an early pension. It seemed like a good deal so I took it. I'm not in the police any more. I've gone straight.

'That's why I was careful when I found where you lived. I didn't want any trouble with the police. And there seemed to be a lot of them around'.

'What people outside our house? No that's just reporters looking for some easy story'.

'No, not them', he said. There's a couple set up in the house opposite. You think I'm a stalker, with the equipment they've got, they're ten times worse. That's what I wanted to warn you about. Somebody's doing some heavy obs. You'd have thought they would have forgotten all that stuff Stephi did by now, forgotten or forgiven'.

Daphne came back into the room wearing her best coat and hat. She was ready to go. So was I.

'What do you want me to do Bryan?'

'Just tell Stephi I'm sorry. Tell her what I told you. Tell her I'm very sorry'.

'All right', I said. 'But no more stalking. This will be the last time we see you'.

'Yes, OK. But just in case, take this. I might just be able to do something to help put things right'.

He handed me a card. 'Bryan Bredley', it said. 'Animal therapy and holistic investigations'. I didn't know what it meant, and I didn't care.

'There's only two Bryan Bredleeys, two Brian Bredleeys. There's only two Bryan Bredleeys, two Brian Bredleeys'.

| *Five* |

Later that day – 7.00pm – Stephi just home, me cooking, wine open.

'Good day?'

'Bit heavy', I said. 'I met that Bryan of yours this morning'.

I'd meant to leave talking about Bryan until we'd at least tasted a mouthful or two of food. But somehow, I couldn't hold back.

'I knew you'd do something. I hope you told him to go walkabout, piss off for good'.

'More or less. But he told me some things you probably won't want to hear. I know I wouldn't. So, brace yourself'.

I handed her a glass of Sainsbury's finest.

'Don't worry, I've got over the sodding bastard. You can tell me what he said. No worries. It's all too long ago'.

'Right then', I said. 'He wasn't Bryan Myers. He only pretended to be. He was a policeman, with Special Branch, and he was telling them everything you were up to – which, by the way sounded a bit more than doing a few charcoal doodles of furry animals – he said you were very creative with your protests.

'Oh, and he was already married'.

Stephi stopped in mid sip. For a moment she stood stock still, taking in what I had just said. Then her face began to contort in a most peculiar way, and I didn't think it was the wine.

I'd never seen an Australian cry before, and it wasn't a pretty sight.

She slumped down at the table, head in hands. I could see she was shaking.

'The bastard', she said. 'The bloody bastard. Everything we had must have been a lie. All those things he said, just an act. He can't do this. He's stolen part of my life. The bloody bastard'.

I was lost for something to say or do. I moved behind her and put my hand on her shoulder so as to pull her towards me; give her a hug. But she shrugged my hand away, stood up, pushing the chair hard against me, and stormed out. I heard her running up the stairs. I thought it better not to follow.

I put dinner on hold. I didn't think she'd want to eat too soon. And neither did I.

Instead I stalked into the sitting room and poured myself a large scotch before slumping down on the sofa.

To be honest, what Bryan had said hit too many cords with me – the ethics of taking on the name of a dead child, of pretending to be somebody I wasn't, living a lie.

It wasn't my choice entirely. I wasn't like Bryan, I told myself. I hadn't wheedled my way into some group so I could grass on them. But I had taken the easy way out; the very easy way out. I was more than all right, but there must be some people around who were not all right on account of what I had done. I'd just shut them out of my mind.

It might have been the scotch, but it didn't take me too long to start thinking there was nothing I could do about it now. What had been done, had been done. I am what I am, I did what I did. There was no going back. I might as well accept it and get on with things.

About an hour later Stephi came down. She was in her sloppy tracksuit bottoms and slippers. Her face, white and a little older looking, poked out from her old grey sweatshirt – the one she liked to wear when she was learning her lines.

'You hungry?'

'No, but I'll have one of those though'. She pointed to the empty whisky glass.

I poured her a healthy-sized slug and did the same for me.

'I feel like I've been punched in the stomach', she said. 'It's stupid. Nothing's changed really and I'd written off that time with Bryan years ago anyway. Even so, it seems something's been ripped away from me. He wasn't the sodding bastard he pretended to be. He was an even worse sodding bastard. What does that make me for being taken in by him – not once, but twice. Once when he moved in and again when he moved out. I must have been a fucking idiot'.

'You weren't to know. And you weren't the only one he tricked. Seems he fooled most of your group. From what he said, some of them got prosecuted for some pretty serious stuff. Sounds like you were lucky you weren't among them. Perhaps there were some perks in being married to Bryan'.

'No, I didn't do much. Nobody got hurt, nothing got burnt, there weren't any cars that got acid poured on their bonnets. I didn't even knock a policeman's helmet off.

'I don't know why I got involved so much. I don't even like animals that much. I mean I like them. But I like to eat them too. It's the way it is.

'I just sort of got caught up in it all. It seemed exciting. And it seemed like a family. I'd never had a family before. We were all in it together. Perhaps that's why what Bryan did seems so bad'.

Stephi seemed a little more relaxed now. She'd got over the initial shock. She seemed relieved to talk about it all.

'What was the worst thing you did?'

'Nothing much really. I poured some sugar into a fuel tank'.

'I didn't know that worked'.

'It does if you use enough'.

She said this as if she'd been calculating how much Semtex to use in a bomb. I could see she was proud of her protester credentials, despite the off-hand denials.

'Whose car was it?'

'It wasn't a car; it was a lorry. We were at the port in Dover. This lorry arrived carrying sheep being taken off to God knows where to be shot in the head. They were packed in like sardines.

'We were all there with our banners, shouting at the lorry driver. He slowed down a bit and a few people jumped over the barrier and laid in the road in front of the lorry. The police tried to drag them away, but the lorry had to stop.

'Meanwhile, I jumped over the barrier and went round the back of the lorry and started pouring sugar into the tank. I'd got to about two and a half bags when I was hauled away.

We had to spend the night in police cells. But the lorry was crooked. They had to unload it and put the sheep in some special pens they rigged up. They were in a dreadful state'.

'Did they press charges?'

'No. They started threatening us with all sort of things. Ten years behind bars, that sort of thing. But somebody, well Bryan actually, had taken pictures of the sheep and sent them off to the BBC and some newspapers. The next morning the pictures were everywhere. There was a bit of a public outcry. I guess the lorry company didn't want any more trouble and the charges were dropped.

'We got off with an official warning. They said it was serious and we'd have police records, but I've never heard any more about it'.

'Until now, perhaps', I told her. 'Bryan said he spotted some cops keeping an eye on our house. Maybe they think you're a threat to national security'.

'Bollocks'.

'Sugar, sugar. You are my candy girl and you've got me wanting you'.

| *Six* |

Friday, 10.00 am, on my way to see Sylvia Slim and a bit pissed off because today was supposed to be a painting day.

Miss Slim had phoned me on Thursday afternoon to say her sleuthing had turned up something that she thought I would like to know. Would I like to come and see her at 9.00 am the following morning? 'No', I said. But 10.30 might just be acceptable.

There was much tutting and turning of pages as she consulted her empty diary before agreeing to my most reasonable request.

As before, only the 'SS' space in the car park was taken. All six other spaces were empty.

I parked the Volvo across two spaces and went in.

'I'm here', I announced somewhat needlessly.

Sylvia lowered her head and gazed up at me, by-passing her spectacles altogether, with a tired expression on her face. I might be a client, I might be her only client and therefore her favourite client, but I was still a tiresome man, as far as she was concerned.

She hustled me into her consulting room, closed the door with the firmness of a prison warden and, without asking, went straight to the coffee machine.

When we were all settled and coffeed up to her liking, she took her seat and pulled out a large green file.

'Green for Green', she said, tapping the file. 'It makes it easier to find'.

I think it was a joke.

'We' – I assumed she was using the royal 'We' – are quite pleased with the results we've been able to achieve on this one', she said. 'I think you might find the outcome very interesting, not to say helpful. Of course, there's more to be done, but I thought you would like to know what we have found out so far'.

I was all ears.

'We've undertaken some surveillance, of course. But that is only part of it. I, we, have been able to follow quite a long and complex paper trail'.

I think she meant she'd made liberal use of Google. But I didn't want to mention it in case it took her even longer to get to the point.

'And?' I ventured.

'Well, as I said, we have turned up quite a story, one that I am sure you will be pleased to hear. But before I launch into that – and I have a report that you can take away and read at your leisure - I would like to remind you of our contractual terms and in particular the privacy provisions.

'Anything I tell you that is not in the written report is not to be used or relied upon. It will only be background information to help you decide how to proceed.

'We don't want to land ourselves with a libel case or give anybody the opportunity to claim invasion of their privacy. And we certainly don't want our competitors to know how we get such remarkable results'. She said this with a conspiratorial half-smile.

'No, no', I said, 'Heaven forbid'. Now please get on with it, I thought.

She did.

'First of all, Geoffrey Porter is not Verdu's son. He is a relative though. In fact, he is, or rather he was, her husband.

Secondly, Jennifer Verdu is not who she said she was. Well, she is, was, but not in the way you would think'.

'So, Verdu was not her real name?'

'Yes, it was, but only because she changed it by deed poll'.

'When was that?'

'Two years ago'.

'And you've got proof of this?'

'Yes, it's all in the report. But there's more'. Sylvia tapped the green folder again. I got the impression she did not often get the chance to play the country house detective, and she quite liked it. She'd had a new haircut in anticipation – a crew cut that any US Marine would be proud to sport – except for the purple hue, that is.

'Good'.

'Would you like another coffee?'

'No', I assured her, I just wanted to know what she had found out.

She told me it turned out Geoffrey Porter was that person's real name. For professional reasons he had not always used it, sometimes being known as Gustave Palmer, sometimes Gregg Potter, and sometimes by other names. He was, in fact, a convicted fraudster.

Nobody except the various Gustaves, Greggs, and Geoffreys knew exactly how much he had swindled out of people, but he had been caught most recently charming old ladies into funding his comfortable, not to say luxurious, lifestyle.

Jennifer Verdu, meanwhile, had been born Jennifer Ian St John James – her father was a Liverpool football fan.

Jennifer Ian St John had not been too good at anything except art. Like me, it seemed.

By hook or by crook, she had managed to get herself into art school and came out an accomplished painter. Looking to set herself up, she took a job as the 'painter in residence; at Letchworth Open Prison. It was here that she met Geoffrey Porter who was at that moment serving out time at Her Majesty's pleasure.

He went to Jennifer Ian St John's art classes and liked them. He liked her even more.

Two years later, when Geoffrey was released, Jennifer married him and a short time after that, she changed her name to Verdu. And two years after that she was knocked down by a bus in Hackney high street. Other than her husband, she had no remaining family and no dependants, and she left everything she owned to Geoffrey.

'This is all we have been able to establish so far', said Sylvia. 'But I am sure you see the implications'.

'No', I said. 'I don't see how it helps at all. It means there was a "Verdu" who was a painter. OK, Geoffrey Porter had a criminal past, but he may have reformed. And there is nothing illegal in inheriting something from your wife, even if she has changed her name'.

Sylvia looked a little crestfallen. She was obviously expecting some wholehearted praise, and perhaps a bonus of suitably large size'.

'It's not that simple', she said.

'I have spoken to Arthur Beaumont, the chap who owns the art gallery in Bond Street that sells all of Verdu's work. He was very shifty about the whole thing. I can't prove it yet but I'm sure he's involved.

This is what I think….'

What she thought was that Jennifer Ian St John had fallen under the spell of Geoffrey Porter and the two had hatched a plan, based on Jennifer Ian St John's natural talent and Geoffrey's persuasive powers, to make them some money.

No doubt Geoffrey did his research to find out which artists were worth copying and where their work was sold. He had lighted upon the mysterious recluse Verdu, about whom little was known other than the quality and price of his work.

The first part of the plan involved Jennifer Ian St John – now Verdu - contacting Arthur. She showed him one or two paintings that looked remarkably like those that had been put his way by the artists' agent Henry Green. They were not signed.

Arthur must have seen the opportunity to make some money. For a suitable commission, say 90 per cent, Arthur might hang these canvasses on his walls. Imagine his ecstasy when the contract he produced was signed by one 'Jennifer Ian St John Verdu'. It was all too good to be true, but it gave Arthur good reason to hang his new painting in amongst the 'Verdus'.

The second part of the plan involved Geoffrey, whom Arthur had never met, posing as a serious art buyer.

While browsing in a certain Bond Street gallery he was particularly taken by some unsigned paintings that adorned the wall. Arthur, who had been hovering nearby, was more than helpful. He explained that this was by Verdu, whose works sold for considerable sums. The particular painting that had caught Geoffrey's eye was unsigned but anybody who knew anything about art could see it was plainly a 'Verdu'. Besides being a delight to the eye, the painting was an investment that was bound to yield an outstanding profit.

Geoffrey was delighted and agreed to buy the painting, leaving a cheque for the whole amount and making sure to take with him an invoice and receipt clearly stating that he had bought a 'Verdu', its size and description. He did not take the painting, but said he would return the following week by when Arthur would have been able to clear his cheque.

Arthur was delighted.

He was not so delighted when Geoffrey returned the following day. He told Arthur the painting was clearly a forgery, he had spotted it right away, and that he had written evidence that it had been sold to him as an original. Clearly Arthur would be ruined if anything of this got out.

Geoffrey said it was certainly a 'Verdu', he had a written contract signed by the artist herself.

Not good enough, said Geoffrey. The painting was clearly not by the real 'Verdu'. He suggested that Arthur might take back the painting for double the amount he had paid. Naturally the cheque he had left yesterday would be – indeed had already been – cancelled.

In other words, Arthur owed Geoffrey a rather large sum of money.

Knowing that he had been rumbled and who had done the rumbling, but relieved that he had been offered a way out, Arthur agreed to the terms. After all, he would only have to sell a few more of the forgeries to make up the difference.

'And then things took an unexpected turn', said Sylvia. 'Jennifer Ian St John got knocked down by a 55 Bus in Mare Street, Hackney. I think Geoffrey was probably devastated. He had lost a wife and an income. In an emotional state he probably let something slip that Arthur was quick to spot. After that there was probably a change of plan. Arthur told Geoffrey all about you and they worked out how they could get some money out of you.

'I might be wrong, but that is what I think probably happened.

'Do you want me to keep working on the case?'

'I certainly do', I told her.

'Then here is my account to date'.

Even with her rather substantial expenses she had not been able to exhaust the funds I had paid her, so I was still in credit.

'When you walk through a storm, hold your head up high, and don't be afraid of the dark'.

| *Seven* |

Saturday. Football. Mid-day because the match was being televised.

'We're always crap when we're on box', said Iain as we took our seats. 'Then again, we're usually crap when we're not'.

It was another six-pointer. There were three teams all on the same points, us, the lot we were playing today, and last year's champions from the division below. We were all in the relegation zone. We were only last by dint of a worse goal difference – minus 33 instead of minus 19. A loss today and we would end the weekend in an even worse position than now. A win and we'd zoom up at least one place – overtaking the team we were playing today, but still at least four points from safety.

We had a new secret weapon. He was a secret to us as well. Jason Obrahmi had arrived on loan in mid-week. He was signed to last year's and probably this year's premiership champions but couldn't make it into their first team. He had been loaned out to another team in our division where he had run riot, scoring in nearly every game he played, but being sent off twice. They had had enough when an argument with their manager had resulted in said person taking a trip to the local A&E to have his broken nose put back in place.

Having had their nose put out of joint, they had sent Obrahmi packing. And now he was on loan to us for the rest of the season.

After ten minutes Obrahmi, tired of waiting for somebody to pass to him, had tracked back to mid-field. Once there he neatly robbed the ball from one of their team, spun round and lobbed it into their penalty area and onto the head of our Jimmy Stitch, who happened to be standing there.

It, the ball, ballooned into their goal. We went wild.

'Jimmy Stich will STITCH YOU UP, STITCH YOU UP. UP, UP, UP.

'Jimmy Stich will STITCH YOU UP, STITCH YOU UP. UP, UP, UP'.

And: 'There's only one OBRAHMI, One OBRAHMI. There's only one OBRAHMI, One OBRAHMI. Oh Oh Oh'.

And: 'We are staying UP. We are staying UP. UP, UP, UP.

At half time we were still leading one-nil.

'I need your advice', I told Iain.

'Yep. Fire away'.

'Well, somebody's using my name. They're trying to use it to get some money out of me. I know who it is. What do you think I should do?

'My idea was to confront them but it might be better just to go to the police. The trouble is, it's all a bit complicated. And there's SIM Card to think about'.

'First of all', said Iain, 'are you sure you just haven't got the same name as this other person. There's millions of people in the world and there's probably a few hundred at least for every name.

'Chances are there might even be somebody out there called Horace Henry Green whose birthday is also 12 May'.

'No, it's not that simple. It's not my actual name they're using, it's the name I use for my paintings. And yes, it is, or was, their real name but only because they changed it by deed poll'.

'What do you mean "was"?'

'Well it was a woman and she's dead now'.

'And you were going to confront her? I know you're bloody amazing and all that, but I didn't know you were a medium as well'.

It seemed perhaps Iain wasn't taking things seriously enough, so I gave him a potted history of what had happened including the letter from Munroe, Munroe and Belfry, how I'd hired Morpeth and Slim to do some digging, and Sylvia Slim's pet theory.

By that time half time was almost over.

'Tell you what', said Iain, 'why don't we go for a pint after the game?'

I nodded.

The second half started. Within 10 seconds Obrahmi had scythed down one of their players and been booked. Mindful of his reputation, he was immediately substituted.

Two minutes from the end, there was a goal-mouth scramble and they scored. The Ref blew for full time.

'You are going DOWN. You are going DOWN'.

| *Eight* |

After the match.

We walked for half an hour or so to find a pub a bit out of the way, the Shipwrights Arms. It was on a side street leading down to the river and what must have been a ship yard at some time in the past. Now the area was all tarted up dockers' cottages that sold for more than any docker would have earned in a lifetime, and new glass and plastic apartments, costing almost as much.

On the way we chatted about the match, but once inside and sat at a table, Iain asked 'what all this about then?'

I told him about how I enjoyed painting and by chance it had turned into more than a hobby. I told him about Arthur Beaumont and Sheridan Boblemheim, I told him about Geoffrey Porter, Gustave Palmer, and Gregg Potter. I told him about Jennifer Ian St John James, now deceased and planted with a headstone bearing the name Verdu. And I told him again about Munroe, Munroe and Belfry, and about Morpeth and Slim.

Iain clearly had his work head on. He listened quietly, occasionally asking for further details. I wouldn't have been surprised if he had brought out a notebook and started talking about proceeding in a westerly direction and apprehending villains and all that.

'Right', he said when I had ground to a halt. 'As a policeman I've got to tell you to take this to the police. If Porter's the kind of guy you say he is, he'll likely as not get the better of you if you go along to meet him. He'll know what constitutes harassment and assault and no doubt, if it came to any sort of slanging match, he'd be more than happy to use the police for his own ends.

'Go along to the police. Make sure you've got copies of all the letters and papers that have anything to do with this: receipts from Beaumont, VAT records, all that sort of thing. The more you have the better it will be.

'Of course, if you do want to see this Porter character to warn him off, you can try that. But if you do, don't go alone. Don't get into a fight. And have somebody there as a witness. Somebody with enough wellie to make him certain it wouldn't be worth his while starting anything physical'.

I knew just the person.

'Thanks Iain', I said. 'I'll think it over and let you know what I decide.

'By the way, how did you know my full name. I don't usually use the "Horace" bit?'

I could see he wasn't expecting this. There was just a momentary look away before he answered.

'Oh, I probably heard it down the station. There's quite a bit of chat about you down there. Or perhaps it was in one of those articles about you. You can hardly pick up a newspaper without seeing your name somewhere in it'.

I pressed on. 'Thought perhaps that was it. But how about my birthday? I don't tell anybody that, especially as you mentioned a day other than the one on by birth certificate'.

Again, there was just the hint of an uncomfortable pause.

'You have two birthdays? What an official celebrity one and a real one, just like the Queen?'

He was trying to make a joke of it but I could see I had caught him out. And it suddenly dawned on me that his sitting next to me these last few years might not have been so accidental as I had thought.

'You don't work for Charlie's lot by any chance?'

It had never even crossed my mind before, but now I had said it, I knew it was true.

'Look, I know we're friends but you have to understand that as a policeman I've signed the Official Secrets Act. I'm not allowed to discuss my work with anybody'.

'You know who Charlie is then?'

Iain was suddenly looking rather sheepish.

'As I said, we are friends. As a friend I'm going to tell you a little story. It's a puzzle really.

'There was this explorer trekking through the jungle. He knew there were two tribes in the area. One was very ferocious. And they were cannibals. Whenever they caught a stranger, they ate him or her. And to make matters worse, they always lied.

'The other tribe was harmless and always told the truth.

'When our explorer reached a fork in the path, he didn't know which way to go. He certainly didn't want to end up in a cooking pot.

'Well the good news was that there was an Indian sitting by the path. The bad news was our explorer didn't know which tribe he was from, the one that always told the truth or the one that always lied.

'But our explorer was a resourceful chap and he thought of a way he could ask the Indian which way to go and be certain he got an answer he could rely on. He went up to the Indian and said: "If I asked somebody from the other tribe which is the right way to the friendly Indians, what would he say?

'The Indian didn't hesitate. "That way", he said, pointing to the track leading to the left.

'"Thank you", said the explorer, and took the path to the right.

'See, if the Indian was telling the truth he would tell the explorer, truthfully, that somebody from the other tribe would lie, and point to the wrong path, which was the one to the left. If he was lying, he would know an Indian from the other tribe would tell the truth and point to the correct path to the right, so he lied and pointed to the left.

'It's a sort of double negative – in this case two wrongs make a right'.

Iain took a glug of beer and placed the glass in front of him. And this time he looked directly at me, without flinching.

'Now, as I said, we are friends and I would not lie to you, but I can't answer your questions. I'd as likely end up in the slammer if anybody found out – or at least lose my job.

'But I think you've got something to ask me', he said.

It took me a minute or two to catch on, but then it dawned on me.

'I know somebody called Colonel, Sir Charlie Aulderton OBE', I told Iain. 'If I were to ask him whether he knew you, what would he say?'

Iain took another gulp of beer. 'He'd say he'd never heard of me', he said.

'And if I asked him if you worked for him, what would he say'.

'Same thing', said Iain. 'He's never heard of me'.

'Thank you', I said.

'And if I asked him if our team was going to avoid relegation this year, what would he say'.

Iain drained his glass and banged it down on to the table.

'He'd say they have every possible chance. It's a near certainty they'll stay up. Might even get into the play-offs'.

'That's what I think too', I said.

'Liar, liar, your pants are on fire'.

| *Nine* |

Saturday, 6.30pm. Home.

I could feel the steam the moment I opened the door. Stephi was home and in the bath.

'I thought you were getting back early today', she called. 'I hurried back specially. I thought we could go out or something'.

I went into the bathroom and sat on the side of the bath to tell her about my conversation with Iain.

'You mean he's been like your minder?'

'I suppose so', I told her.

'You're so up yourself. Do you think they'd spend all that money just to save your ass? It doesn't make sense. You said when it happened, when your parents got killed, they couldn't even spare enough to give you a decent handout'.

'Yes, I know what you mean', I told her. 'That's exactly what I thought. But they seem to have done a reasonable job. I'm still here'.

'More's the pity', said Stephi.

'Well I was going to suggest we try that new Asian crossover place down the High Street. But if that's how you feel, maybe it'll have to be beans on toast'.

'Sorry, only a sick joke. I'll let you take me out for a curried ham sandwich if it makes you happy'.

'I don't know now'.

'Then I hope your chooks lay square eggs'.

So, 40 minutes later we were in the 'Rice and Chips'. There hadn't been a table until the manager noticed who we were and quickly ushered us over to a large round table towards the back of the restaurant and provided us with two glasses of champagne.

The family at the next table – I guessed a grandmother, two parents and three young children - nudged each other and looked our way. The person who seemed to be the centre of their attention – until we turned up – turned round to look. It was Jason Obrahmi.

A broad smile spread across his face as he jumped up and almost ran the three or four steps to our table.

'Good to see you Mr Green', he said in an Australian accent. 'It's great. I've only been in London a few days and already I'm meeting all the famous people'.

I didn't look at Stephi as I shook his hand. I knew what she'd be thinking or probably saying to me any minute.

'Great game', I said. 'You made a big difference. It's really good we've got you. I think we need somebody like you to put a bit of life into the team'.

He shrugged in a sheepish way. 'You were there?'

'Of course, I'm a season ticket holder'.

'No way'.

'Another one of your admirers?' said Stephi after Jason had gone back to his table.

'He played for us this afternoon', I told Stephi. 'It was his first game and he looked quite good. He's supposed to be quite fiery'.

'I thought he seemed alright, even if he does seem to be another of your admirers'.

We ordered our meal and presently one of the children on Jason's table came over with a menu and asked me to sign it. I did.

The boy burst out crying and ran back to his table.

Jason grabbed the menu, looked at it, looked at me, strode over and punched me on the nose. A waterfall of blood gushed out, smothering the front of my shirt.

The manager rushed up with two of his waiters. They grabbed Jason and wrestled him to the floor, where one of them sat on his back.

Jason's mother started shouting. His wife, or maybe girlfriend, started hitting the back of the waiter pinning her husband to the floor, and the children stood and watched.

Stephi had stood up, then taken a step or two back so as not to be splattered by my blood. 'What on earth did you write on that menu?' she shouted in what I thought was rather an accusing way.

By this time, I had my handkerchief pressed against the throbbing flesh that had once been my nose. 'Just that nice phrase you use for me all the time', I gurgled. 'I said "for my little drongo"'.

'You're the fucking drongo', said Stephi and made to march out the door. She might have made it but for the two policemen who ran it at that moment. Somebody at the front desk must have called them, of perhaps one of the other diners in the restaurant. There were enough of them with their mobiles out, mostly held up and pointing at me.

'I'm so sorry', the manager told me. 'I expect the police will want to talk to you, but they must know where to find you. If you want to go, please do – there's obviously no charge. Or would you like me to call you an ambulance or a taxi?'

I said 'no' it was all right. I would find my own way home. 'My girlfriend's a nurse, of sorts, and she will look after me', I told him. 'Perhaps', I thought.

'I thought she was a model and actress', said the manager. He looked a little disappointed. 'I can't keep up with you celebrity types, changing partners all the time. But please come again. Bring whoever you want'.

We left and walked back home.

'You idiot', said Stephi.

'Well, let me apologise straight away for getting my nose in the way of his fist'.

'I don't blame him. I'd be put out if somebody called my kid stupid'.

'I didn't know it meant that. You call me that all the time'.

'Yes, but I'm entitled to call you a dope, you stupid man'.

'Drongo, drongo. Obrahmi made your nose salami, salami'.

| *Ten* |

Sunday morning. !.00 am. In bed. Me propped up on cushions holding my red, swollen, bloody nose.

The telephone rings. We don't have an extension in the bedroom, so I let it ring for a bit in the hope it will go away. It's probably some renegade fax machine spewing out messages.

The ringing continues until Stephi gives me a kick.

'You going to get that?'

'Why me?'

'Because you're awake anyway'.

'So are you'.

'Well, I am now'.

I pad down to the hall and pick up the phone.

'Hi', says a cheery voice. 'Is this Henry Green I'm talking to?'

I tried to think of something sarcastic to say, but couldn't.

'Yes, that's me'.

'Oh great. I was so hoping to speak to you.

'I'm Darleen, by the way. I'm from the LA Post. We have so many readers who would love to hear your side of the story'.

'What story'.

'You know. You English are so funny. Your fight in the restaurant. The one with all that blood'.

'And you're calling me from America to talk about my going to a restaurant?'

'Of course, you've gone viral. That YouTube video has had over three million views already. Everybody wants to know what you did to make that man hit you. Or was it staged? That's what I think. I think you had a bag of, of like stage blood inside your jacket. Is that it?'

Stephi came to the top of the stairs. 'What's going on down there. Who are you talking two at one in the morning?'

'Some bloody reporter from America. She says I've gone viral with my nose, whatever that means'.

'Oh, for goodness sake', said Stephi and stomped back into the bedroom.

'Are you still there', I could hear Darleen shouting down the phone.

'Yes, I'm still here'.

'What time is it over there, because it's getting late here and I've got my deadline to meet'.

'It's gone one in the morning', I tell her. 'The middle of the night', I say.

'Goodness. What are you doing up at that time?'

I put the phone down and pulled the wire out the socket.

As a sort of peace token, although I didn't know why I needed one, I made two cups of tea and took them up to the bedroom.

Stephi sat up and took one.

'I think it's broken, you know'.

'What?'

'You know very well what. My nose. I think it's broken. It didn't use to stick out like that'.

'Don't be stupid', said Stephi. 'You've got a bloody ugly nose. Always have had. It's just a bit swollen, that's all. You're not getting all girlie about it, are you?'

'No, but it bloody hurts'.

'Serves you right'.

'Why? Because my coach in Australian led me to believe "drongo" was a term of endearment?'

'No, drongo. Because you got blood all over my shoes'.

'Red boots, red boots. There's blood on yer boots, blood on yer boots'.

| *Eleven* |

Sunday morning. 9.00 am. Nose throbbing. Groggy from lack of sleep.

I open the front door in the hope that the Sunday papers might have been thrown down our steps. They have, and I take a tentative step outside to retrieve them. Ageing painter, hospital taxi provider and fugitive, is met by barrage of flashing cameras – well two - and shouts.

'Will you be suing? they asked. 'Do you think Jason Obrahmi should be sacked?'

SACKED. What did they think they were saying? He was our only hope.

I ducked back inside and shut the door barely in time to allow a final few shots of a shabby looking resident with throbbing nose clutching his dressing gown about him. Lucky, I remembered the dressing gown.

'It's on the news', said Stephi as I trudged back upstairs with tea and papers.

'What?'

'Your nose. It made the nine o'clock news'.

'What did they say?'

'What? You scared your image might have been dented as well as your nose?'

'No. This is serious. One of those reporters asked me if he should be dropped. That'd be it. We'd go down for sure'.

'But he hit you'.

'But it was my fault'.

'No, it wasn't. You insulted his kid. But that doesn't mean he has the right to go around thumping people and ruining other people's shoes'.

'I knew you didn't know anything about football'.

'Phew', she said. 'That pansy game for poofters. It's not a proper game like Aussie rules. I'm surprised it wasn't his handbag he hit you with.

'Anyway, he won't be sacked'.

'How do you know that?'

'They said so on the news. They said your team couldn't afford to sack him. And there were accentuating circumstances'.

'How do you mean? You said it yourself, people, even footballers can't go around thumping people'.

'Well, I'm only repeating what that policeman said. You know, the one that hauled you in'.

'What SIM Card Simmons?'

'They said he was a detective inspector or something. He had a very nice voice'.

It wasn't just my nose that was throbbing now. It was my head, my ears and probably a dozen other organs. I had to tell myself that it wasn't my policy to throb. That helped a bit – except for the nose.

'And what did this guardian of the law with the nice voice have to say?'

'He said that a twenty-year-old man had been questioned and released with a caution after an incident at a restaurant where a fifty-one-year-old man had made fun of his child who suffers from severe learning difficulties. Apparently, the man had fallen over a chair and hit his nose on a table but had left the restaurant without making a complaint.

'And he said they were questioning a waiter at the restaurant about an assault on a twenty-year-old man, and unlawful restraint and arrest'.

'Fifty-one!'

'That's what he said'.

'I'll sue for defamation – calling a spritely forty-nine-year-old fifty-one.

'And what about all those videos that have been posted on YouTube. They don't show somebody falling over a chair. They show somebody getting smacked on the nose'.

'No, they don't'.

'What do you mean. You were there. You know what happened'.

'Yes, I know what happened. But I've looked at the videos and they only start when you start bleeding – all over my shoes. Then they show that Jason man being pushed to the floor and sat on'.

We hadn't made the papers – the 'incident' had happened too late in the evening – but no doubt there would be some reports in Monday morning's papers. I decided I'd better write to Jason and apologise, and to the football club. We didn't want to lose such a big hitter.

'The minute he walked in the joint I could see he was a man of distinction – a real big hitter... real big hitter. Obrahmi. Obrahmi. Salami Obrahmi',

| *Twelve* |

Tuesday morning. 11.00 am. In the Volvo with Sylvia Slim, heading north through the Blackwall Tunnel.

I had made my excuses and left the hospital run to somebody else this week and decided to call on Geoffrey Porter instead.

'Do you think you would be able to come with me?' I had asked Sylvia when I phoned her the day before. She said she could, and she would.

So here we were, on our way to Hackney, where Daniel DeFoe had once maintained a country residence at his creditors' expense but which was now the haunt of artist-killing buses.

We hadn't contacted Geoffrey; Sylvia said it would be better to catch him unawares and anyway she knew where he lived, having spent a few days sitting in her car just down the road.

'So, who's Morpeth', I asked.

Sylvia looked at me as if I had asked whether her mother was a serial killer.

'My partner?' she said.

'That's the one. Your letterhead says "Morpeth and Slim" but I've only ever met you. I just wondered who is Morpeth and what does he do – work undercover or something?'

Even looking at the road ahead I could tell her serial killer question look had turned into her 'stupid man' look – it was burning into the side of my face.

'It's a she, actually. When we started the business, I'd hoped she would work in it. But it didn't turn out that way. She's kept her job. It makes it easier when we have a slack week, which happens now and then'.

'What does she do?'

'She's a police officer. It's helpful sometimes to have a contact in the police.

'You've met her actually. PC Amy Morpeth. She came to your house. She told me all about it; how they thought you had so much money you must be involved in some scam or other'.

'Isn't that against the rules – talking about people who complain to the police. It must be some breach of confidentiality or something'.

Sylvia resumed her 'looking'. I couldn't tell the variety as I was being cut up by a BMW at the time – Jon, according to the personalised number plate.

'Well, she had a personal interest. Your wife's case was our first. We put a lot into it – it was in her spare time. She's keen on photography, so she took lots of pictures for me.

'I'd only just left the police and we wanted to do a good job, get known; build up a solid reputation'.

'But you couldn't find anything bad about me'.

'No. That was a surprise. But our clients are not always right'.

'So anyway, you still keep in contact with Amy?'

'Of course. She's my partner'.

'But she doesn't work in the business'.

'No. She's not allowed to. She's sort of a sleeping partner. But she's still my partner – my partner in life'.

We didn't say too much after that until we got to Hackney. Sylvia directed me to a back street of terraced houses, probably build in the late 1800s. They were four storied with steps down to basements and steps up to front doors sitting behind flat-roofed porches supported by columns. There was an iron railing to the front.

They were nice houses, built for families with servants, but had suffered when hardly anybody could afford to have servants anymore and the upkeep on such large properties became too much. Most had been divided up into flats at some time.

But now the road looked on the up again. Geoffrey's house, number 63, had been restored to its original glory. No flats here. It was well cared for, with a smartly painted blue front door, complete with brass knocker. There was Jaguar parked outside.

Sylvia strode up the steps and knocked. After a few minutes she knocked again. I began to think the whole thing had been something of a wild goose-chase when the door was opened by a large, shambling, bearded man wearing corduroy trousers, slippers and a cardigan with leather patches on the elbows.

'Mr Porter', said Sylvia, 'we would be grateful for a few minutes of your time on a matter of mutual interest'.

Geoffrey looked Sylvia up and down, almost in a friendly way, as if such a strident approach was a matter of amusement.

'Well, you don't look like an insurance salesman – or I suppose now I should say sales person. So perhaps you're a Jehovah 's Witness or a happy clapper of some other denomination? Either way I have the rather important matter of a pre-lunch drink to attend to'.

'NO, I'm certainly not a happy clapper', said Sylvia. 'My father was Lithuanian', she added for some reason best known to herself. Geoffrey looked doubly amused.

'Mr Green and I are here to talk to you about Verdu. You have made some claims which Mr Green wishes to address'.

'Ah. Yes', said Geoffrey. 'I rather fancied that might be it as soon as I recognised Mr Green. I'm so pleased to meet you' – he said this to me rather than Sylvia.

'Please come in'.

This was hardly what I had expected. For a start he hadn't got Brylcreamed hair or even pointed shoes. He was less Terry Thomas, more Michael Gambon. And secondly, he had not tried to deny he had ever met Geoffrey Porter or that he knew anything about Verdu.

He seemed quite likeable. It was very upsetting.

We followed him into the house and into a comfortably furnished living room. It was hardly an artist's room, not an unmade bed or dissected cow in sight. The curtains were thick and luxurious, as was the carpet, and the sofas, towards which we were ushered, were well stuffed. It seemed as though Geoffrey's old ladies had done him well – well enough to live in considerable comfort.

Above the restored Victorian fireplace hung a large oil painting that looked remarkably like Cezanne's Card Players – except for one detail; the card players were hunched over a chess board.

There was an oak table by the window, too small for a dining table, but large enough for the wooden chess board that sat in the middle. To either side were upright chairs, one of which had been pulled back.

There was a chess game apparently in progress and an opened book, face down, next to it. The cover of the book showed an illustration of a Rook – of the chess variety.

Geoffrey was obviously a chess player and had been working through some game in his book when we arrived.

'Sorry about the mess', he said. 'As you know, my wife died rather suddenly not too long ago and I haven't had the will or energy to wield a vacuum cleaner in as robust a manner as was once the case'.

We looked round. There didn't seem too much mess to us, no dust or dirt to be seen.

'Would you like a drink perhaps? As I indicated, it's my habit to have a whisky about this time. Perhaps you'll join me, it will be a pleasant change not to be drinking on my own? And I often find a little alcohol helps to break the ice, don't you think?

'Speaking of which, I take mine straight but you might like some ice, or soda perhaps? Or there might be some Sherry in the cupboard should you prefer that?

We preferred Scotch with no additions. Geoffrey gave an appreciative nod as he shuffled from the room. There was barely time for us to give each other puzzled looks before Geoffrey was back, bearing a tray with three industrial sized glasses, each half full of highland something or other. It tasted of peat filtered through peat with a peat topping. In other words, it was quite good.

'Now', said Geoffrey, after we had all downed a little of his 1,000-year-old whisky, what is this about Verdu? Have you come to pay me my money? That would be very welcome indeed'.

'No, that is not it at all, Mr Porter', said Sylvia.

'Geoffrey, please', said Geoffrey.

'No, that is not it at all, Geoffrey'.

Sylvia had been magically transformed into some almost consolatory person. 'No, not at all. We think you must be under some misunderstanding about who is the real Verdu. Mr Green has come here with the intention of clearing this up'.

'I see', said Geoffrey, looking straight at me. 'And what exactly does Mr Green think is the nature of this misunderstanding?'

'The nature', I said, 'is that I am the real Verdu. The paintings that bear that name, except for one or two fakes produced by your wife, were all my own work. So rather than owe you anything, I'm afraid it's the other way around'.

Geoffrey allowed a hint of a smile to cross his face.

'I suppose you'll be telling me next that you know I'm a convicted fraudster and that my poor deceased wife, whom you so cruelly called a forger, did not bear the name Verdu?'

'Something like that', I told him.

'Well, I admit it'.

'Pardon?'

'I admit everything. My claim is bogus, a little diversion I cooked up with my late wife. Unfortunately, her considerable talents were never fully recognised and she was more than taken with the idea of being paid a fair amount for her work – as much even as you have been able to earn yourself.

'Of course, what I tell you in the confines of this room will be vigorously denied elsewhere, even, should you be foolish enough to allow this matter to fall into the hands of lawyers, in the highest courts of the land.

'I should think a man with your undoubted business acumen would see the sense in making a reasonable payment to settle this matter in an amicable manner. You could call it a donation in appreciation of the homage paid to you in the form of impersonation'.

Geoffrey was somehow managing to be flattering, sincere, yet menacing all at the same time.

'I'm sorry, we seem to have more than enough to have any claim you make thrown out of court', I managed. 'You have admitted your claim is worthless in front of a witness. So how on earth can you hope to succeed?'

Geoffrey, who was still standing at this point, walked over to his table.

'Perhaps you would indulge me a moment. Let me show you this game. It is quite famous and there are only two moves left to make.

'Please, it will only take a moment'.

Like a fool I stood up and went over to the table. It seemed obvious White was about to win. It had two Rooks, a Queen, a Bishop, a Knight and several Pawns. Its King sat comfortably behind a wall of Pawns.

Against this, Black had only a King, a Queen and a Knight. Admittedly the Knight was quite close to the White King, but was about to be taken by one of the Pawns.

'What do you think?' asked Geoffrey.

'Well. I'm no great chess player, but it looks quite serious for Black'.

'Quite so', said Geoffrey. 'But then you haven't had the benefit of a prison education. Open prisons are quite bursting with outstanding chess players. I was almost reluctant to leave.

'Anyway, what if I do this?' And he moved his queen diagonally from one side of the board to the other, so that it now sat right next to the White King. As it was protected in this position by the Knight, it could not be taken by the King. But there was also a black Rook on the back rank that certainly could take the Queen. 'Check', said Geoffrey.

It seemed a suicidal move.

'Well, surely White can take the Queen with his Rook? He might lose his Rook to the Knight but the black King can then take the Knight. That leaves White with only its King', I said.

'Quite so. But if the Rook takes the Queen, and there is no other choice of move, what If I do this? And instead of taking the Rook he moved his knight the seventh rank of the board. The move placed the White King in check - the White King that was now surrounded by two Rooks and three Pawns and was unable to move in any direction.

'It's checkmate, I think. It's called a smothered mate. The trapped King has nowhere to go'.

'Very ingenious', I told him. 'No doubt chess must have given you great solace when you lost your wife'.

'Oh, I like chess but only as a diversion. I showed you this to illustrate a point. It's that when a game seems over -

done and dusted, so to speak - there's sometimes a surprise in store.

'Now I see Miss Belfry is here. Let me introduce you'.

At this point I saw a smartly dressed woman of perhaps 40 coming up Geoffrey's front steps. He went out to let her in and reappeared a few moments later.

'This is Linda Belfry', he announced. Linda looked, a little lovingly, I thought, into Geoffrey's eyes.

'Linda has been helping me with all sorts of things since my wife was so brutally killed. However, she will tell anybody who cares to ask that she has been here since the beginning of this meeting and has heard every word that has been said. Isn't that so Miss Belfry?'

Miss Belfry, whose garments were entirely black, nodded her approval.

'She was, of course, witness to your boorish behaviour and especially to your threats, both physical and financial, and your ludicrous contention that my poor wife, the artist who painted the masterpiece you see on these very walls, was not Verdu. Isn't that so Miss Belfry?'

Miss Belfry nodded again.

'And now, I think Miss Belfry has one or two things to tell you'.

Miss Belfry sat on the edge of the sofa opposite to us and placed her black briefcase upon her knees, extracting a black leather folder.

'Now', she said, as if she were about to coax her black pyjama-clad, private educated children to resume their nightly nightmares.

'First, I should tell you that we have undertaken a number of legal and other initiatives to protect the name and copyright, and of course the estate, of the late Mrs Jennifer Ian St John Verdu.

We looked suitably interested.

'We have, of course, registered the trade name "Verdu". This protects the signature in the style and colour used by Mrs Verdu and means it may not be used by any other artist.

'The application was filed some time ago and has been suitably advertised in the Trade Marks Journal. As far as we know there were no objections raised.

'Copyright, as you no doubt know, is owned automatically by the artist. But to further protect Mrs Verdu's rights we have formed a number of limited companies featuring the name "Verdu". For example, Mr Porter is now the managing director of Verdu Paintings Limited, The Real Verdu Limited, and Verdu Artwork Limited.

'There are others'.

'We have also purchased various domain names featuring the word "Verdu". Here is a list'.

At this point Miss Belfry took from her folder three A4 sheets of paper, upon which was listed these domain names. She handed these to Geoffrey, who, without a word, handed them to me.

'These domain names are active and linked to a holding page. If you enter one of these names in your browser, you will be able to see the "Verdu" page. It contains links to the various Twitter accounts we have registered and to the Wikipedia page for Verdu. This describes how Mrs Verdu was inspired to use the name "Verdu" and the especially vibrant pallet of colours she favoured after spending some weeks in the Portuguese town of that name. It also contains a critique of Mrs Verdu's work and better-known paintings especially commissioned by us from the art critic Sheridan Boblemheim.

'Finally, we have established a charity devoted to promoting Mrs Verdu's well-known work in the rehabilitation of prisoners. The Verdu Foundation is, of course, registered with the Charity Commission'.

Miss Belfry sat back in her seat as an indication, perhaps, that she had reached the end of her list.

Sylvia sat open-mouthed; her face somewhat paler than when we entered the room. Her hair remained purple. Whether this new arrangement of her features was from fright, admiration or confusion I did not know.

'Now, you can see that we have established absolute right to the name "Verdu". But, of course, we realise that you have some attachment to that name yourself – not least because of your work as his agent', said Miss Belfry.

'In our letter to you we detailed Mr Porter's rights to any unsold Verdu paintings that you hold and, of course, to any money that you hold on behalf of Verdu. We are certain this will be a considerable amount, although the exact figure can be ascertained by an audit. We have a suitable firm in mind.

'However, Mr Porter is a reasonable man'.

Geoffrey nodded.

'He has therefore authorised me to make you an offer of settlement. It is this: for a suitable sum and guarantee that you will neither disclose the terms of the agreement nor pursue Mr Porter in any way, he will allow you to keep the pictures that you hold, to dispose of as you wish. He will also assign to you the rights of the trade name, companies, domain names, foundation and Twitter accounts that I previously mentioned. Further he will allow you to substitute your own text for that which currently resides on the Wikipedia page.

'As I said, Mr Porter is a reasonable man, and although he is saddened that his wife will not receive the accolades that she deserves for creating such memorable works of art, he believes this arrangement will avoid much expensive legal argument between the two of you'.

Geoffrey nodded.

It was like entering another universe, or perhaps the quantum mechanics portion of our own, where it is quite possible for some things to be in two places at the same time.

My own mouth had moved a little to the open position. I snapped it shut.

'Well you have been busy. And how much is a "suitable sum"?' I asked.

I could feel Sylvia giving me one of her special 'have you taken leave of your senses' looks.

'One million', said Miss Belfry. 'This is a very reasonable figure given the price that Verdu paintings currently command and the number that you no doubt hold. But as I said, Mr Porter is a reasonable man. Much too reasonable in my view'.

Miss Belfry gave Geoffrey a sweet smile. Geoffrey nodded.

I could do it, I thought. Why not? It was only a number on a piece of paper. Reducing one number in one column by a one wouldn't make any difference to me. My life would go on exactly as now, and I wouldn't have to deal with Geoffrey any more. We might even become friends.

But then I remembered that Geoffrey had turned the whole thing into some sort of game. And he thought he was winning. He thought he was smothering me. But perhaps I was the one in the seemingly desperate position who could spring a surprise win.

'Well, one million for buying back my own name seems an awful lot to me', I told Geoffrey. 'I shall have to think about it'.

Suddenly Geoffrey was a shade less friendly. 'Well, don't think about it for too long. I'll give you until six o'clock this evening. I shall be out, but you can leave a message on my answer phone. Let me know by then'.

Geoffrey ushered us out.

What do you think?' I asked as we got back into the Volvo.

'I think he's a bastard', said Sylvia. 'I think she's besotted with him. I think he telephoned her as soon as he saw us outside'.

'He may be a bastard, but he's a clever bastard. I sort of liked him. He played his role very well'.

'You think so?' said Sylvia.

'I don't think he was that clever, just smarmy. All that chess stuff. He doesn't know anything about chess. It was all put on for us. To show us he'd thought of everything and we didn't have a chance.

'And that poor girl eating out of his hand. You could see what will happen to her as soon as he gets his money.

She'll get dumped and probably have her career ruined into the bargain'.

'Then you think he's going to get his money?'

'I hope not. Although the way you were talking. It's possible'.

'You think I should call his bluff. Not do anything?'

'Yes, of course I do. I wouldn't give that bastard a farthing'.

'You didn't like him?'

Sylvia gave me one of her 'stupid man' looks. I decided to call Geoffrey's bluff. He could stew in his smothered mate. I'd think about what to do next. Yes, I'd call his bluff.

'I'm bad, very bad. Show your stuff or let it be. Because I'm bad, I'm bad, I'm very bad'.

| *Thirteen* |

Thursday morning. 6.00 am, in bed and asleep beside Lady Brisbanette. There is violent hammering at the door and some sort of commotion outside.

Lady Brisbanette stirs. She is not at her best prior to her first cup of tea of the day.

'What the fuck's that?' she asks, stomping onto the landing and then clomping down the stairs. 'I bet it's those bloody reporters again. What have you been up to now?'

She goes to the kitchen window and shouts. 'Shut the fuck up or I'll call the fucking filth'.

Somebody shouts back.

'We are the fucking filth. Now open the fucking door before we kick it fucking down'.

'There's no need for all that foul language', Stephi says, as she opens the door. I imagine her rubbing her eyes, her hair, her face; pulling her stripy tee-shirt thing more tightly around her.

'Alright then. You've had your fun for the day. You've woken the whole road. What the hell do you want?'

'It's not you love. It's that Green bloke you're supposed to be marrying'.

'How do you know about that? And anyway. How's it your business who I'm going to marry? It's not against the law, is it?'

'You'd be surprised what we know Love. But you're alright. It's him we want. Been throwing his weight around. Gone too far this time'.

Whoever it was, constable Britmouse perhaps, or some other sweepstake winning copper, he must have moved to step past Stephi.

'Woa, Who said you could come in? First, I want to see some identity and next I want to know by what authority you think you can bully people like this. I'm recording all this on my mobile phone, so you better make sure you know what you're about. Or perhaps you would like to make an appointment to come back at a more reasonable time?'

From my warm but suddenly not so comfortable listening post, I felt a sudden rush of pride for the lady in my life. But after all, she did claim convict forebears – although I doubted very much her mobile, which was usually lost somewhere in her handbag and often had a flat battery, was recording anything.

Even so, it was time to get dressed. I got dressed.

By the time I came down the stairs the sweepstake winner had retrieved his warrant card and his warrant for my arrest.

Through the kitchen window I could see a galaxy of flashes as my picture was taken by a host of press-agency stringers.

The policeman stepped forward. 'Mr Green I am arresting you on suspicion of assault. Anything you say......'

I stopped listening at this point. 'I suppose you'll want me to come with you?'

'I'm not sure if you've heard Mr Green, but we are arresting you. That means that, yes, you are required to accompany us to the police station'.

'OK, I said. Do I need to bring anything?'

'No'.

'Stephi', I said, 'please call Charlie and let him know what has happened'.

She nodded. And then she asked the officer of the law: 'Will he be back in time for lunch?'

'I should think he'll be about four years late', said the policeman.

As we left the house some kind of arc light was switched on and a man with what I took to be a television camera moved forward. More lights flashed and various people shouted out. 'How do you feel?' 'Do you deny the charges?' 'Will you plead guilty?' 'What have you got against Geoffrey Porter?' 'Have you ever done this sort of thing before?' 'Did you hit him harder than Jason Obrahmi?'

They pushed me into the back of a police car and we drove off. Then they took down lots of details they already knew and put me in a police cell where I sat for the next four hours.

'You've done it now. You'll pay. You've made a big mistake. A big mistake. Who's bad '.

| *Fourteen* |

*11.00am, at the police station, making my telephone call.
I call Stephi.*

'Well, you certainly called that scum bag's bluff', she says
by way of greeting.

'I was hoping for a little sympathy. Perhaps the promise of
a food parcel or two, that sort of thing'.

'Don't joke, it's serious. It's all over the news. They are
saying you went to his house and beat him up because he
was threatening to expose you as a forger. There are
pictures of him looking pretty bad – Rocky Balboa after
two fights on the same day.

'His lawyer came on saying how he doesn't bear any
grudges. He understands how frightened of exposure you
must have been, somebody in the public eye like you. He
doesn't want you jailed. What you did to him was
nothing. What he wants is justice for the memory of his
poor wife whose life was ended under a bus before she
received the recognition she so richly deserved.

'Blah, blah, blah... You get the picture'.

I got the picture.

'Did you call Charlie?'

'I did. He had to call me back. He's on a golfing holiday in
Scotland'.

'How can a man with one arm play golf?'

'Badly, I suppose. Anyway, he said he'd do what he can,
but you might need to be patient. I think he meant you
might have to spend the night in a cell.

'But listen, I think I've got something that might help you. If they don't let me give it to you personally, I'll leave it at the station. It should be with you in an hour or so'.

Time was up, and I was taken to an interview room where I sat for another 30 minutes or so before SIM Card appeared with Constable Britmouse in tow. The last named nodded to me in what seemed to be a somewhat sheepish way.

SIM Card sat down opposite me and shuffled his papers before introducing himself and PC Britmouse, telling me I had been arrested on suspicion of assault and that I was being formally interviewed under caution. I nodded and said 'yes' when prompted.

'We've heard from your solicitor, Colonel, Sir Charlie Aulderton OBE', SIM Card began.

He gave me a challenging look as if to say, 'try and object to that'.

'He is in Scotland at the moment and cannot be here before tomorrow. Apparently, there is nobody else he can send in his place.

'This leaves us in a somewhat difficult situation. We can lock you up until Colonel, Sir Charlie Aulderton OBE arrives, or we can find you a duty solicitor to take his place, or should you so wish, you can agree to be interviewed without representation when we can hopefully clear this all up in a matter of minutes'.

By his manner I could see he would obviously prefer the last but he doubted I would be so foolish as to agree to it. I was.

SIM Card went through the formalities.

'Now, Mr Green, very serious allegations have been made against you', he continued in his very serious allegations voice. He stared straight at me.

'Mr Geoffrey Porter, whom I believe you know, alleges that the day before yesterday you went to his house with another person – a private detective I believe (said with evident distaste) – and that an argument ensued about your representation of the artist Verdu.

'He has made an official statement and complaint alleging that during the course of this conversation you became violent and struck out at him without warning. He alleges that you punched him in the eye, knocking him to the ground and causing extensive bruising and a cut, and that this might easily have endangered his eyesight had not a Miss Linda Belfry taken him to the nearest Accident and Emergency department.

'Mr Porter further alleges that during the course of your conversation with him, and prior to your unprovoked attack on him, you admitted to forging paintings under the name "Verdu" and selling these for profit – for considerable profit.

'We have been in touch with the hospital concerned. Staff there corroborate Mr Porter's assertion that he was treated there on Tuesday afternoon, and confirm the extent of his injuries – which are indeed obvious from the number of dressings that have been applied.

'We have also taken a statement from Miss Belfry – a solicitor, no less' (at which point SIM Card puckered his lips and raised his eyebrows to indicate the cast iron nature of his evidence) 'which confirmed the statement made by Mr Porter in every material respect.

'Now Mr Green, no doubt there is some simple explanation for this. Perhaps it is a case of mistaken identity? No doubt traffic cameras will find no trace of your vehicle travelling through the Blackwall Tunnel on its way to Mr Porter's house. Perhaps Miss Belfry mistook you for somebody else? No doubt an identity parade would answer that question.

'So please tell me what happened the day before yesterday?'

SIM Card leaned back in his chair as if having just made the winning move in one of Geoffrey's chess games. It was mate in three, no matter how I wriggled.

Before I could answer there has a knock on the interview room door. SIM Card looked irritated – victory delayed – but shouted 'come' all the same.

In came Iain. He did not look at me but bent to talk quietly into SIM Card's ear. He handed him an envelope which SIM Card almost threw across the table to me. Then he left the room with Iain. I could hear them talking just outside the door.

PC Britmouse remained in his seat. He had not said a word so far and looked a little uncomfortable. But, after all, and having no wish to stay in 'traffic' for the rest of his career, he realised it was his duty to guard somebody who might well be a dangerous criminal.

I opened the envelope. The word 'Insurance' was written on the outside in blue felt tip in Stephi's Australian scrawl. There was only one thing inside. It was a photograph of me, sitting in my 'studio' before it burnt down, paint brushes in hand, paint on face and several other places, and a clearly visible canvas. It was The Bee, my early painting praised so grandly by Sheridan Boblemheim in his most respected newspaper column. Never mind that what he wrote was a load of old tosh.

SIM Card came back into the room and sat behind his desk. He shuffled his papers, turned over a page or two, scribbled a brief note. After an eternity he looked up.

He switched on his tape again, told us all that he had done so and that the interview had been resumed and asked: 'So Mr Green, if I might have your version of the events of Tuesday'.

His delivery was less certain, less accusatory. He seemed to be admitting that perhaps, after all, there might be some reasonable explanation that did not include the prospect of a long jail sentence – or even a short one.

I told him. I told him that I had gone with Sylvia to ask him to stop trying to blackmail me over the paintings. I told him about Geoffrey's wife and her change of name. I could tell in an instant that SIM Card was not a fan of Liverpool football club.

I told him about the bus, about the letter from Munroe, Munroe and Belfry. I told him about the chess boards and about Geoffrey's threats.

'And what about Sylvia Slim?' I asked. 'She was there. Why don't you talk to her? She will tell you the same thing'.

SIM Card looked at me. He seemed to be making up his mind whether to tell me something or not. Finally, he placed his pen carefully in front of him and said: 'We have, spoken to Miss Slim'.

'Then surely there's nothing more to say'.

SIM Card seemed almost sad.

'In view of what she said, and in the light of some new information we have, I am putting the matter of the assault to one side for now'.

'Alleged', I said. 'There was no assault'.

'Alleged assault', said SIM Card.

PC Britmouse seemed to be amused.

'But forgery is another matter', said SIM Card with a little more vigour. He must have been thinking: 'If I can't get him on one thing, I can get him on another. He's a slippery so and so but he's not going to get away with it again'.

'I remind you that you are still under caution', said SIM Card. 'As you know Mr Porter alleges that you have been forging paintings, using the name of his wife. And we know that you have sold some "Verdu" paintings and been paid very well for them.

'Verdu was the name used by Mr Porter's wife and he has registered this fact in a variety of ways. Which leads us to believe that you have indeed been forging paintings'.

There was almost a sparkle in SIM Card's eye. Suddenly it was all clear to him. I was obviously the rogue he knew I was all along.

I reminded SIM Card that Geoffrey Porter was a convicted fraudster.

'That may be so, but his wife was certainly not and it is her reputation and her livelihood, I mean her estate, that has suffered'.

'It has not suffered, because there has been no forgery. I painted all those paintings and I signed them "Verdu" because that was the name I used and have always used'.

'We have spoken to Mr Arthur Beaumont, a very respected art dealer who owns a gallery in Bond Street. He told us that you had come to him claiming to be Verdu's agent and he had no reason to disbelieve you. Subsequently he sold quite a number of the paintings you delivered to him, claiming they had been painted by Verdu.

'But Mr Beaumont said that after a while he became suspicious because he had no direct contact with the painter himself. However, with no proof of any wrongdoing he continued to take paintings from you until he received a letter from Mr Porter's solicitors explaining that the pictures were in fact painted by Mr Porter's wife.

'Do you have anything to say to that, Mr Green?'

I certainly did. I told him again that I had painted all the authentic 'Verdus' because I was in fact Verdu. I told him that Arthur was probably being blackmailed by Geoffrey Porter on the basis that he knowingly accepted a painting from him that was not a Verdu but which he had sold as such.

'And can you prove any of this?' SIM Card asked.

'Well I can take you to my studio and show you my paints and canvases. I can show you all the remittance advices from Mr Beaumont. I can show you my VAT returns. But as to the blackmail, I cannot at the moment produce any proof'.

'So, you say you are the real Verdu. Why would you use a name other than your own to sell paintings? After all, you are rather famous and attaching your real name to the canvases would surely have made them more saleable?'

SIM Card leant back in his chair and stared at me, as if to indicate he had made an unanswerable argument. No doubt I was supposed to crumble under the weight of his crystal clear, pristine logic.

'I chose to use another name so as not to draw attention to myself. Believe it or not, I do not court publicity, it just seems to follow me around. But I have some questions for you. When do you think the first Verdu painting was sold?'

'And the relevance?'

'The relevance is that the first "Verdu" painting was sold over ten years ago. I have a cutting that proves it, an article praising Verdu's work written by Sheridan Boblemheim. I also have this'.

At this point I opened the envelope marked 'Insurance' and took out the photograph of myself in my shed, painting The Bee. I handed it to SIM Card.

'And this is?'

'This is me sitting in the shed in the garden of the house I then shared with my former wife. The shed has long since burnt down. The Fire Brigade could no doubt provide you with the exact date they were called to extinguish the flames.

'You will see that I am busy working on the very painting that Sheridan Boblemheim praised so highly'.

SIM Card studied the photograph for a minute or two then dropped it on the table.

'So perhaps you can help me to get this straight. Your proof that you are not somebody who falsely sold pictures using somebody else's name is that you did indeed paint those pictures?'

My 'stay calm' policy was being tested to the limit. I assumed SIM Card was being deliberately thick. It was probably a technique he had used many times to get the people he interviewed to blurt out something they had rather kept to themselves.

It was almost working on me, and it was certainly working on PC Britmouse who was fidgeting in his chair giving his boss an occasional sideways glance.

'No. Surely you understand. When I started producing "Verdus" Miss Ian St John James was probably still in Liverpool. She only changed her name three years ago. She and Geoffrey Porter decided to cash in on my success by pretending to be me'.

SIM Card frowned. 'And you say this photograph, this photograph proves that you started these forgeries before Mr Porter's wife – who of course cannot defend herself against your claims – before Mr Porter's wife changed her name to Verdu?'

'Exactly?'

SIM Card smiled.

'Forgive me for mentioning it, Mr Green, but there is no date on this photograph. It could have been taken yesterday for all I know'.

'Then let's ask the person who took it to verify the date', I said.

'If you can find the person who took the photograph, then that would be a good starting point. You no doubt have the name of this person to hand?'

'I do indeed', I told him. 'It was PC Amy Morpeth. Of course, she was not on duty at the time. I believe she's a keen photographer'.

SIM Card looked up. I clearly had his attention.

'I don't understand. Are you saying that you hired PC Morpeth to take pictures of you? Or are you claiming she is some kind of stalker?'

I put on my most innocent face.

'Neither. Actually, my ex-wife hired a firm of private detectives to follow me. I believe Miss Morpeth knows the owner of the firm and helped out by taking some pictures'.

SIM Card got up and walked out. PC Britmouse eyed me a little uneasily, I thought. I imagined Amy Morpeth being summoned. I didn't suppose SIM Card would be too pleased with her. I didn't suppose she would be too pleased with Sylvia for having disclosed her part in their sleuthing.

After about ten minutes in which PC Britmouse and I pretended not to look at each other, SIM Card came back in. He was a little flushed.

'It seems', he told me, 'that your version of events turns out not to be as farfetched as it first sounded. I still have my suspicions and rest assured I'm not going to let this drop until I get to the bottom of what has been going on. But for the moment that will be all, Mr Green.

'Of course, it is very likely I will have to interview you again'.

He was about to get up when the telephone rang. He grabbed it and pressed it to his ear. 'Not now', he said.

Obviously not now was not good enough.

'I see, I'll speak to him, yes.

'Good afternoon Sir. In Scotland yes. And how is the golf. .... I'm sorry. Perhaps later. The front desk said you needed to speak to me. Should I take this in my office, I'm interviewing at the moment....... Yes, Mr Green.... No, his solicitor could not attend, he is in Scotland playing golf........... Oh, I see. Well no, we won't be detaining him. We have managed to clear up the matter. I will be pursuing the other party....... Yes, vigorously. Indeed.......... No, I understand. Of course not. I could tell that from the start. Just a matter of getting the paperwork right, crossing the 'I's and dotting the 't's.......Yes, that's understood...... No certainly not Sir. Is there anything.....'

SIM Card left the rest of his sentence unsaid. Whoever he was speaking to had clearly hung up on him. He appeared even more flushed than he had been a few minutes ago.

'Well, Mr Green. As I was saying. Everything seems to have been cleared up. We won't need to be bothering you again about this matter.

'Do you think it would be helpful for me to arrange counselling for the trauma this has caused?'

'No, I don't think so', I told him.

I left.

'Who's sorry now, who's sad and blue, and who's crying too?'

| *Fifteen* |

Saturday. Football. Only two games to go before the end of the season and we are second from bottom in the league. We're playing the team that's fifth from bottom, the one we've got to overtake if we're going to avoid relegation. It's raining. Hard.

They've got a new player on loan from Manchester United.

We've got one on loan from Liverpool. Jaomie Obrasti can't make their first team, so it's likely he's only three times better than anybody else who plays for us.

The first half starts and Jaomie gets the ball, sweeps past two of their players and makes a killer pass to Jason Obrahmi, who thrashes the ball into the back of the net.

'Jay Oh – Jay Oh', shouts the crowd. 'There's only Jay two Ohs'. We all feel pleased with ourselves. The drummer starts banging away.

'You're going DOWN. You're going DOWN, DOwn, Down', we shout.

In the celebration, both Jay Ohs take their shirts off and wave them above their heads. Synchronised shirt waving leads to synchronised bookings – both get yellow cards.

Not to worry, we are still in the lead.

Ten minutes later and Jaomie, ball seemingly tied to his foot by an invisible elastic band, moves majestically into their penalty box. Unselfishly he rolls the ball sideways to where Jason has loped. It's another goal.

There's no shirt waving this time. But there's plenty of 'Jay-two-Oh-ing' from the crowd.

Five minutes to go to half time and it seems the Jay Ohs have struck up a striking match made in heaven. This time it's Jason who collects the ball just past the halfway line. He dribbles past three players. There is one defender between Jason and the goal. To his right Jaomie is running in unmarked.

Jason ignores his strike partner and tries for goal. He kicks the ball straight at the defender. It ricochets off him for a corner.

Jaomie extends his hands, palms upwards, as if to say 'what did you do that for?' Jason punches him. Perhaps Jaomie called him a 'Drongo'. Jason gets sent off.

Half time comes.

'What was all that about?' Iain asks.

'I think Jason's a bit fiery', I said.

'No. not that. Your own bit of alleged fieriness with that Porter bloke'.

'He made it up'.

'Yes, I know, his girlfriend told me'.

'You spoke to her?'

'Yes. I did a bit of poking around. Seems Geoffrey's got a history of claiming he has been beaten up. His last so-called attacker was an old lady of 84. Turns out he'd somehow got hold of her building society details and managed to get fifteen grand out before she noticed. When she said she was going to the police he came up with the assault idea.

'It didn't stick, but it might have if the old dear's other boyfriend hadn't been in bed with her at the time of the supposed attack'.

'So that's what you told SIM Card'.

'Yes, and that Miss Belfry had decided to withdraw her statement'.

'And why would she do that?'

'I might have mentioned what I'd found out about Geoffrey to one of those Press guys who sit outside your house. And he might have telephoned Miss Belfry to scare the shit out of her; telling her about Geoffrey's previous and pointing out that if the claim didn't stick, she might not be a solicitor for too much longer.

'He told her that if she gave him an interview, he'd put her in touch with somebody who could help – AKA me.

'She telephoned the station about five seconds later to say it had all been a misunderstanding and she wanted to withdraw her statement.

'I said I would see what I could do. She seemed quite grateful and went off to talk to that reporter chap. Didn't have too much choice really because if she'd refused, he would have printed what he already knew anyway'.

'Well what can I say? Thank you again. I'd probably still be locked up now if you hadn't bailed me out'.

'No worries, it's my job. Or in fact it used to be. I'm moving on. It's been a cushy four years, but it's over. I might have to get back to some real work'.

'Well I didn't know what you were up to for most of the time – which is what you wanted, I suppose'.

'That's it. Anyway, thanks for the ride. It's not too bad looking after you celebrity types.

'Oh, and by the way, Charlie asked me to tell you he needs to see you. He'll be back from Scotland on Tuesday and wants to see you first thing'.

'What's first thing?'

'He said to be in his office at 9.30'.

'9.30!'

'9.30s late for Charlie. He usually gets in around 7.30. He'll be on his third Scotch of the day by 9.30'.

'OK, 9.30 it is', I said.

The game got under way again. We lost three two. We were relegated; there was no possibility of escape.

'You are going DOWN', their supporters shouted. 'There's no captain of your ship, you're allllll SINKING. Allllll SINKING'.

We had to agree. We got up to leave.

'Is this goodbye then?'

'No, I'll see the season out. There's one more home game. I'm a devil for punishment', said Iain.

'I suppose you can't tell me where you're going'.

'Right now, I'm going home. After that? You suppose right'.

'Obrasti, Obrahmi, Obrasti, Obrahmi, Obrasti, Obrahmi – one of them's barmy, barmy, barmy'.

| *Sixteen* |

Sunday morning, early. The phone is ringing and Stephi jumps out of bed to answer it – she is 'on call' this weekend.

I hear Stephi talking to somebody and then going to the front door. After five or ten minutes she comes back up with two cups of tea and the Sunday papers.

'It wasn't work. It was that Sylvia Slim of yours', she says, dumping the papers on the bed. 'She says there's something you should read'.

'She's not MY Sylvia Slim', I say. 'Her heart belongs to somebody else'.

We pick up the papers and start thumbing through.

I find the article Sylvia phoned about quite quickly. There is a news story on the front page pointing to an 'exclusive' report later on. I scan the first and turn to the second and begin reading it aloud between slurps of tea.

The headline was: 'Chess playing fraudster accepts poisoned pawn'.

The introduction explained that the reporter, Josh Hoosemann, had undertaken extensive research to obtain his exclusive insight.

Convicted serial fraudster Geoffrey Porter was found dead at his home yesterday. Police say they are treating the case as suicide and are not looking for anybody else in relation to the death.

It is already clear that Porter, who had a lavish life-style, was deeply in debt.

He had recently been the mastermind behind a scheme to defraud the celebrity Henry Green.

Known to millions as a B-list buffoon, Green is in fact an accomplished painter whose canvases sell for thousands of pounds. He signs his paintings as 'Verdu'.

Porter had devised a scam in which he planned, in effect, to high-jack the name 'Verdu' and hold it to ransom.

But his plans fell into disarray when his wife, Jennifer Ian St John Verdu was knocked down and killed by a bus in a London Street late last year. Jennifer, who had been artist in residence at Letchworth Open Prison when she met Porter, had only recently changed her name by deed poll from Porter to 'Verdu'.

Witnesses said that immediately before she was run down, she appeared to be standing at the kerb, waiting – for what they could not tell. She had jumped out into the road in front of a bus without warning. The driver told the inquest into Mrs Verdu's death that he had tried to avoid her and would have stopped in time had the bus coming up behind not slammed into the back of his vehicle, knocking it forward and killing her.

The jury returned an open verdict.

At this point Porter, who has acted heartlessly to his many victims, became friendly with London solicitor Linda Belfry.

'At Munroe, Munroe and Belfry we are very particular about the clients we take on. It is our duty to know precisely who they are. That meant I knew about Mr Porter's past from the start. It made me very suspicious of him and a little wary, but given his recent loss it seemed a charitable act to take him on as a pro bono client', she said.

'He was very plausible and I admit that at first I had some sympathy for him'.

As soon as she realised, he was using her to perpetrate fraud, Miss Belfry reported Porter to the police.

Porter also tried to enlist art dealer Arthur Beaumont into his scam.

'As soon as he came into my gallery, I suspected he was up to no good. You get a nose for these things in my business', said Beaumont, who has championed Henry Green throughout.

'When Porter claimed to represent 'Verdu' I decided to play along.

'After all, Henry Green is one of my most respected clients. I knew from the start that the paintings he said were painted by "Verdu" were in fact done by himself. As I said, you get a nose for these things. But I didn't let his secret out. I only mentioned it to a few of my buyers.

'Unfortunately, Mr Green did not come to me, or tell me anything of his problems with Porter. If he had, I would certainly have been able to help him'.

The police said they had been aware of Porter's activities for some time and had been tracking his movements. Last week they had conducted a long interview with Mr Green so as to obtain his evidence with view to making an arrest.

'Porter was a serial fraudster who usually preyed on women. In this case, because of the vigilance of all involved, his devious plan failed miserably', said Detective Inspector Peter Simmons, who had for some time been leading an investigation into the planned fraud.

'Porter, no doubt aware of his imminent arrest and weighed down by guilt and his burden of debt, appears, *unfortunately, to have taken his own life before we could charge him'.*

Mr Green was unavailable for comment.

Art critic Sheridan Boblemheim, who writes for this newspaper, has described Mr Green as a promising artist with a distinctive style.

'I think he has made the most of his modest talents and has produced some striking images that sell for extraordinary sums'.

Stephi looked at me. 'Is all that true?' she asked.

'If you call "some time" a day or two, it's not entirely inaccurate. Only mostly'.

'What will you do?'

'I shall sue, of course'.

'What for?'

'He called me a "B-list buffoon" and Sheridan whatshisface said I had "modest talents"'.

'Sounds to me those were the not entirely inaccurate bits'.

'And what about "Mr Green was unavailable for comment?"

'That bit was true too. Somebody called Josh Hoosemann called yesterday when you were at football and said he was a reporter and it was very important that he talk to you. I told him to piss off'.

'And he took his revenge by calling me "B-list" '.

'You're so up yourself'.

'Anyway, look here. It says that judge woman who's heading some public inquiry or other into dodgy arms deals has also been found dead?'

'So?'

'It says "respected high court judge Lucinda Quabert, wife of Lord Liskorge, was found dead at her holiday home in Ayrshire yesterday. It is believed Lady Liskorge died of natural causes. Born Lucinda Plusmeny....."

'Isn't Plusmeny the name of that fellow who's supposed to be your father? You could be related', Stephi suggested.

'Probably am. We aristos are all interbred, don't you know'.

'Shame the French revolution was in France', she said.

'It's not the A-list, A-list. It's not the A-list. It's the B-list, B-list. Looser, looser, looser'.

| *Seventeen* |

Tuesday. 9.30 (A.M.). At the offices of 'Chaucer & Co', Charlie's office.

'Good morning Mr Green'. It was the polished man behind the polished desk. With impeccable style he managed to convey the strong impression that I was an intrusion into his sparkling domain. I felt privileged to be in the presence of such upper class lackiness. 'Mr Aulderton is expecting you. Go right up'.

There was something different about the place. For a moment I couldn't put my finger on it, and then it was obvious: there were other people about. They weren't only about, they were bustling about, carrying stuff — boxes and bits of office equipment.

I went up the stairs. As usual Charlie was already standing at the top waiting to shake my left hand. As always, he was immaculately dressed with his empty jacket sleeve neatly pinned up and his black eye patch as straight as a sergeant major's drill cane. As I reached the top steps, I caught sight of myself in Charlie's gleaming black shoes. In comparison to him, I looked a mess - well, in comparison to most people, probably.

Charlie ushered me into his room. It seemed insulated from what was going on elsewhere in the building. He pointed to the usual chair and, without bidding, walked over to the table to empty the contents of his decanter into two glasses. He gave me one.

Charlie wasn't shaking. This must be serious. 'It's over', he said, taking a cigarette from the silver box on his desk and setting this fire stick alight with his desk lighter.

'I know', I said. 'Geoffrey topped himself'.

'So it would seem', said Charlie. 'But that wasn't the "over" I was talking about'.

'Which "over" is it then?'

'This', he said, spreading his hand in a wide arc. 'The operation is over. You've got nothing more to worry about'.

'I wasn't worried until you said I had nothing to worry about. Now it seems a tad worrying.

'I assume you mean that nobody's after me anymore. But how can you know that? The IRA might have disbanded or whatever, but there must be a few people around who still bear a grudge. Lots of them were my age'.

'Trust me, it's over'.

Inexplicably, I was getting a little angry – hurt perhaps? It was a feeling I did not have too often and it took me a moment or two to recognise it. I could feel myself flushing and there was maybe the start of a twitch in my right eye. It would not have registered on the Jason Obrahmi angermeter, but for me it was boiler-blowing stuff.

'How can it be over? I can't just go back to being Henry Grimond. I've got Horace to think about'.

Charlie raised his one eye. 'Very droll', he said.

'Anyway, all of this can't just be for me. It sounds like you're just ditching me. It's probably some cost cutting exercise and I'm a cutback being left to fend for myself. Is that it?'

Charlie looked me in one eye – his 'England expects' look. 'Trust me. It's over. This wasn't just for you. But it's over'.

'A bit sudden isn't it?'

'Not that sudden. It's been coming for a while. But the final coup de grace was a little unexpected. But there you are, you're free to go about your business. Perhaps now you can become a real celebrity, even a real painter?'

'That's a bit below the belt. Actually, I'm happy as I am, strictly mediocre thank you. But I would like to know what has brought this all about'.

Charlie looked down at this steady hand, then looked up. It was his 'England expected but look what it got' look. He was obviously feeling a little put out.

'I'm sorry, that was unnecessary. You're not the only one affected by this. I'm being put out to graze too. It's not something I care to contemplate', he said.

He pulled open a draw of his desk and took out a bottle of scotch. 'I've been saving this one. It's my last day, so we'd better drink it now', he suggested.

He somehow opened the bottle with one hand, dropping the foil and the top onto his desk. It was done in a flash.

I pushed my glass in his direction. He poured in a hundred quid's worth or so. It tasted only marginally worse than Geoffrey's tipple.

'I've admired you', Charlie told me. Obviously, he was now going to tell me what a shit I was. But no, it turned out to be his regimental pep talk for cannon fodder, MK1.

'I've seen a lot of people face danger – being shot at, having bombs explode near them, that sort of thing. People handle it differently. Some seem to love it. They can't get enough. They get hooked on the adrenaline rush. Perhaps I was a bit like that myself.

'Others, they become detached. They go within themselves, close themselves down. They just focus on survival.

'When it's over, if they survive, they all have a hard time. The one's that love it, want it to go on. They keep putting themselves in more and more difficult positions until something bad happens. And then they have to stop and they have a tremendous come down. Often, they can't handle it.

'Those that have cut themselves off find it impossible to reawaken their senses. They become emotional wrecks.

'You seemed an exception. You seemed to be able to ignore it all. You just became somebody else – somebody who was somehow detached from it all'.

Well, he seemed to have got me taped. I had become somebody else; a person without emotion, an observer of the world. I watched it go by with a wry smile on my face. I was interested to see how it all turned out.

Stephi was wrong. I wasn't up myself. I was just interested to see how I turned out. It wouldn't affect me, whatever happened. I was just an observer.

Meanwhile I observed Charlie rambling on: 'I know it wasn't as easy as that. I know it must have taken its toll. But if you take my advice, I think you should just stay that person you've become and not ask any more questions. But it's up to you. As I said, I'm off. I'll tell you anything you want to know. The buggers can do what they like. What do I care?

'You might think we're not treating you too well, but for your own health it might be better left at that. You're not doing too bad. People seem to like you, you've got a good woman who's prepared to marry you - despite your questionable past. And you've got pots of money. You even managed to get that pushy policeman off your back. What more could you want?'

He might have a point, but the anger and the scotch were getting the better of me. 'I'm sorry', I told him. 'I know what you've done for me. You're probably right. But it's not enough. If it's really over I want to be able to tell Stephi. And I can't tell her if I don't know why or how'.

Charlie poured himself some more scotch.

'OK. You asked for it. I'll tell you what I know. Fire away'.

'Well first, apart from my brother who isn't a relative, do I have any real relatives?'

Charlie looked into his glass, as if consulting a crystal ball. He swilled the liquid around a little.

'You did have, you had a sister – a half-sister - but she's dead now'.

'She wasn't Lucinda Quabert, Lady Liskorge by any chance?' I asked.

Charlie looked mildly surprised.

'Yes. It was her'.

'And all that stuff that Ivan told me, that was all true?'

'Andrei Shubkin you mean? Yes, mostly'.

'And my mother was a spy?'

'An agent, yes'.

'And my sister?'

'No, no, entirely not'.

'So why is this all stopping because my sister died?'

'You're jumping to conclusions', said Charlie in a half-interested way, shutting the folder. He obviously thought he'd said enough; that I'd learned enough.

'Your sister is hardly the only one to have decided now is a good time to depart this world. The dinosaurs are getting old and dying off'.

I wasn't having it. 'Are you really telling me that this is not because my sister died?'

He kept looking down at the folder for more time than it takes me to eat breakfast.

'All right', he said, 'I'll tell you'.

In so many words Charlie told me that after my parents' deaths it had been decided that I might be even more 'useful' to them. That's why they tucked me away somewhere safe. After all, it didn't cost them anything – I was self-funding. The stash of money in the sports bag that they let me keep was off-books.

At first, I had been the threat that kept my father, my real father, on side. It seemed that from the first he had had an inkling of what my mother was up to, but he hadn't been too bothered. And he enjoyed the side benefits. He was very bothered when Charlie's outfit came along and said they knew too.

Given the choice of being prosecuted as a traitor and exposed as an adulterer – not seen in quite the same light in the 1950s as now and potentially terminal for his career (worse still, he might have had to go and live in Moscow) – or helping Charlie's lot, my father chose the latter. In effect he became a double agent. Some of the information he let my mother find out about had been made up to order.

For a while, things went swingingly. Everybody thought they were winning and they all were happy. But then my father got his title and became less important and my mother insisted on going off to Belfast. Her bosses in Moscow were being careful now that Burges and Maclean had been exposed and all of Whitehall was on spy alert.

Once in Northern Ireland my mother, AKA Sonya, began making a real nuisance of herself. It wasn't so very long after the Cuban Missile Crisis and everybody in the West was very jumpy about the prospect of various weapons being shipped around the world, especially if they were likely to end up in places like Belfast. My mother was finding out a lot about what was being done to stop this.

And then there was a bit of good luck, Sonya and Henry Grimond – agent Aleks – got blown up. Charlie's people were able to get rid of Sonya without it being obvious that she had previously been used to pass on some duff data. And with me hidden away, they could go back to my real father and remind him they had living proof of his shenanigans, so he'd better not have any thoughts of blabbing.

Since he'd been funding my upbringing, he knew full well that I was around, but by then he didn't know where.

Scroll on quite a few years and my clever sister gets herself made a High Court judge. By this time, she's married to Bruce Quabert, oldest son of Lord Liskorge. Bruce is ultra-right wing, always banging on about moral obligations, the sanctity of marriage and all that stuff.

It was pointed out to Lucinda that it wouldn't go down too well if Bruce were to find out her father had been a traitor who had fathered a son by his spy lover – a son that looked remarkably like her father and who could be wheeled out at the drop of a hat. Naturally, she was shown my photograph as proof absolute of what had been said.

Like her father before her, she chose the most convenient route and promised her services to her country. We two, her and me, were Charlie's most important charges. And now she was dead and I was apparently off the IRA's most wanted list.

It took about ten or fifteen minutes for Charlie to tell me all this, fitting in his little story between mouthfuls of whisky and lungfuls of smoke. When he ended, I sat for a moment without saying a word. As far as I knew Charlie had never lied to me. He'd told me lots of implausible things but most had turned out to be true. But something here didn't seem to tally. And then it dawned on me.

'Why would you want my sister signed up? She was a lawyer and a judge. She wasn't likely to know too many state secrets. She was too busy upholding the law'.

Charlie looked at me as if I were stupid.

'It's always good to have a judge or two to rely on. You might think the law is straightforward, that people know what it says. They don't. Parliament might pass laws but they often don't know what they mean.

'A clever judge can find arguments and precedents to support almost any interpretation of almost any law.

'And then there's judicial reviews to think about, and judicial enquiries and public enquiries. It's important to have people we can rely on'.

'You mean you stitched her up so she wouldn't come up with anything embarrassing'.

'A bit harsh'.

'But true'.

'There is an element of truth in it', he said.

'And wasn't she heading some inquiry into dodgy arms dealing when she died?'

'If you mean the public enquiry into the Althustian affair, yes, she was chairperson of that'.

'And she died, and a day later you're packing up office. What are you doing? It looks like you're getting rid of the evidence'.

Charlie sat back in his chair.

'Look', he said. 'As I said, you are jumping to conclusions. If you think we had anything to do with her death, you're wrong. We didn't. Except in a round-about way'.

'What roundabout way?'

Charlie frowned and shifted his bottom.

'She might have been finding it difficult to reconcile her responsibilities, that's all. It seems she took her brief too literally and began digging into one or two other little things that it would be unfortunate were they to become known to a wider audience. One of these even went back to the time your father was enamoured of your mother. She found out things that no daughter should know about her father, and it rather upset her'.

'THAT'S ALL. You're telling me you drove her to suicide', I said rather loudly. Geoffrey's decision to part with his mortal being I could take, but for some reason the death of this woman I had never met and probably wouldn't have liked, seemed to be a personal loss.

'Calm down, it won't help. The police say her death was due to natural causes. I think we should leave it at that.

'You know from your own experiences that we deal in some pretty murky waters. Somebody has to. Otherwise the other side would just run roughshod over us. It's the sort of thing we do that keeps people safe. It's kept you safe.

'It kept me safe while I was "useful" ', I told him.

'Over the last ten years only four people have searched your birth certificate. We knew who they all were within a few hours and we knew they were not a threat. If they had been, we would have dealt with it'.

If it was an attempt to change the direction of the conversation, it worked.

'So how do you know only four people searched by birth certificate?'

'Because we had you flagged'.

'So that's how you knew before me about doctor death, about Stephi, about Geoffrey and about Uncle Vanya?'

'Andrei Shubkin you mean. Yes. That's how we knew before you. The system works'.

'It works for you, but what about people who get caught up in it all. What about my sister?'

'Collateral damage happens sometimes. It happened to me', he said, looking down at his empty jacket sleeve. But on the whole the work we do is for the greater good'.

'What, so arms deals are good if we do them but bad if somebody else does?'

Charlie leaned across and refilled my glass. This was the longest conversation we had ever had. I had the suspicion that he might be enjoying it, especially the boasting and self-justification. He hadn't wheeled these out for a while.

'How would you have it then Henry? Would you like any old thugs who disagree with the way things are done in this country to be handed out Kalashnikovs on social benefits?'

'No, of course not. But I would prefer the people who are supposed to uphold the law to stick to it themselves'.

And then another thought struck me, it was about that night in Belfast when my parents – at least one of them – died.

'What really happened that night?'

'Which night is this?'

'I think you know. The night I was supposed to have uncovered a plot. The night that set all this off'.

The scotch was definitely getting the better of me now, but not of Charlie. I knew I had a good point somewhere, but just where seemed to have slipped my mind for the time being.

'You know as much as me', Charlie said.

'I don't think so. I think you were involved. Not you personally perhaps, but whoever it is you work for. You promised to tell me everything. Now I think it is time to tell me everything about that night'.

Charlie looked distinctly uncomfortable. He rubbed his eye patch. He lit another cigarette. He scratched his head. And when he couldn't think of anything else to do, he raised his glass to his lips and gazed at me over a trembling lead-crystal rim with his now slightly watery eye.

'Well perhaps we owe you an explanation'.

'Perhaps you do'.

'It was a sting operation. We'd led the republican lot to believe there was a load of plastic explosives to be had if they had the inclination and the money. They had the first but not the second. To put that right they robbed a bank.

'So far, we'd succeeded in making them look bad. The next stage was to make them look silly as well. We were going to steal the money back from them.

'We knew a couple of likely ships were due to dock in the next few days so we let them know that the deal was on. All they had to do was send along one of their men with a bag full of money. The meeting place we picked was the Fighting Cock. Our man was to meet their man, pick up the money and leave. We were going to wait a while and then, once he had left the pub, pick up the Irish lad.

'With a bit of luck, they'd never know they'd been had until it was too late. They'd just think their man got unlucky and that they'd missed the pick-up.

'But it didn't turn out that way. There was an almighty cock-up. Your supposed father – Henry Grimond, agent Aleks - got wind something was up – we'd kept him as far out of it as possible. But he took it upon himself to set up so many patrols and roadblocks that your Irish friend almost didn't make it to the pub at all.

'When he did get there, our man had already been and gone. He mistook you for the money mule and walked off with your sports bag after muttering something about a fictitious address.

'When the real money-man arrived, he made the same mistake. He thought you were his contact. He left you the money and you kindly told him the address we had made up. When he left, we picked him up as planned and put him in the slammer. Thanks to you the plan worked after all. We – or rather you – got the money and your man was none the wiser that he had been tricked.

'That's all there was to it'.

'So, when did the IRA find out?' I asked Charlie.

'They didn't'.

'They didn't?'

'No. Not an inkling'.

Perhaps I was a little wrong about the Scotch and Charlie. Perhaps he did have a limit after all. Perhaps he had reached it. When I got near my limit, I got argumentative. Perhaps Charlie just got careless. Certainly, I could detect that it was dawning on him that he had let slip something he shouldn't have.

'Well, perhaps a suspicion. No proof, but a good idea'.

'You said not an inkling'.

'A little too strong I think'.

'You said not an inkling, and I've spent the last 40 years or so hiding from an army of would-be assassins who had "not an inkling" that I was involved. In fact, they probably had "not an inkling" that I even existed'.

'No, you're getting ahead of yourself again. We had to be careful, very careful. You don't know what those people were like. It wouldn't have just been you, it would have been your family too. We couldn't take chances'.

He'd done it again. Or was he saying these things to provoke me into asking the right questions? Because suddenly I realised that I had set up the perfect opportunity for Charlie's lot to get rid of my parents, no questions asked, with the people they worked for left unawares that they had been twigged.

'But I haven't got a family. I did then, but somebody killed them off and left me with a crooked sister who'd do anything not to upset the vicar or ruffle her bigoted husband's feathers'.

'Now come on'.

'No, I'm not coming on. If the IRA didn't know what was going on, it wasn't them that killed my parents. Who was it? Tell me that. Was it you?'

'Look, I can't possibly talk about these things. A lot went on then and some of it wasn't very pleasant. People got hurt. There was a lot of collateral damage. That's all I can say'.

I thought back to the conversation I had had with Iain, about his two tribes – the one that always told the truth and the one that lied.

'Charlie', I said. 'You've been great for me. I know I owe you a lot and I know you weren't personally involved in any of this – he flinched – but I have to ask you one, no on second thoughts, two more questions. Then I promise there won't be any more'.

'All right', he said. 'What are they?'

'If I were to ask you what the IRA would say if they were asked who killed my mother and her husband, would they say it was them or you?'

I am sure Charlie understood. It was probably him that told Iain the Indian story in the first place.

All sign of shaking had gone again as he said: 'They would say it was them. And your second question?'

'If I were to ask you what the IRA would say if you asked them if it was you personally who drove that van packed with explosives into my mother's house or if it were some other member of your unit, what would they say'.

'They would say it was some other member of the unit'.

'Thank you', I told him. 'Thank you for telling me, thank you for looking after me. As you say, it's over. I'm just so please that so many of my family, including myself, have been so useful to so many countries and so many organisations'.

I staggered to my feet. He stood up more gracefully, ushered me to the stairs, shook my hand and walked back to his office.

I went out through an almost empty building. I noticed as I left that the 'Chaucer & Co' brass plate had already been removed.

'Who let the dogs out. Who let the dogs out?'

| *Eighteen* |

Saturday football. It's the last game of the season, but there's no Iain. He's disappeared – for good I imagine.

We're already relegated and to top it all we're playing the team second from top. The team leading the league by two points had played their last game an hour or so earlier – it was televised. They had drawn. That meant the team we are playing can snatch the title with a win.

Jaomie Obrasti is playing. He'll have to wear a protective face mask though.

An interview with him is printed in the match-day programme. He has no hard feelings towards Jason Obrahmi, he says. He just never wants to play with him, or even set sight of him again. The club has treated him brilliantly. The doctor did an unbelievably good job on his eye and fractured nose. But this will be his last game here – he wants to go back to Liverpool. It's more gentle up there, he implies.

He's not only a good footballer, he's sensible too.

The game starts and it's obvious the other team are a bit edgy. There's a few late tackles and a few yellow cards. Their manager is doing a Freddie and the Dreamers impersonation – jumping up and down, waving his arms, shouting and whistling to any of his team who look his way. It seems none of them want to.

Ollie Wilson is a rock in defence.

'Ollie, Ollie, Ollie', cried the crowd. 'There's only one Ollie Wil-son, one Ollie Wil-son'.

Damien Onslow is a constant threat.

'There's only one Damien Onslow, one Damien Onslow', we shouted.

'Onslow's not slow. Onslow's not slow'.

Jason Obrahmi is sitting in the stands

Towards half time Jaomie Obrasti collected the ball around the halfway line. He faked to pass to Damien Onslow but instead looped a kick at their goal.

Their keeper, who had come forward to menace Damien, watched as the ball sailed over his head, under the crossbar, and into the goal.

'Jay oh, Jay oh. Why d'you want to go home?' we shouted.

He waved his shirt above his head. One more yellow card.

'Who are yer, Who are yer'.

We went wild. 'Only one Peter Peter', we shouted, 'Only one Ollie Wilson', now 'Only one Jay-oh'. There was only one of everybody.

The score stayed the same until full time. The other side were frantic to get back into the game but the harder they tried the more difficult it became for them, especially, as halfway through the second half, they had two players sent off.

We were relegated, but we all went home happy.

'Coming back next season', I asked the chap who usually sat on the other side of Iain. 'Spose so, devil for punishment. At least the seats might be cheaper. How about you? You coming back?'

'No, I don't think so', I told him.

'We're going down, down, down. We're going down. Ollie, Ollie, Ollie. Peter, Peter, Peter'.

Extra time

Sydney, Australia

Six months later. We, Steph and me ('Stephi', it turned out, was much too long an abbreviation for the Australian market), are sitting outside a café overlooking the ferry terminal. The Harbour Bridge looms in the near background, with tiny crocodiles of people, tied together, trekking across the top of the main span - for pleasure!

'I can't believe it' – it's Steph doing the talking. She's a mouthy Sheila.

'I can't believe it. Why would you do that? You could have done what other past-it men do and gone out and bought yourself a Porsche, or a Maserati. Or one of those huge American things that looks like a four-door car with a truck stuck on the back.

'You could have bought something a bit exciting for a change. But no, as it turns out, you might just as well have bought yourself a sheepskin coat and pair of driving gloves to go with your new car. It's a shame they don't make Rovers any more'.

'I didn't know you knew so much about cars', I tell her.

'A darned sight more than you, it seems. How could you go out and buy a Holden? It's just an Australian Volvo. What colour is it? Don't tell me it's that muddy green colour again?'

'No, as a matter of fact, it's not. It's blue. It's a Holden Insignia. I heard that they're very comfortable'.

'Well, I look forward to being ferried to our new home in comfort then'.

I didn't have a ready answer, I was too busy watching a woman wearing a dark blue raincoat, sashaying her way through the crowds of Chinese and Japanese tourists. She looked remarkably like the woman from Costas all those months ago, the one who seemed to know so much about Steph and me.

Without so much as a nod in our direction, she plonked herself down at an empty table two down the line and ordered herself a coffee.

'You look as if you've seen a ghost', said Steph.

'No, I just thought I saw somebody I recognised – that woman over there'.

Steph looked over. 'Another one of your demented groupies I shouldn't wonder'.

It was left at that. But a while later, when Steph had decided it was time she went and inspected the lavatorial arrangements, I turned around to find raincoat-woman had shifted herself to our table.

'Hello Henry, I'm so pleased to have this opportunity to speak to you alone', she said.

'I'm not Henry', I told her. 'You must have me mixed up with somebody else. My Name's Horace, Horace Steinitz', and my wife, who will be returning at any minute, is Mrs Steinitz'. I don't know why I added the last bit since, if it had any relevance at all, it must mean that I was the self-same person she had spoken to before.

'Yes, yes, yes. 'Stephi', she said rather pointedly, 'will be a little while yet. One of my colleagues is at this very moment engaging her in a gripping conversation. Even so, we don't have too much time and I have something important to tell you – something you need to know. So cut the crap and listen'.

I listened.

'You are both pretty much on your own from now on. You're doing fine. Nothing to worry about. But just be aware, there is no immediate back-up from now on'.

'Yes, I know all that. Somebody who looked after my affairs has retired, but only because he has nothing left to do'.

'How sweet. You think this is all about you. Perhaps a bit conceited of you, I would say, when there's somebody else involved who, in the scheme of things, is a damned site more important you - despite what Charlie and his boy-scout operation might have led you to believe'.

What now? Things seemed to be going off at a tangent that I didn't much care for.

'I didn't know my sister was that much of a big hitter'.

'Not your dear departed sister, blockhead. The world doesn't revolve entirely around you and your family. Things happen to other people too, you know. No, not your sister, I'm talking about Stephi'.

'Stephi?'

'Yes, Stephi – Mrs Steinitz. You've been too wrapped up in yourself to notice what was really going on. That was one of the things that we liked about you. That, and you being so boring. And your so-called art. That was very convenient. It made it easy for us to make sure Stephi was well funded'.

'Are you saying you bought my paintings as a way of getting money to Stephi?'

'At last the penny's dropped. We've got cupboards full of the things'.

'But Stephi? Why Stephi?

I didn't mean it the way it sounded. Of course, Stephi was important – to me. But to the powers that be? If this woman really was a representative of those 'powers that be'.

'And why should I believe you? I don't know who you are or anything. You could be a friend of Uncle Vanya for all I know'

'No, you don't', she said. 'You're right to be sceptical – it makes a change. I know of Andrei Shubkin, the man I think you are referring to, but I have never met him. We are on opposite sides.

'I'm in liaison, that's all you need to know. Now I'm going to tell you something that you must not disclose to anybody, ever, not even to Stephi – she doesn't know anything about this, and she never should. But it's important that you should know, just in case anything happens that seems to be linked. Then you can call this London number. Keep it safe', she said, handing me a business card that said 'Volvo auto repairs, specialists'.

It put the card in my pocket and waited.

Raincoat-woman launched into her explanation.

Stephi's mother, it seems, had been a bit of a rascal – not of the Sonya variety, more a difficult young woman variety who reacted badly to authority of any kind, and who had plenty to react to. She was determined she was not going to be married off to some chinless wonder of somebody else's choosing. Instead she wanted one of her own choosing. And choose she did.

Unfortunately, the choice did not go down too well with the 'powers that be'. Said choice had been married before. Worse still, he had been divorced. And in the 1950s, divorce was a no-no, especially for anybody in line to inherit the throne, no matter if this was a place or two down the pecking order. Had not the last almost-permanent-king abdicated over something similar. Politicians of the day, no matter that there were divorced and re-married men amongst their highest ranks, would simply not allow it.

The UK was going through a difficult time. It was just recovering financially from the war. Meat was still rationed and it was obvious the King was on his last legs. There would have to be a new monarch and the last thing that anybody wanted was another divorcee muddying up the succession waters.

'Nowadays nobody gives a toss, Even the heir to the throne is divorced', said raincoat-woman. 'But back then it mattered. When there was a divorce somebody had to be blamed, somebody had to admit to or be proved to have committed adultery. In other words, they were liars. And nobody wanted a liar or somebody who is married to a liar as there king or queen.

'And of course, the whole thing would have opened up old memories and the shakiness of the previous succession'.

But it seems Stephi's mother was not giving in that easily. She managed to get herself pregnant by her chinless choice. This caused a certain stir.

Chinless choice was threatened with the tower, if not beheading, if he did not absence himself from the scene forthwith. Stephi's mother was persuaded to take a little break behind closed doors, and once the baby had been delivered, to partake of a tour of Africa.

Abortion was illegal and out of the question. Stephi's mother had to do what many other women in much more straightened circumstances than her own were obliged to do; she had to give the baby up for adoption

Stephi was adopted by two long-time lackies who, in return for a suitable sum and the promise of a gong or two for services to the crown, agreed to go off immediately to a suitably far off colony, never to be seen again.

They left the baby behind, to be brought up by a succession of nannies, governesses and assorted carers.

'In short, Stephi is a member of a family that for centuries thought it had the divine right to fuck whoever it pleased. Of course, it was the male side that usually took most advantage of this. So Stephi's mother's antics came as a bit of a shock', raincoat-woman explained. 'She was something of a trailblazer, you could say.

'Had Stephi been a man born in another century she would have been known as a Fitzgerald, a Fitzroy, or some other Fitz. As it was, she wasn't, so she became a Klevity instead. She would have had a "Bar Sinister" on her crest, instead of no crest and the prospect of having to work in a bar.

'It's just the way it goes. It was just bad timing. Everything had to be done to avoid embarrassment'.

I didn't say anything for a minute or two. It was just rather a lot to take in.

'You look after Stephi and you might even end up with a gong yourself – for services to art, perhaps'.

'You mean the equivalent of a "Hero of the Russian Federation"?'

'Something like that. If you don't, or if you let something slip. You might end up with a visit from some people who look remarkably like relics of the Republican cause. It's up to you to do the right thing'.

'Be "useful", you mean. But why are you telling me now? Why are we "on our own now" as you put it. Charlie as good as told me he was being put out to grass because my sister had topped herself and I was no longer much use to them. Surely this hasn't got anything to do with my sister as well?'

'Hardly. This is because of another death. This time it was natural causes. A few months ago, Stephi's mother died. There is now no longer any prospect of her being embarrassed by anything anybody says, or by anything that is uncovered, and all the promises made when Stephi was born have been fulfilled'.

At that moment raincoat-woman's phone buzzed and almost immediately Stephi was back with us. She was looking a little flushed.

'You'll never guess what? I've just bumped into one of the girls I used to go to school with. I didn't remember her very well, but she kept coming up with all these names from the past. We had quite a conversation. Unfortunately, she's on her way back to the UK tonight, so we can't meet up again for some time'.

Stephi seemed to notice raincoat-woman for the first time. She looked across at her in a semi-hostile way as if to say 'are you one of the floozies who's been sending knickers in the post to my husband'.

'Hello Mrs Steinitz', said raincoat-woman. 'I came over because I thought I recognised your husband. It's silly really, but I thought he might be Henry Green. Obviously, a big mistake'.

'Obviously', I said. 'After all, there's only one Henry Green'.

Steph looked at me over the top of her sunglasses.

'Horace, you're so up yourself', she said.

We all laughed, me in a deferential sort of way.

'She's all you'd ever want. She's a lady. She's a lady, whoa, whoa'.

End

Printed in Great Britain
by Amazon

11385891R00201